**Demonic Visions
50 Horror Tales
Book 6**

Demonic Visions 50 Horror Tales Book 6

© 2016

ISBN-13: 978-0-9861114-6-4

Foreword by the Editor

Welcome to the sixth installment of the Demonic Visions series. We have added some talented new writers to the Demonic Visions team. Each new book that we publish will take you deeper into the minds of the writers, and acquaint you with their various styles of prose. So enjoy, and I hope that you will join us for the entire Demonic Visions saga which is intended to last many, many years and span many, many volumes…

~Chris Robertson, author of **Death Dreams Deluxe**

Cover art by Grant Cross, artwork on Facebook: **Grant Cross Artwork**

Table of Contents:

Other Works by the Authors

~~ * * ~~

Matt Drabble - Gated, Gated II: Ravenhill Academy, Asylum - 13 Tales of Terror, Abra-Cadaver, After Darkness Falls Volume One, After Darkness Falls Volume Two, The Travelling Man

Peter Adam Salomon - Henry Franks, All Those Broken Angels, Prophets, PseudoPsalms: Saints v. Sinners

Marc Sorondo - Aurora

Marc Shapiro - Norman Reedus: True Tales Of The Walking Dead's Zombie Hunter (Riverdale Avenue Books), Welcome To Shondaland: An Unauthorized Biography Of Shonda Rhimes (Riverdale Avenue Books), Trump This! The Life And Times Of Donald Trump (Riverdale Avenue Books)

Christopher Conlon - Savaging the Dark, He Is Legend: An Anthology Celebrating Richard Matheson, A Matrix of Angels, Midnight on Mourn Street, The Oblivion Room

Ken MacGregor - An Aberrant Mind

Patrick Freivald - Twice Shy, Special Dead, Blood List (with Phil Freivald), Jade Sky

Mark Slade - The Book of Weird, Seduction of the Innocent, A Six Gun and the Queen of Light, Hellspeak: A Pete Chambers Book, Electric Funeral

Naching T. Kassa - The Venihi, Master of the Shade

Julianne Snow - Days with the Undead: Book One, Glimpses of the Undead, The Carnival 13 (collaborative novella for charity)

J. T. (Troy) Seate - Novels: Valley of Tears, Tears for the Departed, And the Heavens Wept, Collections: Carnival of Nightmares, Midway of Fear, Sex in Bloom

K. Trap Jones - The Charm Hunter, The Sinner, The Harvester, The Drunken Exorcist, One Bad Fur Day, The Crossroads

Shenoa Carroll-Bradd - The Minstrel Angel, The Widow's Painted Room

Rob Smales - Carol of the Bells (a Story Single), and Echoes of Darkness

James Pratt - Cthelvis and Others, Horrible Stories for Terrible People, Vol. I: Monsters, Horrible Stories for Terrible People, Vol. II: Obscura

Vince Liberato - Parental Guidance Recommended, (Upcoming publication via Amazing Stories), Redshifted: Martian Stories, Master Minds, Horror in Bloom

Justin Hunter - Nostalgia, Chet & Floyd vs. the Apocalypse: Volumes 1 and 2

S.C. Hayden - Rusty Nails Broken Glass, Kill Your Idols

Maggie Carroll - Eurydice

Shawna L. Bernard - Darkness Ad Infinitum (Villipede Publications)

JG Faherty - Novels: Carnival of Fear, Ghosts of Coronado Bay, Cemetery Club, The Burning Time, The Cure, Novellas: He Waits, The Cold Spot, Castle by the Sea, Thief of Souls, Fatal Consequences, Legacy, Cult of the Black Jaguar, Winterwood, Death Do Us Part

Johannes Pinter - Beautiful churches of Sweden, 1007, Karmakoma

Stacey Longo - Secret Things, Ordinary Boy, My Sister the Zombie

Rob E. Boley - That Risen Snow: A Scary Tale of Snow White and Zombies, That Wicked Apple: A Scary Tale of Snow White and Even More Zombies, That Ravenous Moon: A Scary Tale of Red Riding Hood and Werewolves, That Malicious Storm: A Scary Tale of Beauty and the Phantom, That Merciless Truth: A Scary Tale of Goldilocks and the Mummy

Rick A. Carroll - Dead Man's Skin

April Bullard - Goody Hepzibah's Harvest Tales, The Sock Thief

Jay Wilburn - The Dead Song Legend Dodecology, The Enemy Held Near, The Great Interruption, The Hellmouth trilogy, Time Eaters

Mike Leon - Rated R, Godless Murder Machine, Supervillainous: Confessions of a Costumed Evil-doer, KILL KILL KILL

Kerry G.S. Lipp - Live Action Hentai

Charlie Jack Joseph Kruger - A Junkyard God With Broken Legs, In Stark Weather, Setting Son, Older Than Gods And Monsters, Spoken Tombstones

D.J. Tyrer - The Yellow House, Acting Strangely

Trisha J. Wooldridge - Bad-Ass Faeries 2: Just Plain Bad, Bad-Ass Faeries 3: In All Their Glory, Epitaphs, Wicked Seasons, The Unicorn & the Old Woman, Mirror of Hearts, UnCONventional, Holiday Magick, Doorways to Extra Time, Once Upon An Apocalypse Volume 1, As T.J. Wooldridge - The Kelpic, Silent Starsong, The Earl's Childe

Sydney Leigh - Baby's Breath

R.L. Ugolini - Quakes

1. TOURIST TRAP BY RAYMOND GATES

"You're sure there's Aboriginal art out here?" Marion's nasal twang made it sound like hee-yah.

"Honey." Douglas turned and pushed his glasses higher up the bridge of his nose, the way he often did when he was getting ready to lecture. Their guide, a short distance ahead, chuckled.

"Too right, love." Steve used his broadest Australian accent, the one he put on for the tourists. "Just a bit further. Bout fifteen minutes or so."

"Fifteen minutes?" Jason's shoulders dropped, his eyes squinted, and a look suggesting he was trying to pass a kidney stone came over his face. "Dad, this sucks! We've been hiking, like, forever."

"Don't speak to your father like that," Marion said. She punctuated it with a mosquito-killing slap of her forearm, and glared at her husband.

Douglas turned to his family and pushed his glasses back up his nose. "Come on, guys! This is fun! We're out in the Australian bush, seeing things most folks back home have never seen beyond National Geographic."

Jason spun his head in both directions, his ear-bud headphones whipping around like the beads on a Tibetan prayer drum. "Uh, I can see trees back home. And mud. And if I go down to the lake, I can get eaten by mosquitoes there too."

"He's right, honey," Marion said. "Why couldn't we just go to the gallery? They have Aboriginal art there."

"A gallery? Are you serious? This is authentic Aboriginal rock art. It's like, a monument to the Aborigines. This is the real deal." Douglas turned to Steve. "Help me out here."

Steve drew the worn and weathered Akubra off his head, lifted his foot onto a rock and rested his elbow on his knee. "You're fair dinkum all right. Doug, is it?"

"Ah, it's Douglas, actually, but yeah, okay. Doug's fine."

Steve continued, oblivious. "Places like this are sacred to the Aboriginals. Have been for thousands and thousands of years. The art that you're gunna see? Most Aussies won't have seen anything like it, much less you lot." He stared at the group. "You're real lucky to find someone like me who can show it to ya."

Douglas held his hands out and raised his eyebrows. Marion and Jason looked unconvinced.

"Plus, the wildlife at the creek's unreal," Steve added. "With the wet we've had lately, could be anything come down for a drink. Platypus. Kangaroos-"

"Oh! Those cute little koala bears?" Marion grasped the camera dangling round her neck.

"They're not bears, mom," Jason mumbled.

Steve grinned. "Oh yeah," he said, nodding. "You'll see koalas all right."

Douglas beamed. "What'd I tell you? Rock art. Koala bears. C'mon guys, this is going to be great!" Marion gave an excited squeal. Jason rolled his eyes and firmly embedded the ear-buds back in his ears.

"Righto," Steve said. "Let's get a wriggle on, eh?" He turned back to the trail and started walking. The family followed behind.

The bushland thickened as they descended deeper into the gulley. Steve chatted the whole time, pointing out plant life, rock formations, and animals that scampered away from their approach. Marion's camera beeped and clicked in time with Steve's revelations. Douglas bombarded Steve with question after question. Jason trudged along, lost in a world of alternative rock.

Before long, Steve brought them to a burbling creek, fed by a low waterfall. A fine mist hung in the air. The place seemed damp and cold, despite the early afternoon sunlight that streamed between the trees.

"What'd I tell ya?" Steve pointed towards the waterfall. "Ain't she a rippa?"

Douglas drank in the surroundings. "This is awesome. Jase, isn't this awesome?"

"Uh, Steve?" Marion asked between photos. "I don't see any rock art around here."

"Not here," he said. He reached into his breast pocket and withdrew a small jar. "There's a cave up behind the waterfall there.

That's where it is." He gave her an odd look. "I'll take yas up there in a while."

"I don't see any animals here," Jason said, and ignored his mother's stern look.

"Don't worry, mate." Steve unscrewed the jar's yellow lid. "You'll see 'em soon enough." He dipped his finger inside the jar, and withdrew a black, tar-like substance. He proceeded to rub the dark goo behind his left ear.

"Honey," Marion said in a low voice, as Steve repeated the process with the right ear. "What's he doing?" Douglas stared at Steve, and shook his head.

"Oh! No way!" Jason said. "Are you serious? We're not some gullible hicks you know." Douglas and Marion stared at their son as Steve applied another black smear to his forehead.

"It's that crap they eat here," Jason explained. "Vegemite. It's supposed to scare off drop bears."

"Drop bears?" Marion asked. The alarm in her voice made Jason smirk.

"Yeah, I read about it on the net. Supposed to be some Aussie legend. Evil koala's that drop down on people unless they smear themselves in Vegemite. It's a bunch of bullshit-"

"Jason!"

"-they feed to stupid tourists."

Steve screwed the lid onto the jar and returned it to his pocket. He stuck the tip of each index finger inside his mouth.

Douglas turned back to Steve and pushed his glasses towards his furrowed brow. "Hey, pal. Just what do you think you're-"

A short, shrill, loud whistle came from Steve's mouth. It echoed around them several times before being absorbed by the bush.

"Douglas," Marion said through gritted teeth. She moved closer to Jason, placed her arm around him, and was avoided his attempts to shrug it off.

Douglas pushed his glasses up. "Okay, Steve. I can take a joke like the next guy, but this has gone far enough." Above him the trees shook as if stirred by an unfelt gust of wind. "I don't know what game you're playing here, but you're starting to scare my family." Several leaves fluttered in front of his face. Steve looked straight into Douglas' eyes, almost straight through them, then turned his head away.

"Okay, you know what? I think you better take us back-"

A dark, furry ball dropped onto Douglas' shoulders. He struck the ground, the air forced from his lungs with a whoompf. His glasses skittered as his nose crunched against the ground. He heard Marion scream behind him. A low, chuffing growl came from it. Teeth clamped onto the side of his face, sending intense, searing pain through his jaw and neck.

"Dad!" Jason froze as the thing chomped its way through the side of his father's head. A warm wetness dribbled down his leg. His fathers' limbs tapped out a spasmodic rhythm against the ground.

"Get away! Get AWAY!" Marion screamed, rooted to the spot. A black furred monster dropped from the tree line and clung to her. Claws like hot needles sank into her breast and shoulder; more dug into her midriff. She gaped at the horrid face inches away from her own. All its features were coal-black: fur, bulbous nose, and Mickey Mouse-like ears. Wicked rows of teeth, like obsidian spikes, burrowed into the soft flesh at her throat.

"Mom?" Jason cried, tears freely flowing. His mother gurgled as her legs buckled and she flopped to the ground. He grabbed a rock and hurled it. The creature yelped and whipped around. Threads of bloody saliva glistened from its jaws.

A branch cracked above him. He looked up and was engulfed by wiry fur. He screamed into a mouthful of it. White hot pain lanced through his shoulder. Mommy! There was a tugging at his back, a tearing. Something in his shoulder popped, and then there was nothing but darkness.

Steve kept his face averted, and his eyes closed, til the crunching, the ripping, and the lip-smacking died away. Uncontrollable shivers ran through him. When he dared to open his eyes his heart almost stopped. An ear lay on the toe of his boot, an ear-bud still nestled inside it, trailing its cord. A black furred head was close. A wet, snuffling sound emanated from it.

"Get out of it!" He kicked out, sending the ear flying and the creature scampering back. Its black face regarded him with cold malice. "Get out of it, ya mongrel bastard of a thing!" Its lips drew back in a snarl and its nostrils flared. Steve saw its body tense and touched his hand to his pocket. It sniffed, snatched the ear into its mouth, and shot up the nearest tree.

Steve let out a long sigh and walked over to the remains. It was mostly shredded clothing, interspersed with unidentifiable crimson globs. Here and there were more recognizable things: a finger, a couple of ribs, and what seemed to be part of the fella's scalp, judging by the hair colour. Other critters would take care of those bits.

He picked up a stick and poked through what hadn't been eaten. Other times he'd found rings, watches, or other bits of jewelry. This time the little buggers had either eaten everything or carried it off with them. And there was no way he was going after them to find it.

He found the lady's camera; a bit of blood spattered and a few scratches on the casing, but still in working order. Likewise the young lad's iPod. They'd clean up alright. Good enough for the pawn shop anyway. There was the fella's wallet: about two-hundred bucks (Australian, thank God), several credit cards, a few family pictures. Steve pocketed the cash, and wrapped the rest up with the remaining clothing and personal effects that wouldn't be worth selling.

Aware of the fading light, he turned upstream and made his way towards the waterfall. He stepped behind the watery curtain into the cave entrance, and tossed the bundle of items towards the back of it. The ochre images on the walls drew his gaze. Stick-like figures seemed to flee from dark blobs with claws and fangs.

Helluva way to make a living, he mused as he headed back towards the trail.

2. THE NEW GOD BY Mike Leon

The new god hangs high in the evening sky, his face stretched into a wide and wild grin with each tooth as big as the moon, if the moon were still there. The new god swallowed it when he first appeared. Now it is only his pale face which illuminates the night, his shadow which brings a shorter night in the middle of the day, and his awful bloodshot eyes which can be plainly seen following his subjects during the other times.

No one knows if the new god killed the old one, or simply supplanted him. All anyone knows for sure is that this new god is here, and nothing is like it was in the old days.

There are about fifty of them, down from a hundred in days gone by, crowded around the camp site. All of them are ragged and dirty, emaciated and torn, with scraps to cover them.

"It's a do-over," says Rick. The forty-something former accountant who stands nearly naked over a pillar of flame that sends acrid grey smoke into the sky. His only covering is a shredded piece of deer skin hanging over his crotch. Most of them don't have any clothes like before. "God was angry that so many forgot about him, so he made us start over, and now we can't ever forget him."

Kelly holds the baby closer to her breast so it doesn't have to look at the world-sized head hovering over them. This baby has no name. She named the last one, and the one before that, and she cried for too long when each of them was lost. She thinks if she doesn't name this one then maybe it will be okay. Maybe if she doesn't love this baby it won't be taken away. So she sits beside the fire and lets the baby suckle quietly, careful never to let the new god see her play with the baby, or caress the baby, or sing to the baby. When she thinks about those things, she has to remind herself she doesn't love the baby. She repeats it in her mind. I don't love the baby. I don't love the baby. It feels more convincing if she takes on a morose tone in her mind.

"It has a body down there," says Montel. He came from the dark only recently, and talks too much about things that may make the new god angry. "Somebody told me once that they went that way real far and they saw its shoulders."

"You mean South? They used to call it South," says one of the others.

"Yeah. South. If you take a boat, you'll see it." No one knows if Montel speaks honestly. His words seem crazy. No one travels in the dark now. It isn't like the old days. Other things own the night now. Better to build a fire and huddle together. The things don't like the light, but even still, some mornings the group wakes to find someone missing; lost when they walked away to squat in the woods, or taken silently in their sleep by some bold and exceedingly quiet entity.

"That's a load of shit," says Jennifer, a woman a few years older than Kelly. She has a young child with her, and used to have another, but it was carried off by something that looked like an enormous botfly. "Everybody knows the ocean turned to blood."

"What? You think boats won't float on blood?"

"It ain't the blood. It's the things in it."

Someone rustles over and nestles down next to Kelly as the others carry on. Without looking up from the baby, she already knows who it is.

"Hey, gimme a taste of that?" whispers David. He smells like sweat. He's filthy and sticky and missing half his teeth. All of them are dirty, but David is worse. He sniffs at her bare left breast like a scavenger.

"No. Don't touch me," she says. It is a familiar argument. The men still want the things men want, but there are only a few women left in the camp. There were more before, but many were eaten by creatures when they were too pregnant to run. Some just disappeared. The things seem to like them better.

"Come on. That thing we brought back tastes awful. Just give me a sip to wash it down." The creature the men killed today is like nothing they have seen before. It looks something like a starfish, with four of its pointed and tube-coated appendages acting as legs, while the fifth contained a face which was feline in appearance except for eight spider-like eyes. The men said it squealed like a rabbit when they stabbed it with the spears. Even on the spit, long after it was dead, it seemed to twitch a little, and the flesh burned off with a stinking purple smoke. It tasted worse than it smelled.

"Get away," Kelly says. She turns briskly away from him, folding her elbow over her chest.

"It's best you give me what I want. Best for that baby too." David's grubby grip closes on her shoulder.

"Don't," Kelly whimpers. She wonders if it would make a difference that it might be his baby. Probably not. She wonders what he would do if she just gave him the baby. Maybe he won't hurt it if he thinks she doesn't care. She must not care. I don't love the baby. I don't love the baby.

"Hey!" A rugged, violent, barking voice interrupts. It belongs to James. The tall man wedges himself between David and Kelly, forcing his feet between them. "She's mine. Get lost."

David slowly turns his eyes up at his adversary. "She ain't yours. You got the other one already."

James doesn't waste time discussing it. He lashes out with an angry fist against David's head. Then it begins. David grabs James' legs and tries to pick him up… James continues pummeling him in the top of the head... Kelly scurries away with the baby as the two of them topple into the dirt… Jennifer shouts "Get him!" but hardly anyone cares enough to stand up and watch.

The fight does not last long. James quickly overpowers David and strikes relentlessly at his face until it is a mess of swollen bruises and cracked bone. He does not stop there. He continues punching until David spits blood, and still does not stop. James' knuckles peel away like latex scratch-off against the cheekbones of David's face, as he hits him again and again. When he does finally let up, David has taken on the stillness of the ground beneath him, and will soon be a part of it.

James sits down nearby and places his hand on Kelly's thigh. "Are you alright?"

"Yes," Kelly says, as she looks at the baby, less to make sure it is alright and more to avoid looking at James.

Again, he wastes no time talking. The big man smells like death, and he hurts her, but he is better than David. The baby cries next to them. She tries to think about the baby, and how much better she will feel when it is back in her arms.

"Blech." James halts the violent motion of his hips to spit a mouthful of translucent white in the soil beside them. She hadn't even realized he was suckling on her. "It tastes like that thing."

"What?"

"That starfish thing. I don't know if it's you or if I've still got the taste in my mouth from before."

Kelly offers him an uncertain glance, then looks down to her breast and the fluid gathered around the nipple. She wipes it away and covers herself with the rotting bra that she has worn as long as she can remember. She closes her eyes as James continues with her, and the last of the evening light fades away.

In the morning, the baby is dead. Things that look like spiders dart from its mouth as one of the men cautiously grips the little body by a foot and flings it into the fire. Kelly cries well into day and curses the new god. She cannot tell if it is amused, or as apathetic as the old one.

3. PRAYER MASK by Mark Slade

Seven tents were spread out in an abandoned parking lot where a 7-11 used to be. These tents were not the rag-tag polyester, rubber, and plastic that I was used to seeing whenever Krieger and I investigated faith healers and backwoods mystics. No, these tents were anything but rag-tag, or weather beaten items. They were made of silk and were dynamic colors of blues and reds, instead of drab, pale whites. The tents belong to John Hammond ministries.

He was a charlatan that Krieger and I had busted many times before. The first time was in nineteen eighty-eight when he and his wife were almost rock star status during his New Age spiritual camp days, pretending to be a thousand year old warrior-spirit by the name of Argo from Atlantis, healing people with plastic crystals anyone could buy at a discount store. We busted Hammond on a segment of 20/20.

We thought he was through, and then he came back in the late nineties, claiming to have found one of the lost books of the BIBLE. His claim was that this particular item was lost in the deserts of Jordan and written by John the Baptist. Not only did that falsehood ruin his name when it was found out that the book was handcrafted by a man in Toronto, but also the credits of several scholars and archeologists. After that, we were sure he was gone for good, with the reports that he'd become nothing more than a drunkard and a hobo. We were wrong.

Now Hammond was back.

That seems to be the way it goes. No matter how many of these fakes and con-men Krieger and I expose, they find a way back into the limelight, emptying the pockets of the innocent, in search of a more enlightened life, or quick fixes to financial and/or health problems. The truth just seems like too much of a bitter pill for people to swallow. It saddens me, but it angers Krieger, who will go on talk shows to try to disprove Alien abductions when he knows it's a waste of time, and those talk show hosts just look at Krieger as a nuisance.

Krieger sent me to see Hammond and his show. Krieger is riddled with arthritis and pancreatic cancer. No one outside of his circle knows this.

One of Hammond's security men led me into a blue tent in the back. On this day, a Wednesday, his ministry was closed down. I had witnessed what he was able to do business wise on the weekend. So it made total sense his healing powers were not on display during the week. Inside the tent I found an office that would have rested nicely with any CEO of a major corporation. A white sofa on a red carpet and a desk made of mahogany, and a painting of himself in a gold frame hung on a makeshift wall. It's nice to know that Hammond had not given up on his decadent splurging expenditures.

"Ah, young Tommy Black!" He came from around his desk, offering his hand. I gave him the limpest handshake I could come up with. He looked at his hand in disgust. "I see the attitude hasn't changed." Hammond motioned for me to sit on the sofa. "Hey! I saw your mentalist act on Comedy Central! What a riot! Krieger taught you well."

"That was my act long before I met Krieger." I was already getting tired of being in his presence. Hammond had that effect on people. He reminded me of that one kid in your school; the mouthy one that everyone beat up or pulled pranks on.

He chuckled, then made some weird, twisted face. "He always liked his male assistants young, hasn't he?"

"I see the expense account has returned," I shot back.

Hammond scurried back behind his desk, pointed at the painting. "That, my friend, will never change."

"Ain't that the fucking truth," I said, slight piss and vinegar in my voice. "And I am not your friend."

"That's evident every time I see you and Carl Krieger." Hammond sat with a shit-eating smile on his face. "Where is the old fruit? He sends his flunky when I set up a meeting? My, things have changed."

"Carl is on business, Hammond." I told him. "What's this all about?"

"I have some….. Oh……this pains me," Hammond dramatically placed two fingers on the bridge of his nose and momentarily closed his eyes. "I have some rotten news for you, Tommy, baby." He sighed, and reopened those two black dots that had always creeped me out. "Here," Hammond pushed an envelope toward me. "Here is something you should see before I send it out as a press junket. Channel 24 is the local station I have become friendly with."

I leaned in and snatched the envelope from the desk.

It took me a few minutes to go over the three photographs of Krieger and another man at a restaurant table. One photo showed Krieger passing an envelope at the same time the man passed one. The next showed Krieger looking inside the envelope as the other man was looking in his envelope, a hundred dollar bill hanging out, stuck to the lip.

Also in the envelope Hammond had given me, were documents of fake I'D's Krieger fixed up for his life partner, Daniel Hoves. Hoves was a Ukrainian by birth, a one time member of a terrorist group that blew up certain parts of Moscow in the early 2000's.

I sighed, rubbed the bridge of my nose. "Why?" I asked.

"Why you ask," Hammond chuckled. "I cannot believe you ask: 'why'. Obvious, isn't it?"

"Krieger is an old man," my voice cracked a little. I found myself getting emotional. That hadn't happened since the passing of my sister fifteen years ago.

I always felt that Krieger's magic and the book he wrote on the subject, saved me from a very unhappy life on the street that would have concluded with a long stretch in prison. Growing up in the slums of West Philly, you had two ways out: dead at twenty-five, or jail at eighteen. I discovered Krieger's magic act on TV the same time I found a copy of his book in a trash can. I found out he was doing a show in Pittsburg, so I stole money from a drunken neighbor, hopped a greyhound and caught the show. I forced my way backstage and met Krieger. I never went back to West Philly, even for my sister or my mother's funeral.

I owe Krieger for changing my life.

"This…. sort of thing…. could ruin him," I told Hammond.

"What's your point?" he said coldly.

"What he has done, yes, not on the… up and up, I realize that."

Hammond snickered. "You-you, do?" He looked at me inquisitively.

"What he did, he did for love—," I tried to say, but Hammond cut me off.

"Spare me the Bryan Adams quote!" Hammond raised his voice. It thundered throughout the parking lot, which rattled me. "You are talking about a man who has in the past, tried to destroy not only me, but several colleagues. He is a menace. All we are trying to do is provide a service—"

"You steal from the unfortunate. You people pass along untruths and misinformation. You prey on the less informed."

"That is not our problem. And it is more… of an opinion that my colleagues and I do not share. We believe—"

"Wait," I stopped him, and let out a small chuckle. "Colleagues? There are others behind this," I stated.

"Of course. In order to fight a man like your hero, Carl Krieger, Sylvia, Gordon and myself, have pulled our resources together."

"A Psychic, a defrocked paranormal scientist, and a used car salesman who can heal. Very credible people. You realize," I tossed the envelope at him. "This stunt is highly illegal. Blackmail."

"No, wait." he said nervously. "Yes. A month ago, we planned to actually release this information to the media." Hammond sniffed the air, thought a second. "Something came up."

"The police came to your mind?" I said.

Hammond laughed and wagged his finger. "No, no. Something better. I admit to a little showmanship in the past…."

"What the hell are you talking about? That so-called showmanship, I saw it on Saturday and Sunday. Still up to your old tricks. Still using the palm of your hand and a sermon that you make up on the spot."

"For my regulars, yeah. They love it. For those who have…. deeper pockets….. I have something else. Tommy, listen to me. I have something that is going to prove to you I am the real deal."

He begged. I laughed at him. Hammond sighed. He shrugged and waved a hand at me. "Okay. I tried. You have passed judgement upon me. I'll never change your mind."

"Close to thirty years, John Hammond, thirty years of making fools out of those that trusted you with their health, money, and ease of mind, not to mention faith. You are scum and that is a stamp across your face as large as the sun." We locked eyes at that moment, and neither wavered for a few minutes until Hammond looked away, nodding as his gaze moved toward that unnerving portrait.

"Well, you've seen the evidence I have. On behalf of my colleagues, I will contact Channel 24 and—"

"That's it?" I interjected.

"That's what?" Hammond chuckled.

"That's all there is to this little meeting and you are going to ruin a man?"

"I offered you a solution." Hammond threw his hands up.

"It was blackmail." I said.

"No," Hammond chuckled. "I never counter offered. I never threatened. I offered a solution."

"What is this solution then?" I was slightly confused. What was his game?

"I just want you to witness a miracle," his voice trembled. "After the miracle, if you are convinced it is a miracle, I want you, Tommy, baby, to go back to Krieger and bring him here to witness another miracle. Then, possibly, he would endorse me."

I laughed again. "You are clinically insane. You know Krieger will never endorse you, faith healing or psychics, or unicorns for that matter...... you know that."

"Just.... witness this once. All I am asking is a little of your time. I will give you that file. Here..." Hammond nervously tossed the envelope to me. "Keep it. I swear. Just, keep it. And if I don't convince you...."

"What about Krieger?" I asked.

"I will bear that cross when it comes. What do you say?" Hammond batted his eyes rapidly, bit his lower lip. Why was he so keen to have me a part of his ludicrous plan? Something was definitely amiss. But he had me on the ropes. No way could I let him release such damning evidence against a man I owed my entire life to.

I threw my hands up in the air. "Okay. Show me what you've got."

Hammond acted like a child on Christmas morning; he bounced over to the tent flap, all the while still watching me. His hands fidgeted with the tent flap, finally it opened for him. He cleared his throat and a black man with a bulging neck peered inside.

"Go get her," he said to the man. "Tell Janie to help you and this time don't forget the hazmat cylinder." Hammond closed the flap, shuffled back over to his desk. "Just one moment and…….. it will start." He mumbled as he sat behind his desk.

During the wait, Hammond just stared at me and grinned. It was more than unsettling, it was bizarre.

A few minutes later, Hammond's second wife appeared through the flap, holding hands with a very tall woman in a white dress that hung down past her feet. Following them inside the tent was the body guard pushing a large yellow can on a flatbed cart. Two bright yellow signs were plastered on each side of can, stating the contents inside were toxic.

The body guard turned to Hammond, "We have a volunteer."

"Who?" Hammond barked at the body guard.

"The young woman that was found in the alley last week," the body guard said.

Hammond chuckled, waved a hand. "Bring her, by all means. Bring her."

I was feeling pinned in. Something bad was going to happen, I could feel it. I stood up and yelled, "I've changed my mind, I'm leaving!"

Hammond jumped from his swivel chair and ran from behind his desk, the chair still turning around and around, long after he'd left it. He placed his hands on my chest gingerly. "Whoa! No, you agreed to this."

"I don't care. Something….. something terrible is going down and I can feel it in my bones."

'You saying you're psychic?" he laughed, and saw that I wasn't amused. "Sorry. Just sit there and watch. Trust me." I gave him a look. He sighed. "You know what I mean. Don't make me beg."

"What the hell do you have that hazmat barrel for?" I asked, and wiped beads of sweat from my forehead.

"Okay. Okay." Hammond motioned for me to sit back down. I reluctantly did so. "I'll explain everything before we begin."

He started to open his mouth, but I interrupted him. "Just tell me what the Hazmat barrel is for. That's all."

"To store something highly dangerous…….." Hammond sighed and rolled his eyes. "Can I just show you? Okay, okay! The woman wearing the veil," Hammond pointed to the woman they ushered in. Strange, all she did was stand there, very rigid. She didn't speak a word. "She is wearing a Prayer Mask."

I let out a nervous, boisterous laugh, and in mere seconds I was almost in hysterics. Finally, I recaptured myself, and coughed a few times. "Prayer Masks have never been proven to be legitimate."

"I swear to you, Tommy. This…. just watch and it will… enlighten you. Mark my words."

"Who sold it to you?" I was interested only so I could tear his world down.

"No one. She… she is my Prayer Mask." Hammond took two steps and removed the veil.

Her face was not gruesome so much it was plain; droopy eyes, a still mouth that turned down, an upturned nose. The skin on her face looked as if someone had taken a cheese grater to it. That was not the disconcerting part. It was the fact that her face was absent of emotion. It reminded me of those death masks I had seen once hanging on the walls of a church in Madrid.

"I found her. Her mother brought her to me to heal. To give her back her soul. She didn't need a soul. Not from what I witnessed. I saw her… bring this sick old man back to life…. the man had died of a heart attack, he fell right at my feet. She gave him her Prayer Mask, and…….. he was alive again. Just as spry as if he was forty years younger.

"Look, Tommy. Throughout history, in every society, there has been mention of a healer, a special healer and her mask. The Mask of Lyvidous, a woman created especially by the Gods to cure disease and death in Greece. Someone who could not die. Someone who is thousands of years old…… that someone…. is in my possession."

"You're making this up, Hammond!" I screamed at him. "People sell Prayer Masks online all the time! Made of plastic, that's all. What, because you put on a piece of plastic and say a prayer, it's supposed to work? The shit doesn't work! God! You people start to believe your own lies!"

"Just…… watch, please." He nodded to his body guard.

The body guard waddled out of the tent, his small legs bent outwards from the amount of weight from the girth of his torso. He slowly waddled back in, leading a naked woman by the hand.

Her body was covered in sores that dripped a dark colored puss, leaving a trail behind her. She was in extreme pain, the hump on her back kept the woman bent forward. There was a small tattoo of a hummingbird just below that hump. She wept. Her sobs were more like whispers, and she shook every time a tear touched an open sore under her eyes.

I sat there quietly, panicking inside. Nothing good could come from this gruesome show. I looked up and saw Hammond watching me, leering at me. I moved my eyes slowly back to the proceedings so I couldn't see Hammond's little black eyes dance around in his head.

The Healer turned to the naked woman, reached out and took hold of her hands. "Let us pray," I heard a voice say, though the healer's lips never moved.

I rolled my eyes and looked over at Hammond. He had his head bowed, and his lips were moving, reciting a prayer. I saw Hammond's wife doing the same, her large curly blond hair had fallen over, covering her face completely. And I also saw Hammond's body guard with his head bowed, he too recited a prayer.

The Healer let go of the woman's hands. She touched her face and dug her thumb nails under the skin around cheek bone, starting first at the bottom, and then worked her way up to the temple of her forehead. Blood dripped on her hands as she removed the skin of her own face. She lifted the thin skin over her features and tore it at her hair line. Slightly, she winced. She was a bloody mess underneath, with sad, large black eyes, little holes for nostrils, and a slit for a mouth.

I gasped, and gripped the sofa cushions harder. I needed to get out of there, leave this Grand Guignol.

The Healer spoke again. "Raise her head to receive this gift."

The body guard roughly grabbed the woman's hair and jerked her head upward. She screamed out in horrific pain. The Healer then carefully placed the skin upon the woman's face, smoothing it over with her fingers. Steam rose from the Healer's fingers and the woman's countenance. The woman yelped at first; then she screamed, and I could hear a sizzling sound as a terrible stench filled the air. The skin was melding with the woman's face, burning into it, like it was being welded on.

In mere seconds, the woman stood upright. Her sores were gone. Her voice trembled as she simultaneously spoke and knelt at the Healer's feet. "Thank you!" she cried out. "Thank you!" She lowered her face to the Healer's bare feet and began kissing each toe.

I was overcome with emotion. I wept.

****

Krieger did not want to leave his house in San Diego and travel a thousand miles to a tent revival show.

"Tommy, you've somehow convinced me to bear witness to a fake miracle and taken me from the comfort of my home," Krieger said. "You could at least have bought me a coffee this morning."

We stood outside the seven tents of the John Hammond Ministries. I looked up to the sky. Dark clouds were rolling in, a strange mystique appearing on an already uncomfortable situation. I sighed and smiled at Krieger. "Carl, you know we promised Daniel that you would only drink mineral water."

"Bah!" Krieger said. "What does he know? I know what my body craves and it craves a dark roasted coffee!" Hammond's body guard opened the flap to the tent that was Hammond's office.

Krieger eyed the man with large hands and screwed up his face. "Why doesn't he build a real office like normal people?" Krieger reluctantly stepped inside. He stopped just short of the entrance and looked around.

I stepped in behind him, and saw everything was in place. The Healer to the left of Hammond, who sat at his desk. Hammond's wife sitting quietly on the sofa. The volunteer stood naked in front of everyone, a man with severe burns all over his body. The hazmat barrel lying down and the top missing. I thought this was very strange.

Hammond stood quickly and trotted toward Krieger, his hand extended outward. "I'm so glad you could make it, Carl." Hammond said excitedly. Krieger only eyed Hammond's hand, he did not accept the gesture or shake it. Hammond frowned and lowered his hand. "Yes. We are all so glad to see you. You have not changed."

"Nor have you! You are still a cretin who spends others' money," Krieger said.

"Ah!" Hammond laughed. "You didn't call me a liar or a fake! Tommy must have convinced you otherwise."

"No he did not! He blubbered about some feats of miraculous height. It was all very embarrassing to see a grown man weep about a magician's trick. I should know, Mr. Hammond. I've seen it all."

Hammond scoffed, shook his head. "Okay. Might as well get this train wreck on the move. Nothing is going to convince this man what we do is legit."

"On the contrary," Krieger gave a wary smile. He pointed his cane at the volunteer. "Please tell this gentleman his services will not be needed. I shall be the patient this woman shall attempt to heal!"

"No Carl," I whispered. "Don't you want to—"

"Shut up, boy!" Krieger screamed at me. My face turned red with embarrassment. "What do you say, Charlatan?" Krieger taunted Hammond.

Hammond had a shit-eating grin on his face. "I say you were reading my mind, old man."

"Then let's get on with it. If indeed this woman and her 'Prayer Mask' can heal, she will remove any cancerous cells in my body. In addition I should be able to walk upright and be pained no longer from arthritis."

"I agree," Hammond said. "Shall you lie down on the couch, Mr. Krieger?" Hammond's wife left the couch and I helped Krieger to it, easing him on his back. One by one, I positioned his legs carefully.

Just as the ceremony was beginning, I stepped away while the others watched the Healer remove her skin from her face. I noticed the hazmat barrel was empty. There were no skins or masks or anything inside. I was momentarily confused until it came to me. The Healer turned around just in time to place her skin upon Krieger's face. I noticed there was a butterfly tattoo under her shoulder blade. She had been the volunteer days before. She was now the Healer! Whoever wears the mask not only is healed, but becomes the healer.

"No!" I screamed as I trotted toward the Healer. Hammond's body guard caught me in a bear hug.

Just then, the flap of the tent opened, and Hammond's colleagues stepped inside: Sylvia the phony Psychic, Gordon the disgraced paranormal researcher. All of them stood there, smiling, enjoying their view of the Healer placing the skin on Krieger's face. Hammond shuffled over to their side, arms folded and his face beaming. All three of them smiled, reveling in their vengeance.

4. FOR THOSE ABOUT TO ROT, WE SALUTE YOU BY MARC SORONDO

"Why are you doing it?" Randall asked neither man in particular.

The three men sat in a triangular formation, all facing inward. There was a low hum that vibrated the walls of their enclosure—a box with no windows and metal hinges at the corners. A single doorway was open on one side; a bare fluorescent light bulb hung from the ceiling.

The man to Randall's left—the older guy, small and waif-thin, the air of an academic or archivist about him—spoke up first. "Cancer…" he said. He sighed. "I could do a few rounds of chemo, suffer for a few extra months, and die anyway, or I could do this. This way, my family is taken care of—the free housing, college tuition to the kids…" He waved his hand as if to suggest there was more. "The same incentives that tempted you, I'd imagine."

Randall nodded. He looked at the other man—the big guy with the gang tattoos and the scars on his right cheekbone.

The big guy grimaced. "Different kind of death sentence." He looked up at the ceiling. When he looked back at Randall, there were tears in his eyes. "I've got people worth dying for too…a little girl. If I die this way she'll have a life I never could give her alive. When the judge gave me this option, I jumped right on it."

Randall and the small man nodded at this.

There was a moment of quiet.

"And you?" the small man asked. "What's your story?"

Randall considered his reasons and decided they wouldn't understand. He'd already lied so much to so many people. He figured one more lie couldn't hurt. "Doctor said I've got three to six months. The headaches will just get worse and worse…soon I won't be able to function at all. Then I'll die. This way I don't leave my family with nothing but debt and memories of my deterioration."

The small man nodded and grunted slightly in understanding.

That had been the way to go, Randall thought. Lying was so often the easier route.

*****

The three men were strapped into their chairs. Three others in long, white doctor's coats prepared syringes.

Randall was struck by the certainty that these men were not actually doctors, that they were, like much else about this process—and life in general—a sham.

At the center of the triangle formed by the seated and restrained men, stood a man in a military uniform. It bared no resemblance to anything Randall had ever seen worn by any branch of the U.S. military. He had introduced himself when he'd entered, but Randall had not been paying attention then—instead he'd been studying the straps that held his arms and legs to the chair. They did not have buckles, at least not ones that Randall recognized. Two metal components had clicked together before the straps were pulled taught, but instead of a button or latch of some kind to release them, there was just a smooth, polished surface.

Randall wondered why such restraints were necessary.

*****

A bit later the three "doctors" had placed strange helmets on the volunteers. Metal at the back and some sort of clear glass or plastic over the face, they covered the entirety of the head except for the mouth. The orifice was completely exposed.

The military guy began to talk then, his voice muffled but echoing in Randall's helmet.

"Gentlemen, I do not know the circumstances that have brought you here. I know the statistics. I know that the odds are that you are either gravely ill or that you have made terrible mistakes. Frankly, I don't care what your reasons are."

Randall wondered if this guy gave the exact same spiel every time. It had the cadence—the smooth, lullaby rhythm—of a well-practiced speech, meant to soothe them even though the words seemed intended to inspire.

"Your reasons don't matter to me, because all that does matter is sacrifice. You are giving your all for your country. Because of you, your friends, your families, your entire communities will live on. Because of you, we can keep the forces of darkness at bay."

The sham doctors took up their syringes. They were full of a substance the color of fresh cream—real fresh cream, from cows that ate real grass: a shade or two off of white with a subtle yellowishness.

For no reason at all, Randall felt absolutely certain that the injections were nothing more than pus scraped from a seeping wound.

"I like to explain things to new recruits before we go through the process. You will each receive a single injection. Within minutes of this injection the process will begin. When we reach the drop zone, this enclosure will be released. Upon landing, pressure sensors at the underside of the enclosure will trigger the release of your shackles…"

Again, Randall wondered why they would bother. Why shackle in the first place? Why open them later? What was the point? They were volunteers.

Randall looked at the criminal and the infirmed man, but their eyes were glazed. Their minds were far away. He wondered if they imagined the short time that remained left in their lives or if they dwelled on a past that was lost to them now.

"There is some variation due to size, metabolism, immune response, and a number of other factors that will influence the length of time required for the process. That being said, within a few minutes of landing, you will all be fully weaponized."

Randall wondered what disease he was being given. So few bugs worked as a weapon. Biological warfare required a perfect balance of virulence and contagiousness with a long enough period of incubation to allow the disease to spread. Too lethal and the agent kills all of its hosts before it can spread very far; too weak and the infected can fight on and possibly even be treated.

The military man nodded to the sham doctors and they approached with their syringes full of pus. They stuck the three volunteers and pushed that sickness down into the flesh of their forearms.

Randall didn't feel anything at first.

The military man waited for the men in white coats to finish and leave.

"Good luck, gentlemen." He snapped a crisp salute to each of them. Then he left.

The door slammed shut. The sound of it echoed twice: once in the confines of the metal box; then again in the much smaller confines of Randall's helmet.

***

Randall wanted to ask the others how they felt. When he opened his mouth, however, it was so dry that he could only manage a low croak.

He felt ill now. The injection site was swollen and fiery red. It oozed a thin, dark discharge. Beneath his skin, the veins in his forearm had blackened, and that darkness was rising. His blood burned as it blackened, and his arm felt hot and ruined.

Moreover, they were falling now.

Shortly after the military man and the sham doctors had left there had been a violent tremor. Had they not been strapped to their seats, they would have been tossed around the confines of their enclosure.

An instant later, Randall's guts had floated up to the top of his abdominal cavity and stayed there. He would have thrown up if his stomach hadn't been empty.

It was empty though, and he was strapped down with that black fire spreading up his arm, so he could only close his eyes and taste bile in the back of his throat.

Then there was an abrupt change in speed, one that jarred the chamber and slammed Randall's sick guts back down to the bottom of his abdomen.

A parachute of some sort, he figured.

Sweat beaded up on Randall's forehead and dripped into his eyes. He blinked a few times, reflexively straining at his bonds in an attempt to wipe his brow. Then he realized the futility of it all and let the stinging drops fall into his eyes.

They were drifting toward the ground like a falling leaf as they succumbed to the unnamed infection. He figured that put him past the point of worry about a bit of saltwater in his eyes.

31

Randall looked through the foggy glass at the others. The big guy had a glossy sheen of sweat on his forehead. His eyes were closed, and his mouth was turned down in a grimace. Again and again, he opened and closed his right hand, the one spider-webbed by blackened veins.

The other guy, the one who'd already been sick, looked as though he'd died. His eyes were closed, and the tension had all run out of his face. The veins in his neck were swollen and black. If he was still breathing, each breath was so shallow as to be visually undetectable.

Randall wished he could call out to him, to rouse him if that were possible. He opened his mouth to try again, but he could only muster up another dry croak.

***

There was a dull thud that reverberated when they hit the ground. If felt like being inside a drum while someone bashed out a tune on it.

There was a loud click that echoed in the chamber and their helmets. With a long groan the metal walls of the container fell away. They slammed into the ground, sending up plumes of dust.

Then there was a series of small clicks before the straps that held them to their chairs popped open and the metal buckles fell away. Randall and the big guy rubbed at the abraded spots on their arms in reflex. The sick guy just sat there, hunched over in his chair.

Unsure what they were expected to do, Randall didn't move. He didn't see anyone. He couldn't hear well with the damned helmet on, but he didn't think he heard anything.

The big guy stood and stretched like a man just woken from sleep. He rolled his shoulder once, then again.

Randall understood because he felt it too. As the blackness spread up his veins, his arm felt hot and swollen. That faded quickly, however, and left his joints feeling stiff and numb. Now his chest burned with black fire, and he figured he wouldn't survive to feel it go numb.

Randall looked over at the other man, the guy who'd been dying before he'd had that shit injected into him. He was pale and his mouth hung open. In the light of the bare bulb, Randall hadn't been sure, but seeing the guy by the light of the sun, it was clear there'd be no rousing him.

Randall grabbed the arms of his chair, unsure if he'd be able to stand without the extra support. He started to lean forward, to let some of his weight shift to his arms.

The gunshots came from behind him. They were tinny, somehow both muffled and echoed at the same time by the helmet.

Randall fell back and tried to make himself small, to hide behind the back of his seat.

The first shot ricocheted off the big guy's helmet. The next several struck him in the abdomen.

The big guy fell back. His butt missed his seat and he fell to the ground, slumped back with his head against the chair. His wounds oozed blood that looked too thick. His eyes remained open, but they were glazed over and unfocused. He looked like a doll discarded by a child who'd suddenly realized they'd outgrown it.

Randall pressed himself back against the seat, as if he could force himself into it and hide there. He felt the thump of impacts against the back of the seat, but none of the bullets made it through to him.

Though the big guy lay there, obviously dead, they kept shooting his body. The other guy, already lifeless before they'd hit the ground, shook with each new impact. Their bodies were riddled with bullets, trembling with each new impact. The occasional shot that stuck their helmets merely bounced off.

Randall didn't understand his own fear. He'd signed up to die. He'd been clear about that from the start, but now…

The small guy's eyes opened. There was life in them again—focus and purpose. He stood, unfazed as bullets slammed into old wounds in his chest, and then walked toward the shooters.

He didn't look at Randall as he passed. His lips were pulled back, like an angry dog baring its teeth, and his hands were bent into claws.

He wasn't dead…not in any sense of the word that Randall knew. He lived on, distorted nearly out of recognition but undying.

The big guy's eyes opened. He sat up and then began to stand. A well-placed shot to the sternum unbalanced him, knocking him back onto his butt. The shot was a meaningless gesture, however, as the big guy began to rise to his feet again as soon as he'd hit the ground.

Randall watched the guy take several shots to the abdomen as he rose to his full, massive height. Multiple shots ricocheted off the clear dome of his helmet and one smashed through the front of his chin, spraying blood, bone, and fragmented teeth across his chest.

A sound vibrated in Randall's helmet, faint at first and then rising to a roar. He looked up as the big guy, his bisected jaw hanging open, strode past. There were two planes in the distance, approaching from the west. While still far away, one plane and then the next released its cargo: a large metal box that fell for a beat before a tremendous parachute opened and slowed its progression.

He watched those two boxes drift toward the ground and realized that he'd assumed his trio of human weapons had been alone; now he understood that he was merely a single bullet in a large-scale assault.

A Molotov cocktail sailed past Randall's seat and exploded into a wet mess of fire that covered the chair the big guy had vacated and pooled at the floor beneath.

The heat off the fire exacerbated the internal blaze that had spread across Randall's chest. He wondered, if he threw himself into those flames, if he would die…really die. He couldn't bear the thought of lumbering into gunfire, mindlessly pursuing anyone that caught his eye. He couldn't let his body go on forever. He'd signed up to die and that's what he intended to do.

He threw himself down into the middle of the flaming puddle, careful not to smother the blaze.

The heat was like being skinned alive. Randall wailed in spite of his dry throat and fought the instinctual urge to roll away.

Bullets slammed into his back, but these were afterthoughts, failing to compete with the consuming fire for his attention.

Then the pain faded. He felt nothing, and he welcomed oblivion.

***

Randall stood, little tongues of flame still clinging unnoticed to his clothes here and there. He turned and took several rounds of gunfire to the chest, unperturbed.

He strode toward the shooters, burning and bleeding and undying.

5. MOTHER'S MILK BY JAMES PRATT

"Do you realize what you're holding?" Currie asked in a smooth voice.

Though the left side of his face drooped and his left arm had been rendered useless as the result of a recent stroke, his speech remained intact. Even with a newly acquired limp and his arm bundled up in a sling, Currie exuded the same vitality which, in the old days, had seemed such a contradiction to his gaunt appearance. If anything, he seemed even more vigorous than before.

Lei studied the thin-necked bottle his old college friend had just handed him. Made of a rough-edged green glass and stoppered with a wooden cork, it was filled with a dark, sluggish liquid. While the unlabeled bottle bore an unmistakable aura of age about it, its most remarkable feature was its absolute lack of remarkability.

"A bottle?" Lei ventured, studiously ignoring Currie's facial tics and the way his friend's left arm twitched in its sling.

"Yes, you're holding a bottle. Very astute. Do you know what's in the bottle?"

Lei glanced at the shelves of bottles all around them. "Considering we're standing in a wine cellar, I'm going to go out on a limb and guess wine."

"Quite the detective," Currie said, smiling. "You know, I always liked your sense of humor."

Lei grinned. "Lacking good looks and athletic prowess, I had to fall back on something."

"The rest of the group somehow came to the conclusion you're a bit of an ass," Currie continued, "but I think you're funny. You've always been able to make me laugh."

Lei's smile faltered a bit. "Um … thanks. Do they really think I'm an ass?"

"Well …" Currie paused to study his glass, the contents of which were a deep, rich purple bordering on black, before answering. "Didn't you wonder why you weren't invited to any gatherings recently?"

Lei frowned. "I … didn't realize there had been any gatherings recently."

"Oh, yes," Currie replied, nodding. "Just last week, Heinz had a bunch of us over so he could show off his latest acquisition."

"Really? What was it?"

"An incredibly well-preserved edition of the1846, November issue of Godey's Lady's Book."

Lei's eyes narrowed. "Since when did Heinz collect old magazines?"

"The edition contains the first publication of Edgar Allen Poe's short story, "The Cask of Amontillado," Currie explained.

"Oh. I … would've liked to have seen that."

Currie chuckled. "Heinz and his books. He treats them better than his own family. Still, I can't help but wonder if he's actually read any of them. He could tell you the age and value of any item in his collection, but I can't recall a single instance when he's mentioned plot, theme, or character."

Lei considered for a moment. "I … suppose you're right. He probably doesn't know his Dickens from his Dostoevsky."

"If it's any consolation, the whole thing was boring as hell," Currie confided. "Heinz will talk about that collection of his for hours, if you give him half a chance. I didn't get away till one in the morning."

"Did Heinz say why I wasn't invited?"

Currie shook his head. "The only time you came up was when Fleishmann made a crack about your driving."

"My driving?"

"There's a certain stereotype regarding people of Asian descent and poor driving skills."

"Oh. Fleishmann said that?"

Currie nodded. "I'm afraid so. The comment was in rather poor taste, even for Fleishmann."

"I … I always got along well with Fleishmann. At least I thought I did."

"Fleishmann is an odd duck. Did you know he masturbates into his wife's shoes?"

"I … didn't. And I didn't realize I was rubbing everyone the wrong way."

"It's not your fault," Currie said before taking another sip. "They take themselves too seriously. One of the dangers of a privileged upbringing is coming to the conclusion one's shit doesn't stink."

Lei flashed a faint smile. "Not only that, they probably save and catalogue everything. Jars and jars of pretentious poo. They probably even keep diaries describing smell and consistency. You know, for posterity."

"Hah!" Currie laughed, nearly spilling his drink. "You're probably right. I wouldn't be surprised if Fleishmann studied every one of his bowel movements underneath a microscope."

Lei laughed in return. "Well, at least you possess a sense of humor, Currie."

"What I have is a sense of perspective. I've always been curious about the things which were forbidden to me. That's why I traveled after college, and not to the whitewashed vacation spots I was dragged to in my youth. Slums, ghettos, anywhere misery and danger might be found."

"Places with character," Lei offered.

"Yes, exactly!" Currie said, nodding approvingly. "You always understood, Lei. None of the others got me, but you always understood."

"So what did you see in these places?"

"Many things. Among them, I witnessed how the other half lives."

"And?"

"Not very pleasantly, as it turns out. My experiences have given me certain … insights."

"Into what?"

The right corner of Currie's mouth curled upward the slightest bit. "The human condition, I suppose."

"Then maybe you could give me a little insight. It's not like I behaved worse than the rest of them. Frankly, I always thought I was one of the nicer ones. I mean, look at Quigley. Remember how we always cringed at the way he treated … well, anyone who wasn't one of us? Remember the time he had that poor waitress in tears?"

"Quigley is a pathetic excuse for a human being. Look, don't lose any sleep over it. You're worth more than the lot of them."

"I … I just don't understand …"

"You're new money," Currie explained. "That's even worse than being poor. It means they aren't obligated to rebrand any of your perceived character flaws as eccentricities, as they are with each other."

Lei grunted in acknowledgement. "Right. Rich people are eccentric while poor people are assholes. Well, poor people and new money."

"Now you understand."

Lei sighed. "I thought they were my friends."

"Why, because you palled around with them in college? Prestigious university or not, they were having an adventure as far as they were concerned. Living dangerously, mingling with the rabble, and all that. You were one of the common folk they magnanimously let into their circle. Now those days are over, they've returned to the safety of their mansions and gated communities."

"I even did their homework for them," Lei muttered. "Entitled bunch of bastards."

"I couldn't agree more," Currie said, raising his glass as if in toast then taking a sip.

"I … I just …"

"Yes?" Currie prompted.

"My college days are some of my fondest memories. Now they've been …"

"Tainted?" Currie suggested.

"Right. Knowing my so-called friends thought so little of me …"

"Cheapens the memories?" Currie offered.

Lei sighed. "Right. That."

"Who cares what they think?" Currie asked, waving a dismissive hand. "They're idiots, and we've outgrown them."

"I … suppose," Lei conceded, watching the liquid in Currie's glass swish back and forth but remain safely ensconced.

"Scratch that," Currie amended. "They're worse than idiots. They're boring."

"That's impressive," Lei observed.

"What's impressive?"

"The way you're sloshing your glass around without spilling a single drop."

"God forbid a drop is wasted. It's a very special vintage. Absolutely life-changing, some would say."

"If you say so. I've never been much of a wine connoisseur. That's more of an old money thing."

"You don't have to be to enjoy it. All you need to do is drink. That's why I invited you over. Not to taint your memories, but to share this most special vintage with my one true, genuine friend."

"That's kind of you to say."

"Think nothing of it," Currie said, handing Lei an old-fashioned corkscrew. "Now pop open the bottle and pour yourself a glass. It's of the same vintage as what I'm drinking now."

"Is the vintage rare?"

"Extremely rare. As far as I know, that bottle is the last one in existence." Currie raised his glass. "I'm about to finish off its twin. Go ahead and pour yourself a glass so we can drink together."

"The last one … Are you sure?"

"Wine is for drinking," Currie insisted. "Fools who hoard it like gold are just as bad as Heinz and his unread books."

Lei did as Currie instructed. The bottle's contents came out thick, almost syrupy, and a curious aroma, both sugary and reminiscent of ammonia, filled the air. "That's a … unique smell. Sort of like—"

"You're stalling" Currie interrupted. "Take a drink."

"If this is the last—"

"It'll put hair on your chest," Currie said with a wink.

"Are you absolutely certain?"

Curried tapped Lei's glass with his own. "I insist."

"Well, if you insist." Lei took a sip. "The taste is … sweet, but … bitter."

"Bittersweet?"

"Right, bittersweet." Lei took another sip. "And the consistency is unique. Does this particular wine have a name?"

"Yes, one as unusual as it is apt. It's called Mother's Milk."

"That is an unusual name. Where did you get the bottles?"

"They were gifts from a most interesting people. Remember what I told you about my travels?"

"That you went to places with character?"

Currie laughed. "Yes, exactly. But I visited more than just ghettos and slums. My curiosity runs far deeper than any of you ever suspected. Nothing fascinates me more than the sheer age of our world, and of all the unknown things that transpired in those vast epochs of time. Even going back to its most distant ancestor, human existence encompasses only the tiniest fraction of the total sum of Earth's history. To satisfy my curiosity, I sought out the lost places where forbidden secrets are kept and forgotten things linger on. In the course of my travels I came across a remarkable culture. Have you ever heard of the Tcho-Tcho?"

Lei shook his head.

"I'm not surprised. Few people have. The Tcho-Tcho are an obscure stone-age tribe, with a society that's remained virtually unchanged for thousands of years. They're very aggressive and hostile toward outsiders, and encounters with them tend to go rather badly. It's probably no coincidence cannibalism plays a large part in their rituals. They're a most fascinating race."

"They … do sound … fascinating," Lei said, swaying a bit.

"So of course, I had to seek them out," Currie continued. "Having studied them in advance, I realized peaceful contact is possible if they're approached in the right way. The tests they put me through were horrific, but I was determined to see things through to the end. That was the only way they would show me their secrets, and they possess many secrets to tell. They're far from the primitive cannibals they've been made out to be."

"No?" Lei asked, his speech starting to slur.

"Far from it. They're the caretakers of knowledge long lost to the modern world. They know where the Old Ones first came through, and where they'll come through again when the stars are right."

"Where the who did what?"

"The Old Ones. A pantheon of prehistoric gods worshipped by the Tcho-Tcho. They are the chosen of the Old Ones, making them a holy race. Humanity's origins are far less auspicious, and so their contempt for us is understandable. Do you know what the Tcho-Tcho call us? All outsiders, I mean?"

Lei's vision was starting to blur. "I don't feel so good."

"Tenak el'kuresh. The name means 'born of dust'. They view humanity as a separate species, and they're absolutely correct. We aren't related to the Tcho-Tcho, genetically or otherwise. We come from a lesser stock, you see."

"What? What are you talking about?"

"The Tcho-Tcho taught me the secret history of the world. I know where they came from, and where we came from. And I know how it's all going to end."

Lei reached out to lean on a nearby shelf. "How … what's … going to end?"

"The world. And in fire and blood, by the way. That's how it's all going to end."

"I …do you hear that?"

Currie leaned forward. "Hear what? What do you hear?"

"Voices. Sounds like whispering voices."

"Ah. It's kicking in."

"What's kicking …?" Lei stumbled back a step. "Did you drug me?"

"No," Currie replied, reaching out to steady his friend. "You're experiencing what I experienced when the Tcho-Tcho performed the final ritual. Consider yourself lucky I didn't make you go through what I did, to prove myself worthy to drink of the sacred milk."

"Sacred milk? What does that mean?" Lei's voice trailed off then his eyes widened in horror. "Oh God!"

"You're seeing something, aren't you?" Currie asked.

"I … I …"

"What do you see?"

"I … I can't …"

"Tell me what you see!" Currie demanded.

"I … a frozen plain, ice and snow as far as the eye can see. There are … things moving across the plain, flopping and oozing like giant, plastic blobs. They … they don't look real, but … they're alive. Not like us, but … in another way. In the way a virus is alive. And they're hungry. I can feel their hunger. Not just for food, but for … thoughts … memories. Now they're stopping. They …" Lei's voice dropped to a whisper. "They see me. They don't have eyes, but they see me. THEY SEE ME!"

Currie slapped Lei across the face. "Get a hold of yourself, man!"

Lei's eyes rolled back then focused on Currie. "You did drug me! You drugged me and I was hallucinating!"

"I didn't drug you, and you weren't hallucinating," Currie said, shaking his head. "You were experiencing the link."

"The link? What …?" Lei paused for a moment, head cocked to one side. "The voices, they're … getting louder."

Currie smiled. "Good. That means the connection is getting stronger. Not everyone is receptive."

"Receptive to what? What are you talking about?"

"The voice you're hearing belongs to Mother."

"Mother? Whose mother?"

"The Tcho-Tcho religion is expansive. Above the Old Ones sit an even greater pantheon of gods. There are three who together form a sort of holy trinity; a creator god, mindless yet all-powerful, an omnipresent god who is one with space and time, and a … sort of mother goddess."

"Mother?" Lei repeated.

"In her capacity is the source of all life. The Tcho-Tcho worship one of her many avatars, the hive-queen of a wonderfully disturbing protean race. The Tcho-Tcho call her Mother in the Black Abyss because she's said to reside in a cavern deep beneath the earth." Currie leaned in close. "Do you want to know a secret?"

Currie's breath brushed his neck. "What?"

"She's real."

"Nonsense," Lei slurred.

"I've seen her with my own two eyes," Currie insisted. "We've been drinking nothing less than her own sacred excretions, by the way. What nourished her children now nourishes us."

"Mother's Milk," Lei muttered.

"It's changing us," Currie said, touching the saggy part of his face. His fingers left a perfect indentation as if they had been pressed into soft putty. "Eventually we'll become like them. Not exactly like them, but something close."

"Like who?"

"Mother's children, made in her own image," Currie explained. "Those boneless shapes you saw on that snowy plain. They're immortal. They've been here for millions of years, watching and waiting for their time to come."

"I … I don't …"

"Remember what I said about her being a hive-queen? Hive-queen, hive-mind. Those 'visions' you're seeing are actually telepathically accessed memories. What one knows, all know."

"I …" Lei flinched.

"What? What is it?"

"The scene is changing. I see a great war, between those oozing things and … beasts? Plants?"

"Do they have barrel-shaped bodies topped with starfish-like growths?"

Gritting his teeth, Lei nodded.

"Then they're a bit of both. What you're seeing are the Masters. They came down from the stars in a pre-Triassic age to colonize this world. Using Mother's spawn as slaves, they built great cities at the poles, which were subtropical in those days, and beneath the primordial seas. But the Masters' enemies made a pact with Mother; with their help, her children cast off their shackles and laid their Masters' cities to ruin."

"The Masters …" Lei gasped. "They're using weapons like something out of a sci-fi movie."

"They were an incredibly advanced race, very wise and powerful. But they were only mortal."

"My head…feels like…it's going to burst. Too much. This is all too much."

"You'll learn to tune it out," Currie said. "Don't worry. I'll be with you all the way."

"You're a bastard, Currie," Lei said, tears streaming down his cheeks. "I thought you were my friend."

"I understand what you're feeling," Currie assured him, "but you're wrong. At first, I too, thought I'd been betrayed. But now I realize what a great honor the Tcho-Tcho bestowed upon me."

"Why did you do this to me?"

"To save you."

"Save me? Save me from what?"

"When the Old Ones came through, they assumed dominion over the universe and fought terrible wars against one another. Some of those wars were the extinction events which devastated the prehistoric world, wiping away all evidence of nonhuman intelligent life. In their hubris, the Old Ones eventually turned against their own masters and were thrown down. Ages hence, this would allow for humanity's ascension. But Mother in the Black Abyss has seen far into the future. When the stars are right, the Old Ones will return and clear off the Earth."

"Sounds like you're talking about a divine apocalypse," Lei murmured. "I thought you were a devout materialist."

"I still am," Currie said, reaching for Lei's shoulder. "Seeing is believing."

Lei cried out as the ceiling vanished, revealing… stars screaming with human mouths as dim shapes fought in the heavens and where the pus-yellow blood of those awful shapes struck the burning earth like doomsday comets, maggoty abominations rose up to feast on the withered flesh and tortured souls of those unfortunate enough to have survived the night when the skies opened up and the Old Ones came home—

"Jesus!" Lei screamed, pushing Currie's hand away. "What was that?"

"A glimpse of things yet to come. But we'll survive, in one form or another, we and the rest of the chosen."

"Why would you want to survive, if it meant living beneath such dreadful masters, and under such hellish conditions?"

"Because I am an avowed materialist, remember? It's not hell I fear, but the idea of consciousness winking out like a snuffed candle at the moment of physical death. For me, hell is the prospect of non-existence."

"But why me? Why drag me into this? I thought I was your friend."

"Of course you're my friend. That's why you're here."

"Did you do this because of that one night? That was a one-time thing. I barely remember it. I'm not even attracted to—"

"No, nothing like that. No offense, Lei, but you're not my type. I was drunk too, remember? But I will need someone to keep me company in the coming darkness. I want you to be my companion in immortality because we will be, as you say, living under such hellish conditions. There won't be much joy or pleasure, so I'll settle for the company of someone who can make me laugh."

"That's it?" Lei asked, the flesh on his face starting to sag. "You want to spend eternity with me because I make you laugh?"

"What I've done is no small thing, Lei. I've saved you from a horrible death, and from the nothingness that follows. You're going to live forever, and see things you never could have imagined."

"Thanks for saving me. Just one question."

"Yes?" Currie asked.

"Who's going to save me from you?"

6. HELL TRAIN BY REBECCA FUNG

They handed down their verdict. The ticket office on Platform Two. The Hell Train.

They ignored my screams and two heavies grabbed me, kicking and wailing, and threw me down the stairway, to the platform. The air was heavy with wet heat and I was beginning to sweat already. Anxiety or was I just getting nearer to the flames? Probably a bit of both.

I was highly aware that They were probably watching. There was no escape.

There was, for one thing, no practical room for escape. The whole place was packed like sardines. I had one fleeting glance at the other platform, the Heaven Train, with its spaciousness and people walking about with orderly grace before I was pushed into my crowd and forced along toward the Ticket Office. The beasts around me were many. A tall woman who had her ticket already stepped back from the office and trod on my foot. "Excuse me!" I said sarcastically, but it was wasted on her.

This was a dark sea of filth, for only the filth were ordered to Hell. I didn't belong here, I told myself. Bad body odor, people spitting and the unruly swearing mob behind me, pushing, pushing, pushing. I was from a finer set of people. I was a finer person. Then one little mistake in my Earth life …

And They, the Almighty They, had dictated the Hell Train for me. Platform Two.

An elbow in the nose, someone's shoulder hitting my jaw, someone from behind smacking my head.

"Do you mind? I can't go any faster," I called out, to everyone and no one.

A glob of spit greeted me in the face and I shut up. I was squashed there so tight I couldn't even raise my arms to wipe it away. There I stood, with a big one trickling down my forehead and some of it dripping in my right eye. Anything had to be better than this bloody queue. Even the Hell Train itself. Or maybe, if I could only get to that Heaven Train. Those people were my sort. I could easily picture myself in a comfy carriage with someone serving me fine wine and strawberries and girls in silk swishing about offering to play me a ditty on their harp … or some other favor.

That is what the Heaven Train would be like. And I needed, with every particle of my soul, to be there.

There had to be a way out of this horror. I was smarter, better than these people, I told myself. Just think. They were watching me, but once I got my ticket, their attention would surely focus elsewhere. So once I got my ticket, I needed to make a run for it. I needed to find my way to the Heaven Train.

Easier said than done. I grimaced as the sound of loud flatulence rang out, low and hot and right in front of me. The fumes rose up and filled my nostrils. Oh god, I couldn't take this much more.

I thought quickly. After I bought my ticket, if I pushed myself out of the crowd and weaved myself backwards, rather incongruously, surely I could weave myself out to the side and away from this mob … perhaps back to where I'd come in and surely then I'd find my way to the Heaven Train? It had been to the side of the stairs – if I could just get back to the stairs somehow I'd find my way there.

That's what I'd do.

Some dullard at the office handed me a grimy ticket with a stamp on it. Then I fought my way back out of the ticket area. This was harder than I had thought. I couldn't see where the heck I was going, there were far too many people, trying to push me back where I'd come from. Their elbows, their waving arms, and their spit smacked me in the face. Someone threw some sauce that smelled of old cheese, and hit me in the eye. I could see even less of where I was going. Push on, I told myself. Push on and keep on. And you'll be on the Heaven Train soon enough. Ignore all those shoves and fingers in your face and in your ear and up your nose and you keep going. That's only for a few seconds. This is about eternity.

I mostly shut my eyes to protect them from being poked out by the relentless crowd surging in the opposite direction, and continued pushing forwards.

Someone said, "You're here dearie. Now hop on."

I opened my eyes and a little old wrinkled lady grinned up at me, showing her blackened teeth. "Platform Two dear. I checked your ticket and made sure you went the right way. You looked like you were almost going in the wrong direction for a while there! Didn't anyone ever tell you to watch where you're going – properly?"

No! Where were the stairs? Where was the Heaven Train?

Her hand tightened on my arm. She was surprisingly strong for a little lady and her nails were sharp.

"This is your train, dearie. Now get on."

I opened my mouth and she repeated, "Get on."

I could smell blood. A little trickle of liquid was running down my arm. God her grip was tight.

"I'll get on," I whispered.

She marched me onto the train and only released me when I stepped inside the carriage. Then she was gone and the doors clanged shut, and I had those little red indentations as a reminder of her.

It was as crowded as the platform and all the seats were taken. Why, oh why, I thought, do people on trains have to be so smelly, sweaty and obese? There seems to be some sort of rule that when you're on a train you'll be sandwiched between two huge guys, and as the train rattled on we were thrown this way and that, or should I say, from one perspiring piece of flab to another.

There's still a chance, I thought. When I got on here the train was mostly full. This isn't the only station and there's bound to be plenty more stations before we get to Hell. The next station … I'll try getting out at the next station. I just need to keep my eyes open. Avoid train patrollers.

A scorching pain on my arm. I tried to jump away, but between the two fatsos surrounding me, it wasn't easy. I turned a little and saw some drongo with a cigarette dangling right next to me.

"You brainless idiot! Keep that thing away from me! That bloody hurt!" I wailed, but he showed no signs of comprehension and exhaled a cloud of smog right in my face. A loud cackle in my ear. I whirled around and saw a large redhead now near me, throwing back her hair, that annoying noise, over and over … and that greasy set of curls dangling in my face. It smelled foul and now I could see the little white things clinging to her hair. A black creature was walking up one strand, and another.

Nits! Her dirty head was teeming with lice.

I tried to lean away from the lice-ridden tangle, but when I leaned backwards, I got a sharp reminder of the careless smoke factory behind me. Ow! A scorch in my back. I instinctively jumped forward and my whole face slammed into that hairy nest of insects. And lice can jump.

Oh no.

I could feel the flesh of the fat guys oppressing closer around me. What little air that I had to breathe was growing hotter and hotter. I pushed my way out from the vermin and forced my head up to gasp a bit of smoggy air, before a rattle of the train pushed me back down again. A bunch of teenagers were on their mobiles making some inane conversation – or monologue, as far as I could tell – punctuated by piercing loud shrieks. How long could I go on like this?

The next stop couldn't come fast enough. I didn't care if there were fifty old crones waiting for me with their claws out, I would fight through the lot of them. I would scream and beg and kick my way to the Heaven Train.

I would endure anything. It seemed I was going to have to. Because over and over the train seemed to swerve and bump, throwing me to the ground which was covered in litter, into someone who gave me a good hit or into some pungent sweaty mass of flesh. The smoker seemed to have an endless supply of lights to scorch me with or to cover me in ash, and now I could feel a creepy crawly marching up my nostril, but I was too busy scratching a couple off the top of my head to immediately swipe at it.

"How much longer," I gasped weakly. I don't know how many times I'd been thrown between people, how many times I'd been burnt or how many lice had crawled over my eyes and into my mouth and nose. "Anyone! When's the next station?"

"No next station," said the woman. Then she laughed.

I had gotten on the last stop before Hell? How unlucky could I be?

"No," I protested weakly. "It can't be. There must be … it must be … there must be another …"

But as I looked around at the others around me, the thin face of the smoker, the wobbling jelly faces, the pitying countenances of the screamers on their mobile phones; I knew it was true. There were no more stations. I was the fool. I wasn't getting off. I would not be making a dash for it.

I hated this bloody train ride. Anything had to be better, even the Devil himself. "When do we finally get there? When do we get to hell? When is the Hell Station coming up?" I yelled.

"No more stations," said the woman. Her eyes widened and those two black dots pierced right through me.

I felt something wet trickle from my pants as she spoke and my legs began to tremble. The train hit another bump and I was thrown from another fatty's sweaty stomach and onto the floor, into my pool of urine.

"This is Hell Train. It keeps on going." The redhead laughed again.

7. THERE IS NO GOD by Peter Adam Salomon

My name is John. I live at 447 Fourteenth Street with my parents and one sister, Jane. My dad works at the library. My mom stays home. My favorite team is the Yankees, of course.

My name is John. I am in the fourth grade at Wilson Elementary in Oak Grove, Tennessee.

My name is John. I live at 447 Fourteenth Street with my parents and my older sister, Jane. My younger sister died of leukemia last year.

My name is John.

There is no god but God. Allahu Akbar.

They'd too many kids, my parents. Electricity in the ghettoes of Johannesburg was spotty on the good days, on bad nothing worked except a hand-cranked radio producing static that sometimes broke into song. Nothing to do but suffer the heat until my turn to be sold.

My name has been John for almost a year now. It was Pierre for the job in Paris, Natalia in Chechnya but that was only for a week. Hard enough to be John or Pierre, being female requires far too much work.

The doctors were rude, busy with their own guards watching every moment of their lives. All the boys tried to help, keeping the mosquito nets patched or the floors swept, hoping to be a guard someday and boss around the doctors. All as dark as me or darker, except when we'd be white or striped or whatever was needed to be the martyr of the week.

Some returned. Most didn't. It wasn't a job for returning. Most that did were carried in, every once in a while they even breathed. Not often.

Didn't matter. The mission either called for death or didn't. The pay was good, better for the former, of course. A little of the money went to our parents, some to us, most to men in black masks with white letters and big guns.

Every boy had the same dream: martyr.

Get a street or, if the job was big enough, a school, named after them in Gaza, Raqqa, or Tehran.

Not that we had names.

All the boys, the same dream. Even the girls were boys. One more surgery and they were boy enough for the job. Unless they thought a girl would be more invisible, then another surgery heading the other way.

The new methods were a vast improvement over the old. Before the chemicals there was Graft Day. They'd be skinned alive, the doctors said, to keep the flesh supple enough to slide over me, sewed up the back and sides until I was white, seeing out of my mask. Alive so the graft would 'take.'

Of course, the stitches had to dig deeply into my own skin, muscles, bones. So the new flesh would work enough to pass. My own immune system, fighting against the grafted flesh as drugs keep us from tearing our new skin off.

That was the old method. The new hurt just as much. In the beginning they tried to transplant the eyes along with the skin but it never worked quite right. We needed to see, to know where to place the bombs. Besides, the blind were as noticeable as the black. Only healthy white boys blessed with invisibility enough to do the job right every time.

All that white skin difficult to get used to at first. There's no difference really, white/black, it's a color, not a person. But white it is, for most jobs. Though striped was a side effect of the new process, the chemicals raw and untested until they learned enough to control it. To calibrate properly.

Now, I'd been dyed so many times my skin retained a trace of white, like an anti-shadow. The reverse of darkness. Not striped, stripes were for parties, where someone too drunk on oil wealth wanted something different and ordered up zebra striped little girls for entertainment.

They never returned.

I was fading, my color melting away. Unless I focused, it was hard to remember I wasn't white. It was just a shade after all,

changeable like gender, fluid and malleable. But the old religions
lingered.

White still retained the power to be invisible. A black boy was
always seen, watched. No one paid attention to white. Not a matter
of doors being opened, but of doors not being closed. So they
dosed me and stained me and until the drugs wore off I was a pale
imitation of myself.

My name is John.
There is no god but God. Allahu Akbar.

No one paid attention as I forgot to take my backpack with me
as I left the school. The mall. The post office. The diner off 95
North a little south of DC. Then, on the flight back home, even as
my body rejected the chemicals, I'd changed so often my skin
stayed white. The lady in the seat next to me offered to share her
crackers with me because I was young and white and not feeling
well.

So I let her live.

A while longer at least, the viral load my sweat was producing
slow acting. Air dispersal would do that.

I could give her the antidote, I guess. Spit a drop or two into
her drink when she wasn't looking. The crackers were good, but
not that good. Besides, who wants to drink spit in soda, even if it
would save her life?

A dozen terrorist bombings, a spree up the eastern seaboard. A
few hundred victims of a short acting virus on a plane bound for
Europe. Another bombing near that silly arch in Paris. Then, a day
or two of rest, purging the drugs from my system.

But none of that matters.

Not the backpacks or the zebra girls with their zebra tails
surgically attached or even the money my parents sold me for to
the men who visited the village to collect as many potential

martyrs as possible. Not even the schooling, enough to pass for American if asked.

No. None of that matters.

All that matters now is they're expecting a black boy, about my size, back in the caliphate any day now. But I'm white. And taller than I was when I left for the states. Heavier, eating a cheeseburger and bacon and every other delicious treat denied me all my life except when on a mission. More American than when I left.

And no one pays much attention to one more white boy walking the streets of Berlin. Or New York. Or San Diego.

They send money to my parents, but in order to do my job they give me money too. I'm to blend in, staying out of sight at cheap hotels. But sleeping on the street is cheaper, easier. Years of missions, saving all that money for a rainy day.

Each backpack, filled with a dozen pounds or more of explosive, or sticks of something that goes boom. Who's to tell the difference at the mall kiosk if eight pounds exploded instead of twelve?

Four more pounds into my safest places. Along with money. IDs the men with guns, and their zebra girls, never provided me, never knew about. Just one more white boy, living on the streets despite all the cash I could ever need to spend, unregistered weapons, demolitions, the skills to use them.

It was never quite time. It was easy work, killing tourists and shoppers and nice ladies on planes. Plus there was nothing I thought worth doing with freedom. Until now.

Until they turned my sister into a zebra girl. She left surgery on all fours, tail swishing the floor with every foot she crawled as the doctors watched with pride.

I never saw her again.

I had other sisters. Younger sisters. Rumor was mom was pregnant again. Bidding would start high if it was a girl. A baby zebra, bidding would be through the roof.

Now it's time.

My name is John.
There is no god but Me.

8. MANNEQUIN BY NICHOLAS PASCHALL

The police tape surrounding the forty square feet of the desert made it easy for Black to find the place, even after driving for ten minutes through the wilds of Death Valley. Several officers were present, along with an ambulance and a coroner. Pulling the cigarette from his lips, he blew out a plume of smoke before discarding the cigarette out the slit in his window before opening the door.

Flashing his badge to one of the rookie officers that didn't recognize him, Black ducked under the yellow tape and made his way over to the scene of the crime. O'Neil and Davidson were standing around the body, an unspecified gender that looked as if it'd been bludgeoned to death. The area was devoid of anything of note, save for a trash can filled to the brim with rusted cans, topped by a mannequin missing an arm.

"So what do we have?" Black asked, clearing his throat as a way of an announcement.

"Well, a nature photographer found the body about three hours ago and called us in," Davidson said, scratching his head. "We questioned him of course, but without any motive we let him go."

"Any idea of who we're looking at?" Black asked, wincing as he stared at the bruised form that the body was composed of; broken bones sticking out from ruined flesh.

"Yeah, we were able to pull an ID from a wallet that was in the victim's pants," O'Neil said, holding out a plastic ID card. "Jessica Martinez, age nineteen. We ran her through the system and other than a few possession charges nothing worth mentioning."

"So we have a woman out in the middle of the desert. Any reason why she would be out here?" Black asked, looking between his fellow officers.

"Maybe she was going to pick up a parcel?" Davidson offered, shrugging. "She has a few possession charges against her, who's to say she's reformed?"

"And we know that some of the traffickers don't like entering city limits," O'Neil said. "There are no tire tracks nearby before you ask."

Black grunted, looking around at the sandy earth. The wind was negligible, so any tracks left behind would be obvious… which was why when Black saw the footprints leading to and from the trash can he looked back up at Davidson. He pointed down at the footprints.

"This didn't find you suspicious?" he asked.

Davidson shrugged again. "It seems a little weird, I know. But what was I supposed to say? The mannequin is somehow involved?"

"Never rule anything out," Black said as he walked over to the mannequin, lifting it by its one good arm from the trash can. He shivered at the cool touch to the plastic, despite the direct exposure to the blaring sun. Hefting out the mannequin, he held it aloft and looked at the head, which rolled to the side.

He was surprised to see a smear of red on the face, a smear that looked suspiciously like blood. Licking his thumb, he rubbed at the smear before adjusting his grip on the arm… only to find his other hand smeared in caked blood. Dropping the mannequin and cussing, Black pulled out a hander kerchief and wiped his hand as Davidson approached him.

"What is it, Black?" Davidson asked, looking at him as if he'd lost his mind.

"That mannequin is evidence," Black growled as he wiped his hand free of blood. "Get the CSI team down here to take a look at it, but it was involved in the killing somehow."

"What do you mean?" Davidson asked as O'Neil radioed for additional CSI personnel.

"The arm is caked in dried blood, and there's blood spatter on the mannequin's face," Black explained, wiping his face with his clean hand. "Jesus, I just grabbed the thing too… my fingerprints are going to be all over this thing now!"

"You had no idea of knowing," O'Neil said. His radio squawked, prompting him to bring it to his lips. "Yeah, Senna and her team would be perfect. Are they inbound already? Thanks."

Black stared at the mannequin, the cheap plastic dented and worn from years of use, burnt in some areas and cut in others. The head had pinpoint holes drilled where eyes would normally be, giving it a disturbing demeanor; Black looked away from the crumpled form and cursed himself for grabbing the mannequin in the first place.

The group waited five minutes until they heard the roar of an engine. Black perked up from his place sitting on the hood of his car, looking over his shoulder as an identical squad car pulled up next to his, parking with a shudder. Three people got out, two men and a woman, all in CSI rubbers and gloves.

"I heard you have yourself a mystery stiff?" the woman said with a smile, her pearly white teeth shining from between ruby red lips. Her long black hair whirled in the breeze as she took off her sunglasses and clipped them to her shirt. "What, the crime in the city not enough for you cowboy?"

Black smiled. "I'm just expanding my horizons, Senna," he said with an easy smile. "I have some evidence I want you to look at along with the body. We can tell she was bludgeoned to death, but we haven't found a murder weapon yet. We were hoping you could give us some insight into what to look for."

"I'll see what I can do," she said as she walked around the ambulance, stopping at the gurney where the body had been scooped up into. She unzipped the bag and winced at the fractured skull that came into view. "Ouch. Well, that certainly looks messy…"

Whatever she was going to say next was cut off by the scuffling of sand and panicked movement. The calm crime scene suddenly descended into chaos as the mannequin, crumpled at the base of the trash can, flipped onto all fours and crawled like a spider, faster than the eye could follow toward Ramirez. Only Black's military experience had him pulling his pistol by the time the plastic missile collided with Senna, knocking her over with a loud "oomph!"

Senna began screaming as the mannequin, straddling her at the waist, began raining down heavy blows on her face. Senna brought up her arms to try and defend herself only to have her left arm snap like dry timber with a careless twitch from the plastic figure. By now the other officers had pulled their pistols and bringing their firearms to bear, with Black unloading a round into the head of the mannequin, blowing a small hole in the back of the head – the exit wound far larger in the front.

What followed was five men unloading their full complement of their combined arsenal into the chaotic doll, splinters of plastic flying from it like rain as the bullets tore through the torso and head – the arms continuing to hammer down on Senna, who shrieked the entire time. Finally one of her fellow CSI agents and O'Neil ran up and grabbed the broken mannequin by the arms, hauling it off of Senna forcibly, the mannequin kicking at her as it was pulled away.

Senna looked a mess, one eye swollen shut with her jaw and nose broken, her left arm bent at an awkward angle. The paramedics rushed to her side and began looking her over, checking her vitals and telling her that she was going to be okay while still keeping an eye on the hostile doll.

Black, reloading his Beretta, walked over to where Senna lay. "Is she going to be okay?" He asked one of the paramedics.

The man looked up, worry etched on his face. "I've never seen injuries like this outside of a car crash! What the Hell is that thing?"

"Take her in this ambulance, I'll radio someone else for the stiff," Black ordered, to which the paramedic nodded. He turned and looked at the mannequin, which was still fighting O'Neil and the CSI agent with surprising strength to get at Senna.

The head of the mannequin was nothing but shredded plastic, blasted apart from countless bullets while the body was held together barely by a long strip running from the left shoulder to the right hip. The arms and fists were covered in fresh blood, with spatter covering the chest and face where visible.

Black wiped his brow. "Well I think we know what killed the hiker," he said.

9. THE VOICE OF GOD BY CHARLIE JACK JOSEPH KRUGER

The room was silent. Silent in that kind of way that Hell may have been, she thought. Silent as a form of torture. Not silent in spite of anything, but willful silence. Sentient nothingness. She closed her eyes, blacking out the glowing hue of the room. Darkening everything to match the silence. Behind tired eyelids she could see her own heartbeat. She could hear it too. The only sight, the only sound, her own.

When she opened her eyes, the sound came back with the light. Like a hard restart. Hell was loud now. Roaring. The airport was real in a new way. A loudspeaker blared information. Flights leaving, people who needed to pick things up. The lights weren't a glowing memory, now they were glaring, screaming florescent eruptions. Outside the bathroom the noise, the lights, the crippling terror would be all the more real. Her moment of separation would mean nothing. That fear was nothing new. It was always like this. An escape for a moment, solace hidden in shame. Then the hammers would come back. Tearing, laughing. Ripping. The sky would ignore her, and there would be no one left to cry for her.

So she kept her eyes open, refusing to blink for the moment, and opened the stall door, stepping into the main room of the bathroom, the sinks were all blasting. Conversations hit the water and sloshed onto the floor, the room was drowning in white noise. Static distortions and lies. It was enough to make her just want to lie down and cry. But it wasn't time for that yet. There would be relief soon. The tears settled in her eyes. Sweat pouring down her temples, sticking her long black hair to her skin, it wasn't time yet. She would have to wait. Hell would dance for her, but there was something better just through the flames. Tears filling her eyes, she left the bathroom and walked into the cold hallways of the airport, not embracing the swirling chaos around her, but being horribly aware of it. Allowing it to exist for the moment. She would tear it down in time. She let the beast laugh.

Flickers of her past clung in the humid air. They clapped against her clammy face and left streaks in the warm sweat. A flash of her father, the smell of his sour breath, the feel of his coarse hands holding hers as she walked into church. The priest, talking through rolled eyes and fevered tongues. Messages of hope, sold behind cans of frosting and government sponsored cheese. There was such a chance, such a worthiness about it all. She could only ever taste it though. Never truly own it. Never consume it. Just pray for it. In an instant she began to wonder, was she sweating now because of the humidity, or because she knew that salvation wasn't just a concept in the murky distance anymore... but something she would hold in her hands soon enough. She put her hand in her pocket and felt the small plastic lump. The rubber button in the middle felt gummy. She held redemption like a simple object. The sweat was beading on her upper lip. She wanted to scream 'hallelujah' and embrace the hope.

"Are you alright Miss?"

A heavy-set employee asked her with facile concern as she moved past him, her eyes rolling around like lost marbles. He had seen her, sweating, eyes widened and overflowing with tears. He felt it was his job to ask, and when she ignored him, he didn't think anything of it. People always ignored him. As he sipped on his soda, surveying the hallway he ignored himself as well.

It felt like months had passed since Darren had dropped her off at the airport. But really it had just been minutes. Not even an hour. A short time. But by this point she had processed so much, feared so much. Standing at the precipice of greatness, there was nothing left to fear. There was no terror left to scrape up in her mind. Things were simply as they had to be. She was chosen, and Hell was already starting to diminish around her. She could feel wings poking through her thin coat. Her shoulders hurt. She was in pain, but a different, new pain.

A gifted pain—some she could remember faintly from her young days fooling around with boys by the baseball field. Her skin felt sanctified. Her wings were starting to grow, she could feel love swirling around in her womb. She was an angel, a messenger of a new savior. More than ever before, she felt herself craving

Darren's hands on her hips. She needed his body, his essence. She wanted to feel him one last time. So she closed her eyes and remembered him. She remembered the way he had looked at her in bed that morning. The smile on his thin lips. She remembered the way he had felt against her skin.

Holding her hand, Darren had read to her from the bible, sharing his visions. She came to know them all, and she shared them with the other women at the church. Darren had picked her to be his voice to the women of the congregation. Through sweat and budding wings, she strained to remember that shameful feeling of pride one last time. The way her father looked at her... so honored, so proud. His daughter was to be the voice of the prophet. And now... here in the airport, she found herself the perfect vessel for The Word. She was now, more than ever, the voice of Darren's god. She screamed. She screamed so loud that the chaos of Hell itself seemed to split. Babylon halted in its steps, shocked at the rupture in the routine.

The heavy-set employee looked up, puzzled, at her. He had known there was something a little off about her. He looked at her just in time to see her pull a small black plastic box out of her pocket. It looked like a beeper. She pushed a button and her small rolling suitcase exploded. Time froze for the employee. He could see the fire swelling, the way it curved and rolled over itself, breathing all the air out of the hallway, making the cold tiles on the walls warm up. The fire moved in slow motion. No one else seemed to move at all. The employee wasn't terrified, there was nothing he could do but watch the engorging fire grow larger and larger. Then he felt the concussion from the explosion. It felt like he had been hit by a car. Now he didn't ignore anything. And the fire didn't ignore him.

She melted in a fraction of a second, her body becoming sprayed liquid and splintered bone. Her very shoulders, where her wings had begun to grow, became shrapnel. Her scream was painted over by the explosion. Everything in the terminal was. Fire and then silence. The whistles, the sirens, the pain from people on the other side of the terminal. The chaos of life. It represented itself

as silent. Hidden sadism. Crying silence. The airport burned. It
looked beautiful on the news that evening.

10. STRAIGHT TO THE KING BY DEVLIN GIROUX

Only a damn fool wouldn't be able to tell by now that I don't like people all that much. Didn't start this way. Wasn't born into it, you know. It's that slow creep up the back of your throat when you know you're sick, but there's fuck all you can do about it. The infection is already there. The pain's on its way. You live with it...and hope you get over it quickly. Thing is, I never did.

Long before I was branded the Suicide King, I was just another idiot kid in a piss pot of a town with no good road out and no future. Yes, I mean both me and the road. I'd spend the endless hours walking that town, passing the same houses from the same hundred miles before. Got to stopping at houses and making up stories about what was happening inside. Stories about coming home to a hot meal. A welcome. A safe place.

But those were just stories.

Tried to find that again. Walking those worn stones of home. Only this time, I didn't have to worry about someone seeing me outside staring into their sanctuaries. Unless I wanted them to see me. Hell, damn near walked through the wall of Mr. Miller's house just to get the undying bastard his last heart attack. Get him back for the rock salt from a lifetime ago.

It hit me hard and fast, that pull from Mr. Gone. Seems us in this game all have our tricks, but his was always the worst, and he liked it that way. The world around me shut off like a shattered bulb. Edges snapped back into place, the wound in reality sealing itself up after violation.

"Good evening, Mr. Montrosse," said Mr. Gone.

Didn't need to see him to know the malignant fuck was in the shadows behind me. He'd dropped me into the middle of a massacre. Three dead. Woman. Two kids. Both girls. Blood. Exposed bone and spent shotgun shells. Still in the air, smell of gunpowder and shit.

"It's a shame, really," came that voice of lice and bile. "There is real talent here. A persistence and clarity of purpose I have to respect. Just look at how many times he shot them. You can see the work put into reloading and making sure to finish the work."

"How many different ways you want me to tell you go fuck yourself, Gone?" I went to fade out, not giving him the satisfaction, only to remain right in place. "Now, what the hell? You can do that?"

"Not me, Suicide King," Gone said. "That's your own work keeping you here. He's in the other room."

Gone wasn't lying.

I found him sitting on the edge of his bed. The same he once shared with the dead woman. The shotgun was across his knees. I was here for him.

"The poor dear just can't live with himself," Gone said, hand to forehead in mock drama. He dropped the act and went cold. "Disgusting. All that beautiful, beautiful potential lost. Why? Sentiment and guilt. Two of the most worthless things in existence other than their progenitors: family and religion."

I always knew what my Takes were thinking once I got close to them. All those not-mine thoughts and memories. Got used to it a little too quickly, you ask me.

"Mr. Montrosse, if I may place a request," Mr. Gone said. "Please, for the sake of consistency, have him use the shotgun. It would make for a nice finish to the evening's festivities."

I heard him, but only as an irritating screech of static behind the thoughts of my Take. Roger. Family annihilator. Debts and another woman. Secrets seen and soon outed. Their lives in ruins. He would save them...and himself.

Roger nodded and turned the shotgun on himself.

"No," I said. Don't think for a moment it was a cry to stop him. It was an order, spoken simple and straight. My hand closed around the barrel.

"Who—"

All Roger got out before I ripped the shotgun away from him. The swing was for the fences, stock catching him right on the blackout button.

"It's really not suicide if you beat him to death," Mr. Gone said, "but who am I to stop an artist in the middle of experimentation."

Not exactly sure where I sent it, but the shotgun faded from my grip. I found Roger's cell in his pocket and dialed.

"Yeah, just trace the address," I said as soon as I heard the dispatcher start her spiel. "Your killer will be in the upstairs bedroom ready for whoever the hell gets here first."

I tossed the phone, still connected to 911, on the bed next to Roger. The look on Mr. Gone's pale, shallow face was perfect, because fuck him.

"This is not how the game is played, Montrosse," said Mr. Gone, voice as cold and measured as an easy murder.

"I didn't ask to play, asshole," I said.

"There will be consequences if you do not Take him."

I felt the fade coming over me. Whatever held me in time and space before had lifted. "Good. This one is marked for me. He gets to live a nice, long life."

Mr. Gone sneered and rushed at Roger in that floating, terrifying way of his. And stopped like hitting a brick wall. For the first time since meeting that creepy prick, he looked astounded. Now, I had no idea if it was going to play out as I wanted, but seeing Mr. Gone slashing away at air was about the funniest damn thing I'd seen in a long time.

"Not...how—"

"Suicide is too good for him, Gone," I interrupted. "He doesn't get a pass."

I faded out, smiling, as Gone tore, ripped, slashed, even bit at whatever I had done to Roger to make sure there would never be a release for him.

No escape from himself.

11. THE AMERICAN BY S.C. HAYDEN

Something large, dark and heavy crashed through the underbrush and into the path ahead. Farther Mancini loosened the machete hanging from his belt. The American's machete was already at hand. The pig snorted, turned and faced them, 200 pounds, maybe three. It pawed the earth several times but did not charge. Red stained the pig's dark skin, darker holes where it's eyes should have been. Blind and bleeding the animal wobbled, staggered, then collapsed.

It was the second eyeless animal they'd seen.

Hennrick, their guide, had spotted an eyeless albino boa coiled in a low hanging branch just the day before. That was when he told them they were on their own and tuned back. He'd taken them as far as he dared. It didn't matter. The dense jungle had opened and the once all but invisible path was clear. Even without the path they would have found their way. They could feel it. Something drew them on. Something wanted them to come.

They hiked in silence for the next few hours. Sister Asty walked between Father Mancini and the American. She had grown up in a village at the base of the very mountains they were climbing. If they encountered any locals, Father Mancini reasoned, she could mediate. But the American knew they wouldn't encounter any locals. They were too close to ground zero.

Sister Asty stopped short and gasped.

The American stepped up behind her and looked over the nun's shoulder. A man hung, arms stretched and hands nailed, in a twisted banyan tree. His abdomen was split and his intestines had been pulled out and strewn about the great tree's branches like party streamers. A crucifixion. The kill was fresh, the smell still thick and wet in the sultry air. Sister Asty fell to her knees. A shrill sigh escaped her lips like a teakettle coming to boil. She shouldn't be here, the American thought. It was a mistake to bring her.

Father Mancini helped her to her feet and hurried her past the grizzly maker. The old priest was stoic. He was guided by purpose.

But the American knew what lie ahead and held no hope that the priest was equal to the task.

All three of them had seen the footage.

***

Three years earlier a man stood before a video camera in a small room in Port-Au-Prince Haiti. The room was filled with the familiar trappings of Haitian Voodoo; bottles of liquor, candles, bones both human and animal, a crucifix. The man wore a threadbare tuxedo and bowler derby. He identified himself as a Houngan, a voodoo priest, and said he was going to channel a powerful spirit he called Mr. Humbaba.

The Houngan placed a live chicken on a chopping block and slit it's throat with a carving knife. The bird squawked and fluttered then went still. The man smeared the chicken's blood on his face. He drank from a brown glass bottle then spewed clear liquid from his mouth over the dead bird, shaking a rattle in the air and muttering some unintelligible can't all the while.

All at once he fell to the ground jerking and flailing and frothing at the mouth. It looked like a standard Tonic-clonic seizure, but it was what happened afterward that convinced the Vatican to take the video seriously.

The spasms stopped abruptly and the man leapt to his feet, snatched the carving knife from the chopping block and slit his own throat. Bright red arterial blood fanned the room. The man, seemingly unaffected, sat cross-legged on a small wooden chair, lit a cigarette and calmly smoked while blood gushed and bubbled from the meaty slice below his chin.

"Let those who suffer come to me and I will make them strong," he said in perfect German. "If a woman is barren," he continued in Arabic, "she need only lie with me and her womb will quicken." He looked directly into the camera and smiled. Blood still welled from his severed arteries. Cigarette smoke billowed from his nose and neck. "Whosoever believes in me," he whispered in Hebrew, "out of his belly shall flow rivers of living water."

The video ended.

After that, rumors circulated of a man who was dead yet walked and talked and performed miracles high in the Haitian mountains. The blind could see again, the lame walked, the barren swelled. Later there were darker stories, stories of mass rape, crucifixion, mutilation, and human sacrifice.

***

The jungle path steepened and the vegetation thinned with elevation. Banyans gave way to palms and thick spiky bushes bristling with hidden thorns. As they crested the final ridge the village revealed itself. Crumbling huts of mud and stick stood neglected in a small clearing ringed by a sea of fronds. In the village center stood a single masonry structure, a small white tin roofed building affixed with a crucifix.

Men and women wandered the village slack jawed and aimless as though shell-shocked. Two men holding ancient looking AK-47s stood near the entrance to the derelict church. Eyes sunken, faces angular, they were skin and bones. They looked as though they hadn't eaten for weeks. Strange when one considered the chickens and village dogs wandering about untended.

Sister Asty, Father Mancini and the American dropped their heavy packs onto the ground and pressed into the village. They walked slowly, carefully, towards the church. Somehow they knew the object of their quest dwelled within.

A haggard old woman with onyx skin, snow-white hair and blood shot eyes sat cross-legged in the dirt regarding the three travelers. As they drew past her she pressed her palms to her face and dug her fingers into her eyes.

Sister Asty gasped. She reached out to stay the old woman's hands but it was too late. The woman pulled her eyeballs out of her head and held them out to the sister.

"Take them," the woman whispered, "I can see so much more without them."

Father Mancini pulled Sister Asty back. Once again, the American wished she hadn't come. Father Mancini crossed himself. He was guided by Christ. The American was guided by a simple truth; energy is power and power is money. The American had no doubt that Father Mancini had exorcized some lower level

69

Demons in his time but the being that inhabited that white church was an entity of tremendous power. A full-fledged Class-1 Demon.

The American looked at his watch. Rather than measure time, his "watch" measured the strength of nearby electromagnetic fields. The meter read 200-tesla, the highest he'd seen in over six years hunting Demons.

The men with the AK-47s ignored the three travelers as they approached the church. If the entity that dwelled within had considered them a threat, the American reasoned, the gunmen would have cut them down. Instead, they stared into space as if they weren't there at all.

The church's interior stank of corruption. There were corpses in the pews. A shifting miasma of flies buzzed in thick swarms around the assembled parishioners. Men and women, eyeless and disemboweled, littered the floor and center isle. The man they had seen slit his own throat in Port-Au-Prince, the Houngan, sat quietly smoking on a large wooden chair at the head of the church. His throat was a dark ragged hole. His eyes flashed blood red in the smoky nimbus surrounding his head.

"Father Mancini, Sister Asty," the Demon said. His English, like his German, Arabic and Hebrew, was perfect. Sister Asty was to serve as their translator but it was clear that her skills would not be needed. Mr. Humbaba was an exceptional communicator. "And who is this? He smells like an American."

"He is a man of God," Father Mancini said, "His name is not important. It's he whose name he comes in that is important."

"Some young priest who wants to play exorcist," the Demon snorted. "How's your faith boy? Is it strong?"

The American remained silent.

Father Mancini wasted no time. He raised his crucifix and stepped forward. "In the name of Christ the redeemer, I revoke you!"

The Demon ignored him.

"Is it true that all priests are pederasts?" the Demon asked the American, "or do you want to fuck Sister Asty? You can have her if you want her. Kneel before me and I'll give her to you."

"Away Satan!" Father Mancini commanded. He stepped forward again, fearless, stalwart, his voice filled the room. "Inventor and master of all deceit, enemy of mankind's salvation, tremble and flee before the almighty hand of God!"

The Demon, eyes like glowing embers, dropped his cigarette and stood. His grin was wicked and the second smile he wore beneath his chin was wickeder still. He raised his right hand and Father Mancini halted his advance. When the Demon's hand became a fist, the priest's clothing burst into flames.

"No!" Sister Asty shouted. She ran towards the burning priest but when the Demon raised his left hand she too stopped as still as stone. The priest, frozen in place, became a burning statue. When the flames rose over his head he tried to scream but all that escaped his rigid mouth was a high pitch squeal.

Sister Asty, frozen, motionless, eyes wide open, was forced to watch him burn to death, just out of reach. More than twenty minutes passed before the old priest fell lifeless to the floor. The American, although not frozen, never moved. His face betrayed no emotion.

The Demon twisted his left hand and Sister Asty pulled her clothes off as though they burned her skin. When she was completely nude she got down on all fours, thrust her ass into the air and hissed. The American watched her squirm. He remembered what the Demon told him. He could have her if he wanted her. She was young and beautiful. Her dark skin, now coated in perspiration, glistened. She reached between her knees with one hand and touched herself. Her mons was swollen and wet, her nipples erect. She moaned, hissed and meowed.

A cat in heat, the American mused.

"Say the word exorcist, and she is yours," the Demon said, "or you can burn like your friend."

The American stepped forward. The Demon smiled. The American reached into his cargo pocket and removed a small silver flask-shaped object with a flashing red LED light on one side. The Demon's smile faltered and the American saw what he had seen so many times before. The moment when a Demon first realizes he's not dealing with a crucifix waving man of faith, but with a cold and calculated man of science; the moment when the Demon's mask of confidence turns into a flash of doubt.

The American raised the silver object and pressed a button with his thumb. The Demon fell to his knees, his flash of doubt now a look of startled bewilderment. The red lights in his eyes guttered, darkened, then winked out entirely. Something that looked like smoke billowed from his mouth and funneled, as though drawn by a vacuum, into the flask like device in the American's hand.

The man with the slit throat toppled over onto his side. The Demon was gone and the carcass of a man over three years dead lay finally motionless on the floor. The American looked at the device in his hand – the LED had changed from red to green and a number flashed on a small screen, 1.8 Gigawatts, enough to power a small city. A Demon as virulent as the one he'd just harvested would probably produce at that capacity for close to twenty-five years.

"Who are you?" The voice startled him. The American looked over his shoulder. Sister Asty looked up at him from the floor, arms drawn tight across her breasts. "You're not from the church." It wasn't a question.

"EnergyCorp International," the American said flatly, "Tomorrow's solutions to today's energy needs."

He placed the device back in his cargo pocket and removed a small pearl handled revolver from another. Again, he wished she hadn't come. He placed the barrel behind sister Asty's ear and pulled the trigger.

It was a shame, but there could be no witnesses. Nuclear power was controversial enough. Demon power would put people in a tizzy. Another shame. It was clean and abundant, the ultimate green energy source. The only byproduct? Bad dreams. In the American's opinion, the EnergyCorp physicist who developed the system deserved a noble prize.

But people simply weren't ready for the truth.

12. DARKNESS, SHE WAS ALONE BY CHRISTOPHER CONLON

Based on an Unfinished Story Fragment by Edgar Allan Poe

1.

I don't know nothin' about it. I never knew nothin' about it. Little bitch anyway.

2.

Alone. She listened to the word in her mind, alone. It had a dreary sound—yet she wished, more than anything, more than life, to be alone, and she felt her spirits reviving already because at last she was truly and thoroughly alone, though someone was with her.

3.

At times there was light and in those times she peered through the cracks and saw, not so very far away and yet as distant as the moon, the lighthouse: and she remembered being in it once, years ago, when she was very small, exploring it, ascending its interminable stairs and gazing down endless distances to the hollow interior of the bottom…But what was she thinking about? Darkness, and she was alone, though someone was with her.

4.

Sometimes from her place in the crate where her father kept her she would peer through the wooden slats at the corner of the basement window which she could just see if she turned right, and she could stare at the white gleam flashing and sweeping from the top of the lighthouse and she would dream of herself as the light, gliding out across the sea to guide men and ships to safety.

5.

Other times she pictured herself in the lighthouse, looking out, doing absolutely nothing all day and seeing only a clear horizon before her, not the slightest speck of a cloud, floating on her island in the sky.

6.

When she imagined herself in these other places she imagined herself naked, as she always was now since her father did not allow her clothes—there was an oily-smelling blanket in the crate and an old phone book for a pillow—but she would picture her skin as smooth and perfect, as it had been once, not torn and scratched and bruised as it was now. She would be beautiful, perfect as light.

7.

And yet she imagined no people with her. Only alone, a passion for solitude, her sole comfort in aloneness. She was here, all safe, and could feel secure in the worst hurricane that ever raged. At times she could be joyful in the crate, feel an ecstasy impossible to describe! But never with people. People never meant happiness for her. Not Sarah de Grät or Julie Orndoff with her terrible gossip—girls she knew, knew back when she knew girls, knew people, teachers and cafeteria ladies and the bus driver, back when Mother was alive, when she spent only nights in the crate, not days too.

8.

The world was the crate and the scraps he fed her in the dark and the slop bucket he walked her out each night to empty in the backyard and the things he did to her which left welts and marks the color of rotting fruit on her cheeks and neck and shoulders and arms and belly and legs and between her legs. She could still remember the other world but it faded each day, swam in her mind, became more and more like the world in her dreams, with herself as light pouring across the ocean. There was no world but the world of her father and the crate and the darkness and the gleam of the faraway lighthouse. Sometimes she heard the sea.

9.

He told her that she was bad bad and she knew she was, knew
that she was the worst little girl in the world and that she deserved
everything she got except that she deserved even less. You don't
deserve to live, he told her night after night with the smell of
whiskey on his breath. He liked to slap her when he said it. He said
it again and again.

10.

Nasty girl without a name. My name is. Was. You don't have a
name anymore, he said. You have nothing. You are nothing.

11.

She remembered TV. Gilligan on his island—he was funny.
Sometimes when she concentrated in the darkness she could
remember whole stories she used to see.

12.

And she looks out and sees the gleam of the lighthouse and
feels the cold, runs her fingers over her skin covered with welts
like strips of leather. It's time, she thinks, time. She stands.

13.

She picks up her blanket from the floor and wraps it around
herself. She moves toward the steps which lead to the basement
door. Looking down, she sees the weak sheen of the lighthouse on
her skin and past that, on the floor itself, the big heap of clothes
collapsed there. For a moment she considers pulling some of them
over her body but decides against it.

14.

She notices, as if it is something she has never seen before,
though she knows that she's seen it, that the heap of clothes is all
stuck through with holes, dozens and dozens of them, and there is a
dark stain around each hole and some of the stains have run like
paint into one another to become a strange pattern in the dark that
looks like the patterns of her own skin.

75

15.

At the far edge of the heap of clothes, sticking out from the top of the shirt, is her father's head. But she would not have known it for her father's head. She would not have known it as the man who climbed on top of her at night in the dark and slapped her face and screamed Little bitch! Bad! Bad!

16.

She would not have known it for her father's head because it is covered in dark swirling liquid patterns and the eyes are collapsed inward like smashed grapes and the nose is a big hole with chunks of something like hamburger around it.

17.

The screwdriver with dark streaks and bits of meat on it is beside her father's head. He had tried to grab it from her when she plunged it into the back of his neck and it was funny, almost as funny as Gilligan on his island to watch him trying to pull the screwdriver from the back of his neck and then getting hold of it but falling, falling down, too weak to keep her from grabbing it from his hand and smashing it through his eye, both eyes, and his cheeks, and his ears, and she heard screaming when she did it but it was not his, it was hers. He never screamed. He said only one word and that word was why.

18.

She is a bad girl and has no name.

19.

She walks up the basement steps into the house where she has not been in a very long time. She takes a look around to see what she can see. It seems in the darkness to be big, unbelievably big, the biggest house she's ever seen, with ceilings so high she can hardly make them out and walls so distant it seems she could run forever and never reach them.

20.

The light from the lighthouse glows through the windows in the darkness. There is another glow too and she suddenly realizes that the TV is turned on. She moves down the hall to the living room where the flickering light plays on the walls. There is no sound. She stares at the images on the screen—sun, blue sky, a man on a white horse—and briefly considers seeing if Gilligan is on. But she does not. She is not sure she remembers how to work the TV. She is afraid it might explode if she tries.

21.
She is afraid that her father will climb up the steps and tell her she is bad, that he might slap her in the face, that she might get sick or worse as he calls her a little bitch, bad, bad.

22.
She goes to the front door.

23.
She steps outside. The night is cold. It is winter, she thinks. She sees the ocean, not too far away, and she sees the lighthouse. The light seems to call to her.

24.
She begins walking. Sand and rocks under her feet.

25.
After a long time she reaches the shore and the lighthouse is only a few hundred yards from her. She looks out into the black water, the light cascading across it like a curtain of diamonds.

26.
Yet she misses the basement. She would like to be in the crate now, in the darkness, alone, where she was safe and always would be. She considers turning back. But no. She knows that her father is alive again, knows that he is waiting for her with his eyes and hands. His hands. Big hands, the biggest hands in the world, everywhere on her, all over.

27.

She looks out into the dark waters and knows where she will
go. She will join the light, the light from the lighthouse, she will
splash out into the water and she will join the light, the beautiful
light, she will swim with the light bathing her in its warmth and
she will become it, become the light, the light that has always
glowed on her at night in the crate, the light that never left her, the
light that never called her bad, the light that loves her.

28.

She shucks off the blanket and moves toward the water. It
rushes up to her toes and they tingle. But it is not cold, as she had
feared. It is warm. Like a bath. She remembers baths with her
mother, forever long ago.

29.

As the water engulfs her she feels the light from the lighthouse
sweeping over her body and as she pushes into the surf she looks
back and it's there, the light, all-embracing, light of silence, light
of love, and she knows that was always the light that was her
friend, her one and true friend, always and only the light, and that
she had been in darkness but it had never truly been darkness, that
she had been alone but never truly alone, and that someone, the
radiant and overflowing light, had always been with her, and
always would be.

30.

She swims down underneath the waves, the water flowing
around her and turning the world miraculous tints of green and
blue and gold. The light from the lighthouse breaks up, reflects,
refracts, shines through the water in dark rainbows and she begins
to see, not far away, things approaching her, beautiful graceful
things like porpoises, but as they draw near she realizes that they
are not porpoises but children, dozens of them, hundreds, all naked
and swimming toward her. Some have missing limbs, some have
big holes in their heads or chests, some have flesh blackened by

fire, some have terrible red stripes on their bodies. But all swim toward her with perfect grace, their faces happy, their injuries and violations seemingly painless now and forgotten in this wonderful world under the water. They reach her. They reach for her. She is enveloped in soft, slippery hands, in joy, in a species of ecstasy impossible to describe.

31.

Voices. A voice. Far away. She hears it. At the last moment she hears it and then she never hears anything in the world again. She hears the voice. Voices. Oh Jesus Christ what the hell did you do to her. What is this place good Lord.

32.

For an instant she is back home, in her crate, her fingers stretched through the slats toward the light of the lighthouse, but she cannot move her hands or head or anything else, she is still, frozen. How can she be frozen? She is. Was.

33.

It's too late, a voice says.

34.

She feels water. Light. Dim. Dimming. The room is gone, the crate. Everything is gone. She is gone.

35.

I don't know nothin' about it, a voice said. I never knew nothin' about it. Little bitch anyway.

13. A KILLER APP BY VINCE LIBERATO

Optimyze is an app that kills people. And despite everybody knowing this, it is also one of the most popular downloads of all time, standing now at three hundred million users globally and growing daily. You're not an Optimyzer… yet. But you've been thinking about it for weeks, and have decided that you're ready to join the largest growing demographic in the world, despite the cost you will eventually pay.

But before you do, you write a quick message and post it in a public bidding forum.

About to Optimyze

Hey internet.

I'm going to become an Optimyzer. If you want me to use you as my sponsor, send me an offer.

Short, simple, and to the point, moments after you post the ad, replies flood in like blood from a split artery. You don't have to remind them that whoever you pick will get to live a little longer. Everyone knows that.

From: Charlie Kopecky

Re: About to Optimyze

Dear friend,

I saw your ad, and was hoping you would consider using my account as your referral when you join us on Optimyze. For this, I would also like to offer you a lifelong weekly budget of $300 on my Shopon.com account. Please take a moment to observe my credentials and a contract (attached). If this is not satisfactory, I can give you a one-time credit of $60,000 to any account of your choice.

Let me know as soon as you can. Others too will receive this offer, so I cannot guarantee it for long.

Best,

Charlie Kopecky

You read over the contract several times, then send Kopecky's email out to a service that specializes in contract and identity verification. Optimyze keeps a foolproof database of its users, and your valuable, non-affiliated Optimyze virginity is not something you will ever have again. While you wait for the update on Kopecky, you read the next response.

From: Hermecita 'Mita' Corazon

Re: About to Optimyze

Hello,

I saw your ad. No doubt you're getting all sorts of offers for the referral. As you know, this will be one of those offers, and what I want to offer you I hope will suit one with your tastes.

You may not know this, but I am the owner of Heartwrech Ranches. And for you making me your referral, I will provide to you a lifelong pass to all of our facilities. This is not something I would normally offer, but our girls (guys if you prefer) have taken a liking to you based off your profile, and for them, I'd do anything.

I look forward to your response. And seeing you soon.

With Love,

Mita

A message pings from a second inbox. It is the reply from the verification agency, letting you know that everything about Charlie Kopecky checks out. There is no need to send them Mita's letter. You've seen her in commercials dozens of times, and actually live a few miles from one of the more famous Ranches. You doubt any of the escorts have seen your picture, but you don't care. All of them are very, very attractive.

You open another message.

From: Keli Adams

Re: About to Optimyze

My name is Keli Adams. I joined Optimyze six months ago and registered with my son, Paul, as my sponsor. He is a good boy, and joined to save one of his friends. While I am proud of him for what he did, he has been unable to find another new person to use his name as their referral, and he has been cut off from the service. Friends and family either refuse or are unable to help, thus I turn to you and your ad. Paul is dying, and I do not think he has much time left.

Please… please save my son.

Forever in your debt,

Keli

You draw Keli's profile up on the Optimyze main page. Her son has a grayed portrait, as does she. You see that she too has been disconnected, which was information she withheld in her letter. It is touching that she chose to focus only on Paul because you know neither of them have much time left.

Depression from Optimyze withdrawal usually takes about ten days before the damage becomes irreversible. Roughly seventy percent of those cut off from the service die, and crippling side effects are guaranteed on any survivors, all left as burnt out husks. After reliance Optimyze for as little as a week, separation from the program causes people to cease eating, drinking, and even breathing after being excluded from it, often passing in their sleep without ever waking up. Or at least that's what happens when users don't go violent. These instances were favorites of the news, always making headlines even though they happened about once a week.

The next letter promises salvation in the afterlife for a sponsorship. It is deleted.

Then another threatens your life if you do not sponsor the sender. You delete it.

A Nigerian prince lays out an offer several times greater than Kopecky's. It finds its way to the trash.

You are called a monster and a prostitute for selling yourself. Then asked to save the sender, all in the same poorly proofread letter. Delete.

Vexed, you create a folder and send Kopecky's, Mita's, and Keli's messages to it. There are several hundred more replies to sift through, and the number is still growing, but you doubt you'll make it much farther due to the repetitive nature of their content.

It takes several more deleted messages until you find another letter worth consideration. The name in the header is very, very familiar.

From: James Pines

Re: About to Optimyze

Hey,

So this is how I find out you're ready to join Optimyze? You're lucky I'm at the end of my current period and need to find a new person for sponsorship, otherwise I wouldn't have seen your ad. But you are fielding offers, so here is my offer to you:

Don't do it.

Yeah, the app is great. And because you were smart enough to not subscribe back when, your sub is worth whatever you can get for it, which must be pretty empowering. But as your friend, I'm begging you to stay away.

I'll be by later. Not to guilt you into saving my life or anything. But I don't think I'm going to make it this time and I want to get things in order before they kick me off.

Best,

James

You think back to when James had first joined Optimyze. He was an early adopter since the two of you were kids/ neighbors/ friends. He was the first with everything, always picking up on things before they took off. James had his Optimyze account hours after the product had hit the market. That night, you remember how he had ranted and raved about how the program was going to revolutionize the way people viewed entertainment.

"It tracks your likes, dislikes, current mood, time of day, prior viewing history and cross checks it against new uploads, the news, the economy, the weather, every other Optimyze user, and dozens of other outside factors. Then, it tells you what to watch or what to play, or what to do with the amount of time you claim to have. And every time, it's perfect. It's exactly what you need at that time. You think social media changed things? Wait until Optimyze takes hold."

In weeks following his praise of the product, you'd see James online, logged onto games for set periods of time, moving up the scoreboards at a meteoric rate. He seemed to have more focus, more motivation, and had accomplished a lot more, which was doubly impressive because he was playing less than he ever had, only winning much more. In addition, every time you did see each other, James had recommendations of shows, movies, and other games that he had been led to through Optimyze.

The memories echo as you transfer James's reply to your folder. That was three years ago, long before Bradley's Law was passed, preserving Optimyze and making virtually all its users transparent to the public. At that time, there were thirty million Optimyzers, and lawmakers refused to be responsible for what would happen to all of them if the service was cut off forever.

Since then, Optimyze's base had grown tenfold, and no cures for its withdrawal or altering of its code were anywhere close to being developed.

From: Carmel Adcock

Re: About to Optimyze

Hey,

Do you want to be on my show? I'm needing a new Op sponsor and my producers are turning it into a story arc for <u>My Awesome and Real Life</u> that is going to document the process. We're raising Optimyze addiction awareness this season, and we think you would be a good fit. Fame. Money too. We're going to the Bahamas to compete in the Reality Games too, so you'll get in on that.

Contract is attached. Let me know soon.

CA

You file this letter as well.

Despite several investigations by the FBI and hackers around the world, the identity of the creator or creators of Optimyze had never been found. It was a modern Trojan Horse. The app came out of nowhere, sent as a gift from the gods of cyberspace, with the consequences and terms of use even laid out in a contract that few read before accepting.

You delete several more messages, and are about ready to make your decision, but one more familiar name flashes across the screen.

From: Senator John Cho

Re: About to Optimyze

Yes. I am an Optimyzer.

And yes. I am going to need a sponsor soon.

So I'm asking you. And offering, in return, the chance to make a difference. I will be forever in your debt, if you only help preserve my life.

And as you know, I always pay my debts.

Senator Cho

There was an attachment and an official government seal. This was the real John Cho. The only exceptions to Bradley's Law were granted for those whose lives would be "irreparably damaged" if their status as an Optimyzer was made public knowledge. Cho, one of the most vocal advocates of shutting off Optimyze permanently, apparently fell under that category.

And for him to be coming to a relative stranger shows two things. The first is that his aides have done their homework about you. Regardless of who you choose, the Senator's secret will be kept safe. The second was that things must be difficult if the senator is reduced to spending his (or his aide's) time and resources for finding people to sponsor him on Optimyze.

You've seen enough.

You go to the site you posted your ad. You rescind it, attaching an addendum for all who replied to read.

Hello all,

After much consideration, I have made my decision. Thanks to all who responded. To my sponsor: You'll get your reply within the hour.

You write another letter and then send your reply. Fifteen minutes later, after creating a new account, you access Optimyze for the first time.

It was not near as great you had hoped it would be.

But after several hours, you still can't pull yourself away.

14. SORES BY DJ TYRER

"That's the third one this week. You're not telling me it's normal." The body lay in a corner of a derelict warehouse.

Stansfield nudged the corpse with the toe of his boot. All the visible skin was covered in what appeared to be oozing pustules. If you looked closely, they appeared to have burst open. A sickly smell rose from the corpse.

He involuntarily scratched his wrist at the thought of it and took out a bottle of hand sanitizer and spread a plentiful amount of the gel over his hands and vigorously rubbed it in. Even having used latex gloves while checking the body, he felt contaminated at having touched it.

DS Peters came over. "These people," he meant the homeless, "are disgusting. They live in filth. It's no wonder they're diseased."

"Diseased? It's more like the bloody plague, you ask me."

Peters chuckled. "When you've done this job a bit longer, you'll understand it's all par for the course."

Stansfield shrugged. He wondered if he stayed a copper a few years, if he'd wind up as cynical.

"I've called the FME," Peter's went on. "If there's no sign of foul play, it's not our problem. You stay and wait for him; I'm going on break."

Typical, thought Stansfield, leave the lowly DC with the non-job. He wished the uniforms who'd found the body hadn't been called away. Understaffing meant he was too often the lowest of the low, these days.

He watched Peters leave, then went over to the far side of the room. The smell wasn't quite so bad there.

He could hear soft skittering sounds in the shadowed corners of the warehouse. Rats. He shuddered. He hated rats. His brother-in-law was in pest control and some of the stories he told... He shuddered again.

If nothing else, Peters was right about the filth. This place was a dump.

The stink seemed to have slithered over to him with the sound of the rats, although it might have been some other unpleasant smell; blocked sewers and dead rats could be every bit as nauseating as a pustule-covered corpse. He took a handkerchief from his pocket, pressed it to his nose and tried to ignore it.

Something seemed to brush against the side of his boot and he jumped in surprise. He looked down, but could see nothing.

"You're getting jumpy," he told himself and checked his watch, wondering just how long the forensic medical examiner would be.

A rumble of thunder told Stansfield he'd arrived: the sheet of corrugated iron that did for a doorway had been pulled back and the FME was ducking under it, medical bag in hand. His assistant followed after, gamely fighting to get the gurney in through the recalcitrant gap.

"Morning," he called, hastily hiding the hankie, lest mockery be directed his way.

The forensic medical examiner glanced in his direction. "Oh, morning. What have we got?"

"Homeless person, possibly a junkie. Same sores as those other two. No sign of violence, so, unless you see anything, I'll hand it over to you."

"Do you have a name for them?" the FME asked as Stansfield joined him by the corpse.

"No. No ID. Looks like your typical down-and-out."

The FME approached and pulled latex gloves on. "We've had the odd banker or executive, down on his luck, end up in the gutter and die of an overdose, or even exposure. Don't assume they weren't someone and haven't been missed."

Stansfield shrugged, not caring. "All I want to know is if your initial examination says suspicious death or natural causes."

The FME knelt beside the body and carefully looked it over, then stood and said, "No evidence of injury and obvious signs of disease, I'm happy to give 'natural causes' as my preliminary cause of death."

Stansfield sighed in relief. "In that case, I'll sign the body over to you and be on my way."

The forensic medical examiner snapped off his gloves, wipes his hands on a wad of tissue and took out the paperwork. Stansfield sighed again for very different reasons: it seemed as if nine-tenths of his time was spent either form-filling or compiling reports. Just handing over the body of a diseased tramp seemed to require a good deal of paper. He was just grateful there was no evidence a crime had been committed: a crime meant a crime scene and a crime scene meant scene-of-crime officers bagging and tagging everything after a fingertip search, and SOCO meant even more paperwork, with the prospect of a trial or inquiry at the end of it, and even more damnable paperwork.

Signing his name, he was done. He handed the forms back to the FME and said, "I'll be off, then."

The FME nodded absently as he and his assistant worked to get the body onto the gurney.

Stansfield was glad to get outside into the fresh air and away from both the smell and the sound of the rats scampering about in the darkness.

He headed over to his car, an average-looking mid-range model, neither too old nor too new, and climbed in. That was the one thing that could be said about the area, aside from a few junkies looking for somewhere quiet to shoot-up; virtually nobody came here, the recession having killed any dreams of turning the warehouses into luxury riverside apartments. Not that the change of use necessarily did much to discourage the vermin. Idly, he wondered if finding a banker moving into one of the disused shells they called home had the rats and what-had-you scurrying off in search of a new domicile.

Back to the station and a stack of paperwork and news that the terror alert had been raised another level.

"What does that make it?" he asked an Asian PC in the canteen as he hunched over a coffee. "We're doomed?"

"You tell me; you look like it's been keeping you up nights."

"I think I'm getting the flu." He gave a demonstrative sniff and scratched his wrist.

"Lovely," said another PC over her sausage roll.

"Maybe it's 'space flu'," said a PCSO.

"What are you blathering about?"

"It was on the news, last night. Earth passed through the tail of a comet a few days ago and they had on some scientist saying some illnesses might reach Earth like that, floating down into the atmosphere."

Stansfield coughed out "Nonsense," swallowed the last of his coffee, then got up and left the canteen.

"Must be the full moon," the custody sergeant said as they passed in the corridor. "Had a scabby whore in who was going mental in the hospital."

"And, that's why I'm glad I'm out of uniform," Stansfield called after him, before coughing violently and swearing.

"Sounds like you're going to have a lousy weekend," the custody sergeant replied with a laugh.

"Yeah." He sighed. It did. He filed his last paperwork of the day and headed out into the car park, enjoying the cool of the evening air on his skin.

The drive home was a nightmare. The polyester in his cheap suit had got him itching and his head was hurting. He wasn't sure if it was his sinuses or a migraine, as his sight seemed to be blurring; he nearly rear-ended a mini when he didn't notice it slowing.

"Honey, what's wrong?" asked his wife.

"Flu," he croaked.

"Poor baby." Her voice sounded rather husky and her cheeks were red like they'd been slapped. He'd read about it in the papers: slapped-face syndrome or something like that; he couldn't recall the proper name for it. A virus. He guessed they were both rundown: too many late nights, too many drinks, too many takeaways and too much stress. They needed to regain the balance in their lives.

She was scratching herself as much as he was.

"Polyester," he told her, sagely.

She shrugged and said, "Pizza for dinner."

He went upstairs and changed out of his suit; he noticed he had a rash. He'd see how things went over the weekend – no point relying on the out-of-hours service unless desperate – and make an appointment on Monday.

While his wife fetched the pizza from the kitchen table, he settled himself down on the settee and put the TV on and turned to the news. Leave the eating healthily and sitting up at the table for another day. Slump and relax tonight.

Just bad news. Always the same. Corruption. Sex scandal. The terror threat. An outbreak of norovirus closing a hospital. Ebola resurgent. Celebrity divorce. The comet the PCSO had mentioned. Syria. Always Syria. He snorted and called up a box set instead: something to munch pizza to.

His wife settled down beside him on the settee and put the pizza box on his lap before helping herself to a cheesy slice.

Stansfield found he didn't much fancy anything to eat, but he gobbled it down out of habit, and barely noticed that he scratched himself all the way through the meal until his wife declared she was off to bed.

"I'll be up in a minute," he said. He could do with a sleep.

There was a sudden crash, but no scream, just a low moan.

He headed upstairs as quickly as he could, head swimming and legs wobbling under him; he barely had the strength to take the steps.

He could hear quiet sobs: inarticulate, phlegm-rich sounds. They were coming from the bathroom.

He almost didn't approach. He knew it was his wife, had to be her, yet something primal told him not to.

He staggered over to the half-open door. There was a horrible smell and a splash of blood and yellow-green pus visible on the tiles. He heard something scuttle. He couldn't hear the sobbing anymore.

Stansfield turned and headed for the stairs, his only thought being to get away. From what, he'd no idea. He tried to remember where he'd left his phone, but his mind was just a blur or terror and pain. He needed help.

There was an unpleasant rippling sensation beneath his skin, as if his muscles were twitching of their own accord. But, it was more than that, he knew...

He tried to call for help, but his voice was just a gurgle. He swayed, then slowly fell forwards, and began to tumble down the stairs. His last conscious thoughts were to wonder if it would be Peters who'd find his body and whether the illness really had come from space and how many more were affected.

Then, his neck snapped, mercifully ending his life as his skin began to bulge and split.

15. BLACK BARN BY HANNAH CLARK

"You ready, sister?"

I glanced up from my sorting job in the trash can. The man before me was not my brother. He didn't look like anyone's brother. He watched me with wide, gray eyes, like he had scooped them from the sky behind him. Heavy clouds hunched over the Baltimore skyline. He broke my line of vision, like a ragged mountain between the skyscrapers. I straightened up from the trash can. My backpack leaned on my leg, and I reached down for it.

"Ready for what?" I asked.

"For the snow."

His hands were jammed in the pockets of his huge brown coat. He moved them around while he spoke, and they looked like twin aliens writhing in his gut.

"Big snow coming. Are you ready?" he said again.

I felt the strap of my pack with my thumb. If I swung it over my shoulder, I could probably run to the tracks and lose him.

"I'm ready," I said. He laughed. His whole streaked face lit up with beautiful white teeth. I paused.

"Nobody's ready." He chuckled. "Especially not you, skinny."

I closed my fist and considered knocking him for the last comment. He smiled again, and his teeth made me pause. My own mouth looked like the city sky behind me, dirty and poorly built. All of him, his coat, his heavy boots, his wild eyes, screamed wanderer, like me. But his mouth… that was built with money. I eyed his arms. Maybe he was hiding a fancy watch in those moth-eaten pockets.

"What're you selling?" I said, trying to sound tough. Trying to sound like I didn't have a thin sleeping bag and an overpass to protect me from the storm.

"I only sell to people with money. I give to my sisters."

He stepped towards me, and I raised my bag, ready to swing it at his head. He lifted his hands out of his dark pockets, showing two, weaponless palms. He smiled again, and I watched the perfect masonry of his mouth form the words, "just take this, and when it starts snowing..."

He reached one hand back into his coat, this time drawing it out closed. He slowly extended the fist toward me, like the branch of a tree, and opened his hand. "...you'll know where to go."

It was a rock.

I sighed and let my shoulders relax. Just another nut. A funny nut.

I took the rock from his smooth hand. The gray stone sat neatly in my palm and had a solid, comforting weight.

It could probably pack a good fist.

When I looked up, the man had gone. I looked across the street, and up at I-95, roaring on the overpass above. Nothing.

I was grateful he didn't give me a shelter card, or a church flyer, or something stupid like that. "Homeless advocates" were always sneaking around, trying to herd you.

I slipped the rock into my pocket and lifted my pack. I had to tell Yaga about this guy.

***

I found the old stump of a woman behind a line of dumpsters by Back River Housing. She had flipped all the dumpster lids open, so they rested at an angle against the building. Beneath this lean-to she had stacked wooden pallets, two feet high, and I found her sitting on the pallets with her shopping cart parked next to her.

I peeked into her palace and whispered, "Can I come in?"

She sat with her eyes closed, cross-legged, on piles of torn tarps and bags.

"Leave your pack in the cart," she muttered, without opening her eyes.

I did so, and crawled up onto the pallets and under the dumpster lids.

"Is this for the snow?" I asked, squeezing besides her. She smelled like fish and smoke and magic, but maybe that was the dumpster.

"I'm making an igloo," she opened one eye long enough to wink at me. "I'm going to stay here, and no pigs will move me, because they are all running from the snow."

93

She giggled, a high, old woman laugh, and then snapped both of her eyes open to stare at me.

"What've you got?"

I smiled and dug a hand into my pocket.

"Something funny. A nutty old guy gave me a rock today. He said it would show me where to go from the snow."

I opened my hand to show her.

"Oh, wait…" I muttered, looking down at it. I hadn't noticed it before, but the rock had black letters on it, like someone had written on it with a sharpie. The small, jagged letters spelled out The Black Barn.

"This must have been on the other side," I said. "I didn't really look at it."

Yaga stared down at the rock. I felt a heat rise in my stomach. That guy wasn't a funny bum. He was trying to get me to come to his shelter. Or worse, his house.

"Ugh," I grunted. I made to toss the rock away from me, but Yaga caught my hand.

"It's just some shelter shit, by a poser," I said.

I pulled my hand away from Yaga. I knew his teeth were too perfect.

"They dress like us," I said, and squeezed the rock in my hand like it might pop, "then they try to pull us into shelters to stroke their own egos."

I raised my hand to throw the rock away. Yaga grabbed me again.

"No." She lowered my wrist and gently pried my fingers apart. "No, this is not a trick."

"I'm not going to a shelter," I said, a little too loud.

Yaga winced and looked up at me.

"I would never let you," she whispered, "but this is different."

She slipped the rock from my hand and studied it, turning it over in her hands.

"What did he look like?" she said after a few moments.

"Like us, I guess."

I watched a rat scurry up the side of Yaga's pallets. I kicked my foot and it squealed, running back under the dumpster.

"He had smooth hands, though, and rich teeth, so I know he was posing."

Yaga's deep, creased eyes widened. She pressed the rock back into my hand.

"You've been picked."

I felt laughter bubble up my throat. I released it in a long, slow laugh.

"Picked to be harassed?"

She shook her head, still staring at me. I felt her warm, rough hand around mine.

"You remember my daughter?"

I remembered a small girl, with big, soft arms and a red face. I'd only met her twice, right after I left my dad.

"This same man found her, last March. And gave her a way out of the cold."

None of us, the people under the bridge, had seen Yaga's daughter after that March storm. We figured she froze.

Yaga gazed out of her hovel at the road. The snow had started to fall. I watched the flakes spin in slow circles before the wet street consumed them.

"She told me, just before the storm, 'I'm going to the Black Barn.' And she looked so happy."

I stared down at the stone, heavy in my palm, and felt a sudden desire to destroy it. I flung it away and heard it crack against the pavement.

"No!"

Yaga scrambled out of her tarps. Her small legs carried her across the alley, and she knelt over the rock.

"You broke it…" she called back at me. "Oh, my…" her voice trailed off. I pulled myself out of the lean-to and moved to her. The stone lay on the ground, cracked in half. I reached down and picked it up off the wet ground. The stone came apart in my hands and I gasped.

The inside of the rock was hollow and beautiful. A sharp purple lining of crystals coated the interior. The shimmering points of the purple crystals melted into a deep blue and then fused to each other at the base. The center of the rock was a cathedral of color and light.

There was also a piece of paper.

"How the hell…." I pulled the paper out of the stone, the solid stone, which held it.

"He must have glued it together…." I muttered, but Yaga wasn't listening to me.

"Read it," she hissed.

I fumbled to unroll the scrap of paper. It was thick and yellow, like a piece torn from an old book. I pressed it open with my fingers and read, Emily, we have a place for you.

I dropped the scrap of paper. Yaga snatched it out of a puddle. She stared at the writing, then up at me.

"How did he know your name?"

I shook my head. A gust of wind tore down the alley, sending white snow into my face. I turned back to the dumpsters.

"Can I stay here?"

Yaga had already pulled my pack from her cart. She pressed it into my hands.

"You have to go," she said. "This is something uncanny. And if we ignore it, it will just follow you."

I watched Yaga hobble back to her lean-to. She looked back, once at me, and I thought I saw tears streaming down her cheeks. I wanted to shout, call her a senile crone, but instead I shouldered my bag and walked into the blind snow. I wasn't going anywhere.

My feet carried me down the deserted streets. Everyone had already holed up for the storm. I passed a few promising spots, park structures, sheds, and a few dumpster tents, but every time I glanced in, a huddled figure told me it was taken. My ears and nose felt like ice, and I was losing feeling in my fingers.

I wandered past the train yard and down to the riverside. I figured the bridge might have room. As I turned out from an industrial park, I paused. Someone had spray-painted small black letters on the side of a cinderblock wall. Black Barn. I looked up at the wall, which belonged to a warehouse. The featureless building loomed up through the snow. I glanced around for a door. One stood just to the left of me. I hadn't noticed it before. On a whim, I tried the handle, and it turned. I eased the metal door open, and a dim interior stretched before me. I considered turning around, but a blast of wind pushed me inside. I stumbled over the threshold, and the door slammed from the gust. I turned to push it open again, but it was locked.

I wiggled the handle again and pressed my shoulder into the door. Nothing.

I stood in the darkness, listening for movement. The room was warm, but I couldn't tell how large. I felt at the wall, but found no switch. I pressed my back against the door, like an anchor, and slid into a seated position. If anything, I could wait out the storm here, and then someone, eventually, would come turn on the lights. Eventually.

I had no watch or flashlight. The only sound I heard was the wind, howling outside. I set my pack in my lap and dug around inside for something to eat. I found some dried apricots, picked from the trash can earlier this morning. I nibbled like a mouse and waited. The minutes, or hours, stretched into the darkness. I twitched at every noise. Somehow, my eyes never adjusted to the dark. It stayed an inky abyss.

After a while, I returned to my bag for more food, but I found only crumbs. My hand brushed against a length of rope I used to tie my tarp down. I pulled it out and felt the fiber in my hands. Standing up, I set my pack against the door and tied one end of the rope to the door handle. Then I tied the other end to my belt loop. My tether in place, I started feeling down one wall, touching along its warm, smooth paint. After about ten feet, the rope tugged at my waist. I hadn't found anything on the wall. I doubled back and reached the door, walking in the other direction. Ten feet later, the rope stopped my progress. Nothing.

I extended my hands in front of my face and stepped out from the wall. Keeping the rope taut, I moved in an arc through the darkness. Slower this time, I waved my hands before me, taking small, uneven steps. I felt like an astronaut in the void of space.

I kicked something. I felt a slight impact on my foot and froze as I listened to a clinking metal object bounce away from my foot.

I knelt down, feeling around my feet, but I found nothing. Thinking it had landed ahead of me, I crawled along the floor, feeling damp concrete under my hands. I moved about a foot before my hands brushed against something soft. I jumped back, and then slowly felt at the space before me. My fingers met smooth fabric, like a blanket, with something soft and thick beneath, like a sleeping bag. I pressed more. Something was underneath. Something long and solid. I felt in the folds of the blanket.

Something with legs.

I recoiled and grabbed the rope. I pushed myself backwards until my back hit the wall. Arms shaking, I felt along the interior until the found the edge of the door. I reached for my pack, and found nothing. The wet, bare concrete met my hands.

I reached up and pulled at the door handle. It rattled like the wind outside.

"Help!" I shouted, and immediately regretted it. My voice echoed into the blackness, bouncing across the void and betraying enormity of the room.

Then I heard a response.

"What do you want?"

The voice echoed like mine, but without the fear.

I could only think to say, "light."

Immediately lights clapped on. A blinding whiteness erased my vision. I raised my arms and squinted until the room materialized. In front of me, rows and rows of red blankets lay, draped over long mounds. The blankets stretched lengthwise, hiding narrow, pointed forms.

I could tell they were bodies, because one lay ten feet in front of me.

A red blanket covered the form, well, covered most of it. One corner lay, peeled back, and beneath it I saw a face.

"I'm glad you came, sister."

My head snapped up. The man from the overpass stood between a row of red blankets. He had the same brown coat, the same hidden hands, the same pearl mouth. I watched him walk, like Moses through his red sea.

"Do you need something to eat?" he asked. I just stared at him. He stopped, about three steps past the uncovered man.

"Everyone needs to eat," he continued, moving his pocketed hands so the front of his coat twisted like a growling stomach. "The problem is," he paused, smiling down at me, "where to find food."

I looked past him for an exit. At the end of the long, white warehouse, I saw another black door.

"You weren't ready for the storm, were you, Emily?"

I refocused on his gleaming mouth, but stayed quiet.

"That's why you came here. That's why they all come."

My eyes wandered without my consent, down to the edge of the body on the floor. I looked, finally, at the pale, sunken face.

My breath stopped, and I saw that his eyes were empty, hollow sockets, and his mouth…

I screamed.

His mouth gaped open, brown, with black holes where his teeth had been torn out.

The man above me smiled.

"Do you know what they keep in barns, Emily?"

I pushed off from the ground, bolting past the man, running for the door.

But I forgot the rope. My waist snapped back, jerking my head down and feet off the ground. I landed on my side and my head hit the ground. Stars exploded in my eyes, and through the blur I saw a black figure eclipse the light above me.

"Cattle," he whispered.

The lights snapped off.

Through the darkness, I thought I saw a perfect row of white teeth, growing larger as they neared my eyes.

16. INQUIRY BY JAY WILBURN

I don't remember if I shoved the kid or not. I'm not giving that answer though.

Stanley Baker swallowed twice as he looked around the room. The principal of the junior high school, Dr. Liza Bell, was there as was his assistant principal, Ms. Kimberly Darn. All his bosses were women and divorced. It was Ms. Darn pronounced as a "z" and not an "s." Liza was spelled with a "z." The kid's dad, Mr. Harrach, was there and sitting too close. The kid Mr. Baker didn't even teach was there smiling like the king of the world.

Why isn't the police officer in this meeting? Kids and parents run the school.

Mr. Harrach jumped right into the action. "You're lucky I don't come right across this table at you."

Mr. Baker coughed hard into his elbow before he responded with a voice breaking on every other word. "I want the police officer present for this meeting."

The principals looked at each other.

Dr. Bell mumbled. "The officer is at training today. Mr. Harrach, refrain from threats or there will be no meeting."

"I'm just saying he's lucky I don't. Not that I'm going to."

Stan Baker watched the kid smile wider in the corner of his vision.

You're lucky I don't come over, you sawed-off punk.

"Tell your side of the incident, Mr. Baker."

The assistant principal scribbled her notes.

Baker pictured himself snapping her pencil with the plastic flower bobbing on one end. Everyone gasped at his presumption. The sawed-off punk and his father nodded thinking this proved the teacher was the monster. Then, Baker jammed both broken ends into her eyes. The balls burst and leaked like boils. Her screams filled the room and one of them vomited. Baker turned slowly and dared Mr. Harrach to come across the table because Baker was the lucky one.

Baker croaked. "I'm not aware of an incident."

Mr. Harrach demanded. "Last Thursday when you yelled at my son."

Mr. Baker coughed before he answered in a breaking voice. "I came back from having flu on Thursday. My voice is lower and more strained from being sick. It probably sounds different to the kids. This may be the one point in my life that I'm not capable of yelling."

Mr. Harrach snorted. "Are you losing your voice from yelling at kids?"

"No," Baker answered low and rumbling. "It's the flu."

Ms. Darn added. "It's true. We interviewed him on Thursday. He has no voice."

That's actually not true, but I'm thankful for your bad memory, boss lady.

The kid whispered. "He's a liar."

Everyone seemed to ignore it. Stan Baker could not. He looked. The elves crawled out of the candy dish on the table. They nodded at Stan and lifted their tiny blades. They crawled up the kid's chair. They leapt from the table. The kid tried to swat them away, but they kept coming. They held his head back by his hair and pressed their blades into his exposed throat as he cried.

What the hell is that kid's name anyway? Try to get his name before you slice him, boys.

Mr. Harrach ignored the attack. "You spit on my son with the flu?"

"No"

"My son says you spit on him."

"He did," the boy choked out.

"Let's not do this," Baker demanded.

The elves stopped and withdrew their knives without drawing blood. They were disappointed. They waited along the back of the kid's chair incase Baker changed his mind.

"Are you calling River a liar?"

River … what a name for a kid. Not raising a future president, are you? Yes, River is a big, lying liar with a stupid, gullible, worthless father. Next question.

Baker coughed. "River does not like being told what to do. He has a father that believes any story he tells. So, he tells a story instead of just doing what he is told."

"What do you mean?"

"He was slamming lockers and throwing book bags. I told him to stop."

Mr. Harrach shook his head. "He says you shoved him into the locker, told him to stand by the classroom, spit on him, and then threatened to give him a referral."

"After twenty years of teaching, you're saying I shove a kid, but then tell him where to stand. I spit on him and then my biggest threat is that I'm going to write what he did on a piece of paper and turn it in to the office?"

A drawn silence filled the room. Mr. Harrach breathed in bursts with his arms crossed.

How would you like me to cut an extra hole to help you get more air? River can watch how real men solve problems.

Dr. Bell broke the silence. "Sometimes I spray when I talk. It is not really spitting spitting."

Mr. Harrach looked from the principal to the teacher. "Is that what you did? Was it an accident?"

Mr. Baker shook his head. "That sounds like a terrible condition, Dr. Bell, but no, that is not what I did. I did not spit on anyone. That did not happen."

Mr. Harrach grunted. "I guess we're just going to have to agree to disagree on this."

The principals were nodding and starting to get up.

Mr. Baker growled. "No."

Everyone turned and stared at him.

He pictured a copy of himself standing up and taking the letter opener from the desk. The copy drove the blunt point into the soft flesh of Mr. Harrach's throat before anyone knew what was happening. River jumped up. The elves wrapped up his ankles and dumped the kid back in the chair. They held his shoulders and pinned him to the upholstery with their tiny blades as they giggled. Mr. Harrach struggled, but the copy of Stan climbed into the man's lap and twisted the letter opener inside the sucking wound.

The copy looked at the shocked principals and smiled. "Bad day for training the resource officers! Now, I want this jackass dead. He wants to live. I guess we'll just have to agree to disagree, right?"

The original Mr. Baker continued in the quiet, bloodless room. "We're not going to agree to disagree about me committing a crime. Teachers only have reputation and you're not taking mine because your son doesn't want anyone telling him what to do. You can pretend like you don't know, but this isn't the first time he has lied to you to stay out of trouble and you know it. I'm done with kids making accusations with no consequences. This inquiry is done. If the lie continues, I'll be the one suing and I won't stop until we are both broke. You have far more to lose in this than I do. I assure you."

Dr. Bell said, "We should probably take a break. Maybe—"

"No," Mr. Baker cut her off, "we're finishing this now. I thought the camera was working in that spot and that's the first thing I asked for when they brought me in about this nonsense. All this is for want of a working camera. Fix the camera! I didn't do anything, but to tell your son to behave which is my job and which is his job. If Dr. Bell thought for a second that I was shoving kids, she would fire me before you could get in the parking lot."

Dr. Bell nodded. Mr. Harrach's jaw worked the muscles along the side of his head. Blood gushed out of the hole in his throat. The copy of Mr. Baker lifted the letter opener and offered to go at the man again. Mr. Baker shook his head slightly at the copy while no one was looking.

"Then, I guess we are done," Mr. Harrach stood up and extended his hand.

Mr. Baker stood and coughed into his elbow. "I don't want to take a chance of passing off this sinus infection. I wouldn't wish this on anyone this close to the holiday."

Harrach shrugged. "Suit yourself, stranger."

He turned and shook hands with the lady bosses.

The copy licked the blood off the letter opener as he waited. The original Mr. Baker could taste the metallic, salty blood as he swallowed several times.

Mr. Baker walked toward the door of the office and stepped out into the hall. He turned back and looked through the doorway at River still pinned to the chair by the Elvin blades. The boy shook his head at Mr. Baker.

Mr. Baker arched his back so the working camera in the office hallway did not pick up his face. He smiled at River and spit on the tile at his feet. River looked at the other adults talking and then back at Mr. Baker. The boy lifted his hand below the table and stuck up his middle finger.

Mr. Baker nodded and walked up the hall.

He whispered to himself and to the copy that walked to his right and just behind him. "Remember, the camera over my room isn't working."

The copy nodded and licked the flat side of the letter opener again. Mr. Baker swallowed several times on his way back to his classroom.

17. YOU SHOULD'VE CUT THEIR HEADS OFF

BY KERRY G.S. LIPP

I woke up blindfolded and handcuffed to a chair with no memory of what got me there. My memory felt as dark as my blindfold. It smelled normal, even pleasant but I heard several people around me shaking their handcuffs, the metal rattling against wood. Some were screaming, demanding to be let go, asking what was going on and all the other stuff people would say waking up bound and blindfolded in a strange place.

"Shut up," a voice yelled and when multiple people didn't shut up, I heard the unmistakable sounds of fists striking faces. Everyone got quiet pretty quick after that.

"Now," the same voice started again. "Who you are and why you're here is completely irrelevant. All you need to know is that in a few minutes you will be knocked out again. Each of you will awaken freed of your bonds with a kitchen knife in your hands. The last one left alive, will be the only survivor, and that survivor will be supremely rewarded. We're watching. Anyone who leaves with someone in here still alive will be greeted with a bullet in the head when they step out that door. Get out or die trying. I don't care if you have questions. I won't answer them. If you're the last one alive, you'll get your answers."

A few people sobbed, but no one protested.

"Release the gas," the voice said.

I heard something hit the ground, a hiss, and smelled something weird. It was hard to tell when I actually passed out, but I did, already thinking about what I could do with my knife upon waking.

***

Through luck or fate, I woke first, though groggy for a moment. I looked around to get my bearings. It all came back to me as I saw five others slumped around the table, heads down, nodded off like bored husbands during a Sunday sermon. I didn't recognize any of the others but I did notice that we were a rainbow.

105

Three women and three men including myself. All different races and ages. Thank God there were no children, but even if there were, I would've killed them without hesitation to get home to my own.

This must've been some kind of sick social experiment or some kind of test. We were seated around a dinner table in mock family fashion. Everyone looked like they'd just passed out after their third helping of Thanksgiving dinner, but then I laid eyes on the glint of the giant butcher knives in each of their hands and remembered my own.

I looked at it. Squeezed it. It felt good. Felt right. Familiar. I wondered if it was a coincidence or if whoever set this up knew that this weapon, and especially this style, was my armament of choice.

After shaking the haze from my head, I felt fine and jumped up. I'd killed a whole bunch of people before with a knife just like this one, and I could have these other five slaughtered before they awoke. Even though I loved a challenge, I wasn't crazy about the odds, and had the knife in the throat of the woman sitting next to me before I was even out of my chair. She didn't flinch as the blood shot across the table and spilled down her shirt.

I grabbed her knife from her lifeless hand and my own easily came free from her neck. I thought I might have to saw it out, but it slipped out smooth, a perfect cut. I wound around the table and stabbed and sliced and killed. I didn't know who they were and I didn't care.

The spray of blood from severed arteries and veins never ceases to amaze me. Abstract patterns and splatters covered the walls, highlighted the table, and in the end, even dripped from the ceiling.

I slashed all of them before they woke up, except for the last one. A man, not white, but otherwise I could not expound. When he opened his eyes and saw me coming they didn't show fear or desperation, they showed rage, hostility. Not many people would react to a man drenched in blood wielding two big knives coming at him that way, and it made me wonder just who he and these others were. I didn't have much time to think that through though, and I jammed both blades into his angry eyes.

Looking around at the mess of the dining room, I thought about how lucky I'd been to come around before any of the others and wondered if this scenario had somehow been rigged. I guessed I'd find out soon enough.

I wiped the blood from my face and headed to the front door, and swung it open. I took a deep breath, enjoyed once last whiff of spilled blood and went outside for some fresh air and some answers.

When I stepped onto the porch, I saw laser sights all over my chest, some stinging my eyes, blinding, making me squint. I dropped my knives and shielded them.

"I'm out. They're dead. I won," I said from behind my hands.

"No, you lose," said a man about fifty yards away, pointing a rifle straight at me. It was the same voice that spoke while we were blindfolded.

I poked my head over my hands to see him. He shook his head. Other men surrounded me from a distance, all with guns drawn.

"What the fuck are you talking about and what the hell was that anyway?" I shouted. "They're dead."

"Not all of them," he said and took a couple steps forward. "Two are alive in there still bleeding out. You should've cut their heads off," he said and smirked at me. "You failed, and we don't reward a job done halfway. Looks like no one wins this time. Pity you couldn't follow simple directions, we could've used you."

"For what?" I asked.

"If I told you I'd have to kill you," he said and smiled, flexing his finger over the trigger.

Then he told me.

The guns fired.

18. STRANGER THAN FICTION BY ROB SMALES

Gunshots erupted in the darkened living room.

Linda glanced through the doorway from the kitchen. "Billy, what are you watching?" Most of the big television was visible over the back of the couch, currently showing close-ups of shambling, rotting people being cut to pieces by flying bullets. A lump of shadow stuck up over the couch back, a silhouette against the lighted screen outlining ears and a baseball cap.

The silhouette spoke. "The Stalking Dead." On the show, the view shifted to a ragtag gaggle of people, looking pretty similar to the shambling horde but for the fact that they weren't actually rotting, all firing guns again and again, some stopping to take obvious aim, others merely spraying lead. There were pistols and rifles, a couple of shotguns, and one man with a big revolver who fanned the hammer like he was in an old-time western.

"Oh, honey," Linda said, dismayed. "You're only twelve. You know I don't like you watching this kind of thing."

On the screen, zombie heads exploded like decorative pumpkins being hit with baseball bats two weeks after Halloween. Gore and chunks of meat and brain spattered the surrounding crowd of undead, who didn't seem to notice. Linda felt her stomach twist, then rise a little.

"Aw, Mom." The silhouette shifted, the head turned, and Billy's face came into view, a half-moon hanging over the couch back, one side lit by the flickering light from the television, the other cast in shadow. Even more than the images on the screen, this strange view of her son made Linda shudder.

"I'm out," said the revolver-wielding man, raising his smoking gun toward the sky. "Me too," said one of the rifle-bearers, then two women with pistols also retreated, cursing. "Step aside," said a skinny man with a hillbilly accent, stepping forward and drawing an old cavalry saber with flourish. "I ain't gotta reload this." With a rebel yell, the swordsman charged the small army of zombies, followed closely by a man and woman carrying what looked like fire axes.

"Baby, don't you have some homework to do, instead of watching that stuff?"

"Can't I do it after?"

Linda shook her head. "Now, please."

Billy sighed. "All right." He picked up the TV remote as the dryer buzzed loudly. Linda went through the kitchen to the laundry room, scooped the warm, dry clothes into a basket and headed for the bedroom. Passing through the living room on her way to the stairs, she was shocked to see the big screen now showed a pair of men next to a cement highway on-ramp. Though strategically-placed digital blurs covered their groins, they were obviously naked, and one man was—nausea twisted her stomach again, harder this time—crouching over the other and eating his face.

"I thought I told you to do your homework." Her sharp tone was slightly spoiled by the bile packing her throat, but it was still enough to make Billy jump.

"I am," he said, lifting a notebook and pen into view. "It's for civics. I'm supposed to write a summary of a current news story."

Linda strode right to the back of the couch, laundry basket on one hip. "What are you—" She could see the bottom of the television now, see the local Channel Seven News graphic and the clock in the corner of the screen. "This is . . . this is real?"

"Yeah," said Billy, balancing the notebook on his lap and readying the pen to take notes. "They think he's on some kind of drugs. Salty-something."

Jesus, she thought, he sounds so matter-of-fact about it.

Gunshots sounded, and though a bullet punched a hole in the crouching man's leg, he kept right on eating. The scene suddenly shifted to a split screen, the crouching cannibal on the right, the local news anchor on the left.

"Police were forced to fire into the assailant multiple times, wounding him fatally. Though the victim's name is still being withheld, said assailant has now been identified as . . ."

And this guy sounds bored! No wonder Billy's so—

Billy's pen was scratching across the page.

"Don't do this one."

Billy looked up. "Huh?"

"Don't do this one," she repeated.

"But I—"

"I don't care, and I don't want any argument." She moved toward the stairs. "Do something else. See what's on channel five, instead."

From the couch came a sigh worthy of a full-blown teenager; Linda ignored it and went up to the bedroom. She folded the clothes quickly, automatically, her mind filled with the images she'd just seen. I had that same assignment when I was his age, she recalled. Christ, I did mine on a presidential speech. Times sure have changed.

When she got back downstairs, she was pleased to see the inside of a bright courtroom filling the widescreen, a white-jumpsuited old man in center stage. Well, this is better, I guess, she thought, moving up behind the couch to see Billy busily scribbling away. "What's the trial ab—" she began, but the commentator's voiceover cut in.

"Seventy-nine-year-old Jieming Liu is charged with killing and eating his wife, Yuee Zhou, age seventy-three. The crime was discovered when the couple's son went to check on his parents in their apartment in Shrewsbury, Massachusetts. Zhou's body was discovered in the back bedroom, where Liu, who suffers from dementia, had begun consuming her left ar—"

Linda scooped up the TV remote, and her thumb came down on the channel button.

Billy's head popped up. "Hey!"

"Not that. You can't do that." Her thumb came down again and again, the TV finally settling on Channel Nine News.

"Twenty-six people—twenty students and six adults—were shot and killed at the Sandy Hook Elementary School in Newton, Connec—"

She mashed the button, then again, going straight back to Channel Seven News, hoping they'd moved on to something other than the face-eating man. They had.

"—a midnight screening of The Dark Knight Rises and opened fire with a semi-automatic weapon, killing twelve and wounding—"

She punched back to channel five.

"—twenty-one-year-old Morgan State University student, admitted to police to killing his roommate and eating his heart and brain—"

Back to nine.

"—opened fire in a Seattle, Washington coffee shop, killing five people before turning the gun on hi—"

She punched two buttons, going directly to one of the higher channels. On the screen, the revolver-wielding man, dirty and blood-spattered, waved an arm. "Come on! We have to stick together!" A group of ragged, gore-speckled people filed past, including the man with the saber and the couple with the axes. Linda tossed the remote onto the couch.

"But this is the—"

"I know what it is," Linda said, the words rough in her throat. "You just watch this while I go pick up a newspaper. We can do that homework when I get back."

"All right!"

On the screen the man with the revolver was making some sort of speech, but it suddenly pixilated, then went blurry. She turned to go get the car keys, wiping the tears from her eyes. At least in fiction, she thought, we're not doing it to ourselves.

~ ~ * * ~ ~

Author's Note:

Each of the news stories mentioned above are real items I made note of in 2012: all in the United States, all in the same year. In 1981, when I was twelve years old, any one of these items could have been called the News Story of the Year. In 2012, it was just . . . the news. In the words of Linda in the story above: times sure have changed.

19. GOT MILK? BY JOHN ALFRED TAYLOR

"Now paint in little white eye sockets," Colin told Briony. "And teeth at the bottom." He'd already had her draw India-ink crossbones under the big black mole.

"You're sure this won't piss-off your dermatologist?" Briony asked, squinting in concentration as she bent to her task at his left side.

"Not Doc Schulmann. He likes his laughs. Should have heard him joking when he snipped off the tags in my armpit."

Colin hoped he and the Doctor would still be laughing two hours from now, but wasn't going to bother Briony with gloomy possibilities. At least his mole had smooth edges and was still all one color.

"There," she said, standing up. "Give it a few minutes to dry before you put on your shirt." With Briony wearing nothing but a running bra and a thong, Colin began to wish that he didn't have an appointment.

She went down to the garage with him. Must be worried too, he decided. Couldn't have that, so he slapped her on the ass cheek that had a tribal tattoo, and grinned his widest. "Back before you know it."

Briony smiled back uncertainly.

Doctor Schulmann stared and pursed his lips for a second, then chuckled and shook his head in admiration. "How long did it take you to think that up?"

"Not long," Colin said. "Gallows humor comes quick."

"Yeah, and it's the only thing that keeps us going sometimes," said the Doctor, looking at the mole for a second as if he was trying to memorize the decoration before he scrubbed it off. "You know what we call kids in burn wards?"

"No."

"'Krispy kritters.' And old people who're a bit out of it are 'gomers'."

"And I thought you guys in medicine were humanitarians."

"Oh we are. That's why we have to talk rough sometimes. So tell me about this mole."

"I've had it for years. But then it got bigger, and started sticking out."

"Like when?"

"The last two or three weeks. I thought you ought to look at it."

Schulmann nodded. "Glad you came in."

"It's malignant?"

"Not at all." The Doctor palpated the mole, while Colin tried not to recoil. He measured its length and width with a short plastic ruler, wrote on his clipboard, then looked at it admiringly again. "It's benign. Just a bit unusual. Which is why I'm glad you came in—I might want to write it up."

"So what is it?"

"Are you ready for this?"

"I don't know till you tell me."

"It's a supernumerary nipple."

"A what?"

"An extra nipple—not as rare as you might think. Mostly they're rudimentary. Though I've never heard of one developing like this."

Colin cringed inside. "Can it be removed?"

"No reason to. If it's not broke, don't fix it."

"But it's growing."

"So it is. Which is why I want you back here in a week."

"You just want to write me up."

"That too," Doctor Schulmann admitted.

After parking the car, Colin walked to the end of the garage he was using as a temporary studio, and stared at the roughed-out shape of The Nurturer standing among spalled chips and shavings of walnut. Her great tits had lost some of their appeal.

Upstairs, Briony rose from the futon sofa as he came in. "You're all right—it isn't bad?"

"It isn't bad, but it's weird. Really weird."

"Weird?"

"You won't believe this."

"Try me."

"It's a nipple. Doc Schulmann says supernumerary nipples aren't as rare as you might think."

"Can't he take it off?"

"No need. But he wants to see me in a week—I think he wants to write it up."

She grinned. "I don't know of any single-cup bras."

"They're called yarmulkes," he said, remembering an old joke about what you got when you cut a brassiere in half. "Yarmulkes with chin straps. But a big Band-Aid ought to do."

"I hope so."

That night Colin woke just enough to realize he was uncomfortable sleeping on his chest, turned onto his right side and went back to sleep.

And dreamed. The sun was setting, with long shadows sliding across the lawn and creeping up trees. But these shadows were absolute, containing no hint of light or color, sliding together like puddles, merging into a rising tide, a flood of utter blackness—

He jerked awake. He'd been sleeping on his chest again. He turned and shifted till he felt easy, then fell back into the dream. He was drowning in darkness, except now he wasn't drowning, but rather swallowing the thick stuff as if it was air.

"Sweetie," Briony said. "You've got ink all over your top."

Colin stared, the bit of fried egg on his fork stopped before his open mouth. "Can't have. Haven't written or drawn anything since two days ago."

"Whatever. But there it is."

Colin finished his breakfast before he went to look in the bathroom mirror. There were dark smears on his sleeveless sleeping shirt, and he saw why when he pulled it up. The stuff oozing from his new nipple did look like ink. Briony had followed him in and was looking at the mirror over his shoulder, reaching around him and running her finger through the blackness before he snagged a bathroom tissue.

"Don't!" he said as she first smelled it and then licked it, but Briony laughed and reached around again for another sample. This time she popped her finger in her mouth, sucked it clean and smiled.

"It's milk, silly."

He shook his head. "Whoever heard of black milk?"

"Black or white, it's just milk. Taste it and see." She picked up more on her finger, offered it to him. He turned his head away in revulsion; bad enough to be lactating, but worse to think of actually tasting himself. He wiped the stickiness off, but more welled out within a moment. Colin reached for another tissue.

By afternoon that side of his chest was aching, with the dark overflow dribbling down his stomach, till Briony had him stand over the kitchen sink while she milked him. That was short-term relief, but finally she gave up and left him standing alone at the sink, saying they needed something more.

Colin heard the car start up, and squeezed his new breast as well as he could, spattering the white porcelain with leopard spots. He kept working the new nipple; what else could he do till she came back?

At last Briony was coming up the stairs, then she was taking the electric breast pump out of the box. "Please," he said. "Please hurry."

"Gotta read the instructions," she whispered, then muttered "Oh fuck."

"What's wrong?"

"This thing was made in China—instructions don't make sense. Says we have to plug it in to an electrical outlep—I should hope so, even if we don't have any outleps—and the cone has suckiness. So forget the instructions. I'm going to plug this in, outlep or no outlep, and you put the cone where it matters, and tell me if it has suckiness."

Briony plugged it in, and ohgodohgodhowgood the cone had suckiness.

"We ought to save some," she said, lifting the pump away. "Save it in the fridge."

"Why?"

"Nursing mothers do."

Colin couldn't help frowning. "I'm not a nursing mother."

"Of course not. But your doctor will want a specimen."

"Oh yeah." He'd been too busy to think of Shulmann till now, but this was a genuine emergency—no need to wait till next week, "So you save some for the Doc, because I'm going to see about another appointment ASAP."

Briony emptied the breast pump's receptacle into a glass, crimped foil around the top for a lid and put it in the refrigerator. While she rinsed things, he admired her cool for a second, even if it was lots easier for her than him.

He speed-dialed Shulmann's office. All he got this late in the day was a tape-recording of the receptionist explaining office hours.

The Doc's home phone number wasn't in the book, but information found it. At least it's not an unlisted number, though he wasn't sure it was right because the answering machine voice was anonymous. If it was Shulmann's, he hadn't bothered to change the message and record his own greeting. When the tone came he gambled, blurting: "Doc, this is Colin MacIntire, the guy with the extra nipple. Things are happening…" He really couldn't say what to an answering machine. "…and I need to see you right away."

He felt a rush of power and pleasure when he had to use the pump again. Much more than relief, which explained the expression of the nursing mothers in so many pictures.

Doctor Shulmann didn't call back till half-past nine. "So what's happening if you have to see me this instant?"

"I'm giving milk."

A long silence till Colin wondered if they'd been disconnected. Then Shulmann almost whispered, "Really lactating?"

"I'm even using a breast pump. But the milk's black."

"Black milk? You're joking. I can fit you in before anybody tomorrow. I'll be at the office by 7:30. And bring a sample."

Colin was still washing down a stale Danish with orange juice when he looked in the fridge.

The specimen wasn't there.

He went into the shadowed bedroom. "Hon…"

Briony made a wordless noise.

"What happened to that sample for Doc Shulmann?"

"That? Threw it out… middle of the night… cause it went real sour."

His new breast was hot and rock-hard, but no time to drain it now. Colin put a loose jacket over his lopsided chest, scooped up the parts of the breast pump, and hurried downstairs. He looked them over in the passenger seat to make sure he had everything before turning the ignition key.Maybe this was good luck; now Doc could watch him produce a fresh specimen.

He didn't have to knock. Shulmann was waiting at the outside door, and led him down the dim hall to his waiting room, then through to an examining cubicle fierce with light.

"Dumped the stuff we saved," Colin said as he assembled the breast pump. "Thought you might like a fresh sample." He shucked the jacket, pulled off his t-shirt.

Doc Shulmann stared at the puffed and dripping nipple. "Black all right." He rolled an examining stool next to the counter for Colin, gestured for the cord of the pump, and plugged it in, then watched in fascination.

Colin centered the cone and switched on the pump. Pain for a moment, like lancing a boil, then relief, followed by a warmth he couldn't define until he felt a swelling in his groin. He glanced at Doc Shulmann, with the sensation becoming a flush of embarrassment, wondering if he'd noticed.

But no fear of that. "How often do you need to use the pump?"

"About every five or six hours so far."

"And the secretion's always that dark?"

Colin nodded.

"Then how do you know it's milk."

"My girlfriend tasted it."

The doctor tilted his head dubiously. "Let's see what the lab says."

"What did he think this time?" Briony asked as she poured him a second cup of coffee.

"Just go on the same another day, keep using the breast pump, see how things develop… he's sending a sample I gave him to a lab, and wants to see me again tomorrow afternoon. Says my hormones probably don't know what to think."

"I sure don't," she said. "But I do know you're hungry."

"Doc said I would be." He had two more pieces of toast slathered with butter and raspberry jam.

Then he needed another session with the breast pump. Now that he accepted the nature of the pleasure radiating from his nipple, he wallowed in a warm erotic fog till he was almost dizzy, seeing nothing but a red pulse through his half-closed eyes.

Once or twice Colin opened them enough to see Briony sitting on the futon, waiting. Afterwards he took a shower while she washed the pump.

He put on fresh clothes, and went down to the garage to look at his rudely-blocked statue of The Nurturer with renewed interest. Great tits all right, and worth finishing. Soon, but it could wait— right now he was too hungry.

Briony was in the bathroom when he came back upstairs. Wasn't there ice cream… butter pecan? Though as soon as he opened the freezer door he remembered eating it the night before. Cold cuts and cheese? Only uncooked bacon in the little drawer for snacks. Colin stooped to rummage in the next shelf down. Pickles and relish, a cardboard container of chicken broth, apple sauce. And then he found the three jars in the back, and realized what they held before he brought one out.

He lifted the jar as Briony entered. "Why didn't you pour this down the drain?"

"Because I need it."

"You said it was just milk."

Colin couldn't tell whether Briony was grimacing or smiling. "Oh it's milk… your special milk. It tastes like milk, but it's more.

One drink and you'll know." She reached for the jar with such certainty he gave it up without thinking.

Briony twisted off the lid and drank, then extended the jar to him. He sniffed before lifting it to his mouth. Black perhaps, but it was fresh and cool.

"It changes everything," she whispered.

He swigged from the jar, held it in his mouth for a moment before swallowing—very rich milk, but nothing more. "Doesn't change a thing."

"You'll see."

Then the room rippled and came back, only now the colors and shadows were brighter, the outlines sharper. He was one with the room, everything flickering with excitement and possibility, and he was powerful and calm; the hot dark source the world revolved around now that he knew what he could give.

He could see the swelling of Briony's lips, the tiny beads of perspiration on her skin. He knew what she was thinking. He owned her, he realized as he raised the jar again. More than that— he contained her, surrounded her.

She was the first.

Shulmann was next. Colin guessed the reason when the Doctor called that afternoon to tell him the lab had screwed up and needed a new specimen, asking if he could come after hours. He was sure the moment he stopped the car and felt the waves of need from the open clinic door.

Because the Doctor had drunk the first specimen, his mind was open; a satellite to a dark star. Colin used the pump in front of him, and made him beg for a drink. "Master," Shulmann said afterwards, nuzzling his god's hand with a mouth stained black.

From then on Shulmann came to him. Every night the three of them would eat a simple supper; Chinese takeout or a pizza out of the freezer—it didn't matter because Colin was the dessert. Being milked was pleasure, drinking himself at the same time was ecstasy. Being in the others' minds to feel the joy and power they were ingesting from him was even more wonderful, but best of all was knowing Briony and Shulmann were his, now and always his.

When another nipple appeared on his hip the Doctor talked about feedback, suggesting it resulted from drinking his own milk. Colin didn't know, but was glad to have the new teat, confident he could supply whatever milk was necessary.

Soon more was. One evening the Doctor brought his receptionist Nadine—no surprise, because the possibility had been in Shulmann's thoughts the night before and Colin already knew they had a thing going.

Emboldened, Briony introduced a friend from high school to their little circle. Then Shulmann recruited a plump nutritionist to watch Colin's diet. Next the lover of Briony's high school friend appeared, and Colin developed another nipple just in time.

Rituals grew with the group, beginning with a ragged hymn they sang before the communal meal.

> "We gather together to share Colin's blessing,
> His flowing is growing and makes us all glad—"

Colin was embarrassed at first, but soon began to consider it his due. Who else could give them the black milk? Let them express their gratitude of their own free choice.

Tonight was even more crowded. Most had had to stand for the love feast; deli potato salad and cold cuts passed around on paper plates, and now Colin's bodyguards were forcing a path for him. Finally he reached his throne through the throng that was trying to touch him. Before he sat down he turned and raised his hands in benediction.

He'd painted the Nurturer's nipples black after he had it brought upstairs, and now it stood beside him in a sea of votive candles.

Dressed in his white doctor's coat, Shulmann began the invocation, but Colin didn't listen because Briony had handed him the grail and bent to operate the breast pump. Being milked while swallowing his bounty always made him blind with pleasure.

And the more he drank the more he could give; in the last week five new nipples had appeared on his body.

Doctor Shulmann was filling cups from a pitcher of his milk and passing them to the worshippers. They waited patiently in line despite their eagerness for the black sacrament, content to be near the source, a god who was one of them.

His flock had grown past the point where he knew their names. There was Nadine's roommate Joyce, there was Marge the dietician, there were the Johnson twins who smiled in tandem, there was Ted the bartender, but there were others he barely recognized—the phalanx of blue-haired widows, the mechanic with grubby fingernails, the thin young man who wore sunglasses after dark. So many in fact, Shulmann was looking for a larger place to rent.

And right now the newly initiated ones were leaning across either arm of the throne, the thin girl suckling the teat under his shoulder blade, and the old man with the mustache moaning as he drank joy from Colin's upper arm.

At the rate new nipples were erupting Colin was sure he could supply all who came. He remembered a picture of the Magna Mater he had seen: her upper torso covered with breasts like a cluster of grapes. Perhaps in the end he could outdo Diana of the Ephesians—more would worship him…

20. BETTER THE DEVIL YOU KNOW BY MATT DRABBLE

The world turned slowly for Dr. Henry Loomis. It was slow, and it was black. He slept, he spooned differing foods into his mouth and he drifted.

The investigation was short and concise. His wife and son were butchered in their home. Their safe haven against the world had proven no haven at all. The monster that had ruined all of their lives had proven to be no great arch enemy. The man was no Lex Luther, no ex-psychiatric patient returning from his past seeking bloody vengeance. The monster in question was simply a random act of unbearable foul luck. Greg Barden was a drug addict lost beneath a crumbling system and high on whatever he had been able to cram into his already overloaded system. He had simply stumbled onto Henry's street looking for a house to burgle. The police had wasted no time in snatching him up and extracting a confession.

The next few months ran by in a hazy whisper for Henry. The funerals, the arrest, and subsequent trial took their time, but he could remember very little of it. His heart was broken and his days were black and empty; he merely existed and waited. His already shattered world was about to take a further devastating blow when the case against Greg Barden collapsed.

Henry sat in a CPS office and had it explained to him by a well-meaning but overstretched prosecutor.

"I don't understand," Henry said as the sticky heat from the office seared through his body.

"It was a cock-up, Dr. Loomis," the woman said with professional sadness. "The police had a warrant to search Barden's premises, which they did. During the search they discovered what they assumed was the murder weapon. The knife was covered in … shall we say … DNA evidence. Unfortunately there was an overnight period when the knife wasn't fully sealed and protected when it was in the lab for testing. Some technician was in a rush and didn't protect the knife properly. The defense was able to successfully argue that the evidence could have been tampered with, however ridiculous that sounds. The knife was the only direct link to the crime and when it was thrown out, we had no case. It's a technicality, Dr. Loomis," she had explained blandly. "Barden confessed on the basis of them finding the knife; without the knife being admissible, then his lawyer was able to have the confession retracted and the case was dismissed."

Henry had only been able to stare at the woman but his mind was already turning.

He waited until after dark before he drove to the hospital. The roads were deserted, and the night was appropriately stormy. Blackwater Heights was perched above the small fishing village of Ermsby; its presence was ominous as the Gothic spiked railings high on the roof pierced the black night sky.

He pulled up to the guard hut and was waved quickly through. If the guard was curious as to his reasons for visiting work so late, he knew better than to ask.

He reached the room that he wanted and used his keys to open the cell; he stepped inside and closed the door behind him. Everything that he was now doing went against all hospital rules and regulations, but he was hell and gone from caring.

"Ah, good evening, Doctor." Albert's voice drifted out of the dark room.

Henry could see the figure lying prone on the bed; the room was gloomy at the best of times during the night time, but Albert just seemed to swallow the light around him.

"Albert, we need to talk."

"I was wondering when you would arrive. I saw the news. Such a messy business," Albert tutted. "Such a messy business all round," he smiled. "I was so terribly sorry to hear about your unfortunate turn of events," he commiserated.

"Thank you, Albert," Henry replied stiffly.

"Oh, yes. I have been following the case with such avid interest, Dr. Loomis. All of that mess, all of that unnecessary mess," Albert said sadly. "And to have it all topped off by a blunder from the police; I can't imagine how you must feel, Dr. Loomis."

Henry peered through the gloom towards the motionless figure. He couldn't see Albert's face, but he could feel the aping of emotion from the monster within.

"I wouldn't think that there was much in this world that you would be incapable of imagining, Albert," Henry parried.

"Oh, you might be correct there, Henry; you just might be correct."

Henry noted the first time that Albert had referred to him by his Christian name. "What are you, Albert? I mean really, deep down, just what are you?"

"I'm just a man, Henry, nothing special - two arms, two legs, and all that."

"No, Albert. I think that you are much more than that. I think that you are a monster. Not of the Grimm Fairy Tales variety - you are human. But you are a monster all the same."

"Sticks and stones, Henry, sticks and stones," Albert chuckled. "And just what is it that you want from a monster such as me?"

"I need… I need…," Henry faltered

"I know what you need, Henry, and I can give it to you," Albert said, rising from his bed.

Henry watched as Albert stood with his hands folded behind his back in a school teacher's pose. The dim light caught the frame of his thick glasses. Henry could see the amusement in the monster's eyes, and for the first time he could see the real Albert standing before him: all preening and posing was gone, all emotional faking was dropped, the mask was set aside, and he shuddered before the presence. He reached for the hate, for the vengeance, he grasped for the hands of his wife and son beyond the grave. He shut out the thoughts that screamed at him to turn back, that pleaded for sanity, the voice that told him that it still wasn't too late, but he knew that it was. His mind was set and the decision was made. Tomorrow was for doubts, tomorrow was for consequences and repercussions, but tonight was for making deals with the devil.

***

It was the following morning when the discovery was made. The routine rounds check found Albert Day sleeping late in his room, his body wrapped beneath the thick blankets. It was only when breakfast arrived that the orderly noticed that Albert still hadn't moved. A patient lying unmoving was always a cause for concern, even for those who weren't on the suicide watch list. The orderly called for assistance and the three burly men entered the room cautiously.

Dr. Henry Loomis was found curled up inside Albert Day's bed. He wore Albert's clothing and had kept his face hidden beneath the blankets for as long as he could. The CCTV footage was carefully studied and found Albert casually leaving the hospital wearing Henry's clothes, the long heavy coat and hat obscuring his features. He had used the doctor's keys to open all of the necessary doors and Albert had driven the doctor's 4x4 out of the grounds with no one bothering to check. Despite a massive countrywide hunt, Albert Day was never found again.

***

Henry waited; he had plenty of time now to wait. He ignored all of the pleas and interrogations, he ignored all the tests and the gentle probing of what once were his colleagues. He was found to be not competent to stand trial for his actions, and after a successful plea from his lawyer, he was remanded to Blackwater as a patient.

His life now was just to sit and wait. He checked the newspapers that they allowed him to read, and he pored over them every day for news from across the country and beyond. He had made a deal with the devil. Not the fictional red monster with pointed horns and a tail - he had made a deal with Albert Day.

They had bartered and bargained for several hours, offer and counter-offer, until eventually they had reached an agreement. A number was finally agreed upon and it was a number that Henry would take to his grave. It was a number that would have to be paid in the blood and tears of strangers. Albert would take that number of new victims; only when he reached that number, would he turn his talents and attention to Greg Barden, the man who had taken Sarah and little Andy.

125

Henry studied the news for possible victims, seemingly accidental deaths, missing children, discovered bodies; every one of them he knew was a potential step closer. It was another piece of silver paid and another nail in his own coffin. He waited for the day when it would be Greg Barden's obituary that he read, and he could only pray that Albert Day was a man of his word.

21. JACK BY A.S. McDermott

He sees her standing at the corner of Osborn and Whitechapel. The whore. He has been following her all night and she has already had three customers. She lies down among the rats and the filth without a care in the world. He decides to make his move before she finds a fourth.

He walks up to her, forcing the mask he wears into a smile. He tips his hat and her tired face smiles in return. Under the gaslight her skin is blotchy and sickly pale.

"Hello, luv," she says, her speech slurred by whiskey. "Looking for some company?"

He nods.

"It'll be a bob. Show me you have it and Polly will take care of you."

He takes his money out of his pocket. It's more than she asked for and her grin broadens, bathing him in her foul breath. She leads him down a side street to Buck's Row. They stop in front of a stable entrance. He looks round to make sure no one is watching them. Even if they are, it matters little as the street is unlit and the moon provides scant illumination.

She lifts her skirt and petticoat, revealing the dark shadow between her legs that is of no interest to him. His hand tightens around the object in his coat. He stares at her silently.

'Come on, luv. Do your business. I ain't got all night."

He withdraws his hand and whips the blade across her throat from left to right and back again. Her glassy eyes stare at him in disbelief as her blood gushes out. She then crumples to the ground.

He crouches down by the body. The blood flow slows to a trickle, most of it soaking into her hair and the ground around her. She is already dead, but his work is not done.

He presses his hand through her clothing, searching for her abdomen. He slams the blade down into her left side, ripping clothing and flesh. He wrenches the blade free and jabs it several more times into different parts of her abdomen. He stops, unsure how to proceed. He has been anticipating this night for a long time, but now feels strangely . . . dissatisfied? It's almost as if-

Suddenly, a shadow falls over him. He springs to his feet and turns with a snarl, ready to silence any witnesses.

Standing in front of him is a tall, bearded man, wearing a dark overcoat and hat much like his own. The man has a pistol clutched in his hand, but it looks quite unlike any pistol he has ever seen. It is shiny and compact, almost like a toy.

"Hello, hello, hello," the stranger says. 'What's all this, then?"

'You a copper?" the murderer asks. "I just found this poor bird dead."

"Don't bother," the man says, flicking the pistol in his direction. "I've come a very long way to find you, and time is of the essence."

"Find me? Why would you wanna do that?"

"To solve the greatest mystery in history. Who was the man who murdered at least five women in Whitechapel and was never caught? Who was Jack the Ripper?"

"Never heard of him. Me name's Charles Cross." He hopes the stranger will accept the false name.

"Well, Mr. Cross, my name is Dr. Frederick Carlton. And I have come here from the year 2020."

"You're a bloomin' nutter." He backs slowly away, trying to decide between fleeing or fighting.

"That may well be, but I'm not the man standing over a dead prostitute with a bloody knife in my hand, am I?"

Cross quickly hides the blade behind his back. "It weren't like that," he protested. "She led me on."

"Tell me why you really did it. The truth, please. Or I will shoot you in the head."

Cross licks his lips nervously. "It's the whores, sir. They have to be taught a lesson. Me poor old mum was left by me dad for a whore. She died penniless and I was taken to an orphanage."

'Sounds to me like you should blame your father for that, not these unfortunate woman trying to make the best of their lives."

Cross's face twists in anger. 'What do they know about real work? Laying on their backs for a shilling while I work hauling meat all day long for little more than nothin'. They all deserve to die."

Dr. Cartlon frowns. "This is disappointing. I came here expecting to find greatness. But you're just some idiotic butcher. You have no concept of what you've started, the legend that you'll become."

Cross stares at him, uncomprehending.

"I chose to come to this time, you see," Carlton continues. "I'm what you might call a Ripperologist – a big fan of yours. I know more about your work than even you. Other men might choose to see the age of dinosaurs or the building of the pyramids. But this time, more than any other, is where I wanted to be. Your actions will inspire both killers and detectives for generations to come. And the killings will also bring much needed attention to the terrible conditions of the people living here. I came here to see where it all began."

Cross notices the pistol is no longer pointed at him, and the man who claims to be a doctor is staring off into space, apparently deep in thought. In an instant the murderer decides that he's had enough of the stranger's insane ramblings.

"And here's where you'll die!" he cries.

Cross lunges forward with his weapon as fast as he can. He hears a muffled gunshot, and his momentum carries him forward, stabbing the man in the arm. Both fall to the ground. Blood flows.

***

He sees her standing on Hanbury Street in the early hours of the morning. He tips his deerstalker hat at her and beckons her into the yard where he waits. Her name is Annie and after some small talk they agree on a price.

He thinks at first that he'll be unable to do it, but then remembers how important it is that things go exactly as planned. He has no choice.

The blade that he took from Cross's body comes out, and he slashes the woman's throat before she even has time to see the knife shimmer in the dim light.

He rubs the wound on his arm. It still aches, but he must work through the pain.

129

He crouches down beside the dead body and lifts her skirt and undergarments. He slices open her abdomen and probes her bloody cavity with his gloved hands, removing her intestines and draping them over her shoulders. He then carefully cuts out a portion of her uterus and places it in his doctor's bag.

"Forgive me" he says to the corpse quietly, and then leaves the scene of the crime.

He knows there are three more ahead of him, and he hopes his strength will not fail him. History depends on him. Only once the work is down can he safely return to the future, preventing a paradox that would unravel the world as they know it.

It's not easy being Jack.

22. A LONELY WIDOW WOMAN BY R.L. UGOLINI

My hand turned the rusty metal crank, sifting a pinch of salt into the flour. My knuckles, swollen and unlovely, complained at the effort, but I bore them no mind. What was one more care at my age?

I would have to get used to a cold, empty bed again – that was sure. Come winter, I'd go back to shaving just the one leg, growing out the long hairs on the other, in the still of the night, their downy softness suggestive of a man's company.

"There are worse things than being a touch lonely," I said as though he cared what I thought or wished to interject an opinion. Wasn't much for conversation or consideration. Mostly, he liked to take up space in my kitchen and make me rue the choices I'd made. However, his lack of parlay meant nothing to me anymore. I knew Mush For Brains heard me well enough.

"Be useful and hand me that pastry cutter." As if what I wanted mattered to him – I knew I might as well be talking to myself. Rapt he was, standing like a stump in a beam of dirty sunlight. Shadows played across his face, accentuating crevices that deepened every day. Though he had noticeably shrunk from his early days, when he still connected with his roots, his presence here had only grown – infiltrating, trespassing. He smelled ripe.

"Come on now, you'll take root. The pastry cutter," I reminded him. The butter, farm fresh and churned by hand, waited for me in the icebox. "Vex me and I'll feed you to the goats."

Cruel of me, but I was ornery. His attention was elsewhere of late, and no amount of charm or incantation could turn him. That being, I resorted to common oaths to needle him like some overgrown hoodoo. Everyday words, but powerful still. Luckily, I knew him to be particularly afraid of my small herd – and with reason. Those mohairs were greedy little devil dancers, always looking for their next meal and even I considered him a banquet.

He rummaged through the drawer with twining, ineffectual fingers. "No goats," he mumbled as he handed me the pastry cutter.

I took it from him carefully, avoiding the slightest glance of his touch. His body was a shell of what it had been under the mid-summer moon. Carbuncles and sunken, pulpy hollows pocked the flesh that was so recently golden, warm and taut.

The butter cut into the flour mixture with ease. The dough came together as though fulfilling the desires of the base ingredients. I floured the butcher block and rolled out the crust. My motions were rhythmic, practiced. The act of Making had always come as natural to me as it had for my Ma and Gran before her.

Still, I had an inkling they would not have looked kindly on what I'd done last winter, but they weren't around, were they? Twas nothing crafting the toby. A little blood flower root. A fistful of red clay. Two egg shells. A tooth, lost then found. Took more patience to make a crust come out flakey than to bind the whatnots and nitty-gritties called for making a man. When I was done, I wrapped the earthy bolus in a snakeskin sheath, hung it from the eaves in a westerly wind, and…nothing.

Truth be told, these days I avoided rootwork, as the digging aggravated my arthritis. I stuck mainly to spells in my day to day, and on my web page. Land-locked, house-poor soccer moms with high-speed internet and lingering regrets kept me in pizza money. Love drawings, blessings, cleansings, what have you. MasterCard and Visa accepted. I shipped glad tidings in the form of candles, oils, and honey jars anywhere in the continental United States. I was not without skill.

So, when nothing happened with the toby, it was embarrassing, like I was no better than some cut-rate doodle-bugger. I told no one, not that there was anyone to tell.

Then, one blustery day, when spring had almost blown itself out, I went to collect the laundry from the line and saw a comet-like smear of bird shit soiling my best linen sheet. Filthy carrion circled overhead, rubbernecking their desecration. Should a read the omen right there. At the time, I only saw – among the slick, chalky smear – a seed. A gourd of some kind, mayhap a pumpkin or butternut squash. I planted it in a freshly turned hummock.

Within days, leaves broke the surface of the earth. The vine that grew forth, thick and bristly, insinuated itself into everything – the chicken coop, the gutters, the compost bin. And then, from one perfect butter-colored blossom, came an offering like no other.

Smooth bronze skin pulled firm over hard, rippling flesh. Tall and broad, with clear eyes that drank in the sun. I called him Jack.

I draped the dough in the pie plate and trimmed the excess. Flecks of butter freckled the crust and reminded me that there were things yet in this world to fill me as no man ever could. The plate went in the icebox to chill.

Jack returned to the window. In the dooryard beyond grew a patch of sunflowers heavy with seed, their ample heads bowing under their heavy fertility. He watched them with the single-minded fascination of a lover, which was particularly irksome considering that such devotion was all I had really ever wanted from him.

I set out the sugar and three large eggs. Heavy cream. When making a custard, one should not skimp. A little nutmeg, some cinnamon. And of course…

I eyed Jack. It was time.

"Now, go on. Out to the garage with you. Help a lonely widow woman and get me a good-sized pot." I held my hands out, measuring off an expanse the width of his once broad shoulders. "About yay big. Go on, fetch. Don't you worry – I promise, I won't let the goats get you."

Blinking through a bloody haze, Sam Isaac looked down at his mangled prosthetic tangled with the brake pedal. He didn't remember the actual crash. His leg hurt. His leg, not where it attached to the prosthetic. He knew about phantom pains, but that was all he felt. The rest of his body was numb. He was afraid to look.

"Hello, Sam."

"Too...soon..." He didn't look at her. The Not-Rita Rita that he sensed beside him. Did she sit in whatever little space remained between the passenger seat and the glove box puke of collected inspection receipts, renewed registrations, the origami bridge of car manual pages, and whatever else might have gotten stuffed in there in the past five years? Or did she perch on the dash beneath the red-lined spider-web cracks? Did it matter?

"Welllll," the demon disguised as his dead wife drawled in her same deep voice. "It's complicated."

"Haven't drank... Haven't... touched a-a drop since..." His words caught in his throat like the shattered glass around him. Why hadn't the air bags worked? Hadn't he been wearing his seatbelt? He thought about moving his arm to feel for the belt but couldn't seem to find his arm. He blinked his eyes open. The deflated balloon draped across the steering wheel, almost artfully crimson in his unfocused vision.

"Oh, I know. Quite the model life you've lived since our first deal," Not-Rita said. "Upstanding citizen, good worker...model father..." She drew out that last bit.

Sam wanted to shake his head. Shake it hard. No, no, this wasn't fair. Couldn't be happening. He couldn't feel if his head moved at his will. The phantom pain in his leg was creeping up beyond the amputation in growing throbs. "Deal... we had a deal..." It occurred to him that he couldn't feel his mouth moving to make words, though he sensed he spoke. He couldn't leave

Matt. Not now. The deal was for him to stay and care for his boy. They were all they had left for each other, truly. "Rita..."

"Oh, honey, you know I'm not really Rita. She's not coming to this realm any time soon. This is just how your mind perceives me."

Rita had been dead already when he awoke in the first accident. A person doesn't wake up when half their skull is caved in from the back corner of a tractor trailer. She'd been more sober than he that night, but she shouldn't have been driving. He should have just called a cab, but he hadn't wanted to spend the money. It had taken both of them scraping together the money for their first "date" in years. Sam had just gotten back in touch with his half-brother who'd offered to babysit six-year-old Sam. It was just going to be a few hours...

"Our deal...? Did...everything...everything like...like it said..."

He'd almost lost his son from the accident, from the DUI charges, from possibly not being able to care for the child due to the loss of his right leg and potential brain damage. From the smearing campaign of the parents of the teens who'd died in the other car Rita'd spun into before hitting the tractor trailer...

Those parents had said he and Rita belonged in Hell for killing their children. Sam had believed them, accepted their accusations. They had killed three kids; Hell was what they deserved—Sam mostly. Thou shalt not kill. Do unto others... But he wasn't giving up on his son.

The book had been on the traveling library cart the teenaged volunteer wheeled around the hospital. He still had his vision, and though he'd been having a hard time remembering his therapy instructions, he made certain, certain he'd followed the directions he'd found. Down to blood sacrifice. He'd told Matt it was their secret, but he could imagine no purer blood than that of his young son.

"Not quite, actually... And we did make sure you got everything at first. The donor for your leg, the affordable yet unbeatable attorney, custody of your son right with your 'miraculous' recovery. The 'silence' of those pesky parents..."

"Then...then what? Till he grew up. Till he was an adult...could take care of himself. He's only...only...eleven..."

"See...that's where it gets complicated, Sammy. There are a few old-school folks from my parts that would say he qualifies as an adult at this point."

"Wh-what?"

"I mean, if I'm to be honest, we shouldn't have even honored the original contract as far as we did. We were quite generous actually. His blood that you offered wasn't exactly pure."

"Wh-what?"

"Well, he certainly wasn't a virgin anymore..."

In that moment, Sam felt his body. That fleeting shiver of pain, however, could not compare to the sinking illness in his stomach that pulled him to an eternal pit of Not-Rita's revelation repeating over and over and over...

Matthew Isaac sat in a pentagram drawn with bloody entrails. The remains of his half-uncle and aunt were arranged, in pieces, outside of the circle. Killing them had not taken as long as he'd expected nor had it been as difficult.

He was surprised at the lack of any emotion, actually—no anger, no relief, no triumph, no hatred. Nothing.

Matthew doubted he would see the dawn of his sixteenth birthday, and he was at peace with that. He would not return to his bed...or any bed in that house, that prison. If the spell did not work, he would sleep in the bloody pentagram.

When he'd gone with his half-uncle to identify the body of his father, killed in a T-bone collision from a drunk driver, he'd seen the cute volunteer wheeling around the cart of books. She'd paused, offered condolences upon hearing of his father's death, and asked if there was anything she could do. He asked if he could borrow a book since he'd be there for a while, as his half-uncle answered questions to a police officer—like if his father had started drinking again and if he'd gotten permission to drive with his prosthetic leg. The girl told him to take any book he liked and not to worry about returning it. The dark, old-looking book called to him and he nearly snatched it from the rolling cart, barely remembering to thank her.

He took the book home, but didn't find the spell until the next day. Even on the day his father had died, he was not given peace to hide, alone, in his room. Matthew hadn't been surprised; he'd gotten nothing but pain and fear the night his mother had died and his father had lain dying in the hospital.

The touching, the...everything. That had started the day his parents had left on their date.

When his father had asked Matthew to keep a secret about taking his blood, it was not the first secret he'd been told to keep. His half-uncle and aunt had said that Matthew's "behavior" with them would hurt his father more, keep him from healing. His father had said his blood would help him heal faster.

Matthew had wanted his father to heal faster. He'd wanted his dad more than anything.

Now he just wanted to be with his parents. Even at six years old, he knew he'd never forget the horrible things people had said about his parents from the first accident.

He'd studied this spell for five years. Five long years. At eleven, he'd been powerless to fight against them. It had taken five years of studying to fight, of getting into playground brawls, of stealing money to take MMA classes while saying he was getting math tutoring.

But he'd finally done it. He'd stopped them, and he was ready.

"Hello, Matthew."

The teenager blinked, inadvertently wiping his eyes with his bloodied hands and giving the candlelit living room a reddish hue. "Mom?"

"Not quite. But I'm here. What do you want?"

"I want to be with you and Dad."

His not-mom blinked. "Do you know what you are asking?"

Matthew looked at the corpses of his caretakers for the past five years and nodded. "I do. That's where I belong."

She was silent for a long minute, still looking quite surprised.

Standing carefully in the gore-smeared circle, Matthew held out his arms as if he were a child again—though he was taller than the woman he addressed. The woman who wore the face that had grown hazy in his memories after so many years. He welcomed a last, clear vision of that face, though his heart knew it wasn't her. "Take me home, Mom. I want to be with you and Dad. That's all I want."

The demon wearing his mother's face walked into the pentagram and embraced the boy. "I'll take you home," she whispered, and kissed him.

The kiss, at least, felt like a real mother's kiss.

24. FROZEN TEARS by Rick A. Carroll

Sometime after midnight, Paul slipped out of the library, checking the door to make sure it locked behind him.

Snow drifted lazily from the night sky, a light fall that had only just begun to stick. It covered the pathways of the college, giving the sidewalks an ethereal quality under the lamplight. When he moved to Santa Fe, he would never have imagined how much snow a desert city could get. A native of south Florida, he had never even seen snow outside of television until moving here.

He pulled his phone and checked the time, cursing when he realized how late it was. Bus service had long since stopped. He brushed aside a snowflake as it fell on his illuminated screen. Monica would be happy to pick him up, he was sure, if he could get to her before leaving for the bar. He stood by the roadside, watching a couple of students make their way across the parking lot before disappearing into the dorms. After a few minutes of waiting, he sighed and put his phone away, looking in the direction of town.

St. John's College lied in the high hills east of Santa Fe proper, distant from the press of downtown and surrounded by the richer estates along Old Pecos Trail. While this gave the small college a quiet and secluded feel, it also meant that only the wealthy could afford to live nearby. He considered calling a cab, but put his phone away and started to hoof it down Camino Blanca Cruz. He lived downtown, at most a thirty-minute walk.

A car shot past him as he walked up the access street to the college. Paul yelled out for them to slow down, even though they couldn't hear him. He knew firsthand how treacherous the roads could be. A chill ran up his spine as old memories surfaced, the squeal of brakes and the flash of red lights. He stopped and took a moment to compose himself. It was why he didn't drive any more. In fact, it had taken more than a year before he could even sit in a car as a passenger.

The snow fell harder, heavy flakes drifting lazily from the sky as he passed the soccer fields before coming to the terminus of the road. A small residential area separated him from the wooded hills, where an arroyo ran deeper into the city. If he kept to the streets, he would have to loop down before making it downtown while the arroyo was a straight shot. In the summer, he wouldn't even have considered taking the streets, but at night and in the snow the ground would be treacherous.

Unsure, he looked at the street and then back to the dark houses.

"Fortune favors the bold," he said, crossing the street and slipping between the residences. A dog barked at him from a couple of yards down, followed by its owner yelling for it to be quiet. Paul quickly hopped the wall behind the house, moving into the shadows of twisted scrub trees. His boots crunched in the snow, the old fall iced over under fresh powder. He took each step carefully to avoid twisting his ankle, using tree branches for support and dropping into the arroyo below.

The arroyo was enormous, easily fifteen feet across and six deep. Branches and mounds of dirt poked up from the snow covered floor, and Paul took great care navigating his way down. Even still, he slid the last couple of feet down the steep embankment. He gathered himself, took a step forward and froze in place. On the far side of the arroyo, a white figure with ice blue eyes stared at him.

His heel slipped out from under him, dropping him to snow covered earth. When he looked up again, the figure was gone.

"You're losing it," he said. The warmth of his breath misted in front of him, swirling in the night air as it mixed with snow. For a moment, Paul could see eyes in snow, and then they were gone.

He took a deep breath and steadied himself before standing and brushing the snow free. It was falling harder now, a lot harder. He took out his phone to check the time, but found the screen shattered.

"Son of a bitch," he said, lifting it to his eye line. Light spilled through the cracked glass, but the display was just jumbled pixels.

He hit the power button, and as the light faded, he could see a woman standing behind him in the reflection of the broken glass.

Paul spun around, but there was nothing behind him except for the bank of the arroyo. He backed away, stepping deeper into the channel.

"Who's there?"

Light washed over him. He spun to his right and threw his hands up, blinded by headlights racing down the arroyo. He froze in fear, only managing to scream as the car bore down on him. His scream mixed with the roar or the engine, closer and closer…

And then silence.

Paul opened his eyes, alone and in the dark.

He turned around, looking for the car, but there was nothing there. No tail lights, no tire marks in the snow, nothing to indicate that it had ever been there. His heart pounded in his ears and he dropped to his knees, a hand over his chest.

"Paul."

He looked up. A soft, feminine voice. Or was it the wind? His hands shook from fear or cold, he couldn't tell. His teeth were chattering.

"Paul." His name again, carried on the wind.

Then he saw her, again. A lady in white at the edge of the arroyo, her hair as dark as the night and eyes like stars.

"La llarona," Paul whispered. An urban legend, an old New Mexico tale. La Llorona walks the waterways, looking for lost children.

He inched back, fingers clawing at the frozen ground. The figure lifted her hand and pointed directly at him before blowing away in the wind, falling apart as if made of snow. Paul screamed and turned, scrambling down the gorge. In the trees he could see faces, children screaming, a woman crying. Paul yelled at each nightmare, following a twist in the arroyo before skidding to a stop.

A car had crashed into the trees at the edge of the arroyo, its rear end crushed.

"No," Paul whispered, walking to it, his hand outstretched. He stepped over a Land of Enchantment license plate in the snow, past pieces of metal and plastic, across broken glass over pavement that had not been there a moment before. He walked to the rear passenger side of the car, where the vehicle had been hit. The hatchback door had taken a direct blow, crushing inward and spearing through a child seat' strapped into the back.

"No," Paul said, tears falling down his cheek, his eyes locking on the yellow diamond hanging in the ruins of the rear window, letting him know there was a baby on board. He put his hand on the wreckage to steady himself, but it broke apart, the vehicle breaking into thousands of snowflakes and blowing away in the night air.

A hand touched his shoulder. "Paul."

He spun around stepped back, seeing himself. But not as he was now, but as he had been three years ago. The unkempt hair, the look of shock. He could smell the gin on his breath from a faculty mixer.

"No!" He screamed and fell away from himself, turning to run. He scrambled up the side of the arroyo, the flesh of his palms and fingers tearing as he dug the cold ground for handholds, pulling himself away from the channel. He fled through the trees, trying to outrun the wind. It carried his name, screaming it in his ears, mixing with the sound of a child screaming and an engine roaring. Paul yelled as his foot caught on a root, slamming him back to the earth. Everything went silent, all save for one sound.

A mother weeping. He closed his eyes and cried as well. He could hear her weeping in court, the day the Judge let him go. The day his attorney argued that the little he had to drink had not been enough to impair him, that anyone in those weather conditions would have lost control. The day the state let him kill a child and then walk away.

He rolled onto his back, and the woman in white stood over him.

"What?" His voice cracked as he spoke in the bitter cold, his tears freezing to his cheeks as they fell.

The woman pointed at him again, and from her side, Paul watched as the ghost of a boy stepped from behind the white woman.

"What do you want?" he whispered.

The boy reached out and placed his icy hands on Paul's cheeks. When Paul sucked the next breath in, it froze his lungs and throat, sending his body into convulsions and drawing the heat from his blood until finally his body grew still.

When the boy spoke, it was through Paul's frozen lips.

"I want my Mommy."

"So, whatchya think?" Bob Harrison opened his beer and took a sip, a cat-ate-the-canary smile on his face.

Sid Chambers felt a twinge of jealousy, but didn't let it show. Instead, he gave a low whistle. "Sweet."

"Yep, picked 'er up yesterday. The W-9. Dealer gave me a great price, too. Knocked six grand off for the trade in."

"No foolin'? That much?"

Sid couldn't believe Bob had gotten that for his W-5; hell, it had been ten years old. He leaned down and grabbed a beer out of the cooler Harrison had sitting on the garage floor. The temperature outside was already approaching ninety.

"You oughtta think about getting rid of your old clunker, Sid." Bob nodded his head in the direction of Sid's house, where Shelly was out in the driveway washing their car. "My Pop used to say, 'high mileage means high maintenance.'"

Sid sighed. "I don't know that we can afford it right now, not with Sid Junior starting college in a year." He glanced at Bob's W-9 again.

Gotta admit, it's a helluva lot nicer than mine.

He drained the last of his beer and tossed it in the trash. "Well, I gotta get goin'. Good luck with her, Bob."

"You think about what I said. In the long run you're just costin' yourself more money and getting aggravated by hanging on to something that don't perform the way you want."

Sid waved without looking back as he crossed the street. But that night, as he lay in bed, he did think about it.

High mileage means high maintenance.

He thought about it a lot.

***

"Whoo-wee, look at you, Mister Fancy."

Sid turned around and found Bob Harrison standing across the street, getting his mail.

144

"Afternoon, Bob." Sid couldn't keep the smug tone from his voice, or the smile from his face. In fact, he'd been smiling all day, ever since he signed the papers at the dealership.

"Looks like you took my advice and then some." Bob walked over and joined Sid at the end of the driveway.

"You were right. I figured out the maintenance costs, and I decided to do it."

"Is that a W-10?"

Sid was sure he heard a note of envy in Bob's voice.

"Yep. Hadn't even been test-driven yet. Practically right off the truck."

"Ain't that sweet."

"Comes with a ten-year warranty, too. Anything goes wrong, they fix it for free."

"Well, this calls for a celebration. Why don't you'n the missus come over Friday night for some beers and barbeque?"

Sid tapped his mail to his forehead in a mock salute. "You supply the burgers, we'll bring the booze."

"It's a date."

He headed up the drive just as Shelly came back out of the house to get the last bag of groceries. She smiled and waved to him.

"Hi, honey."

"Hey, babe. What's for dinner?"

***

"Sean, please pass the potatoes." Shelly Chambers held out her hand for the bowl. Next to her, the lanky, long-haired boy kept his gaze steadfastly on his plate.

When it became painfully obvious his son wasn't going to acknowledge Shelly's request, Sid cleared his throat.

"Sean, pass your mother the potatoes."

The boy looked up, his brown eyes narrowed and his nostrils flaring. "She's not my mother."

"Sean!" Sid slammed his water glass on the table. "You watch your damned mouth."

"Well, she's not. So I don't have to do what she says." He threw his fork down and pushed his chair back. "You can't make

145

me!" He stormed down the hall. A moment later came the bang of his bedroom door slamming shut.

Sid sighed. Ever since he'd brought the new Shelly home, Sean had been acting up. It didn't make sense. Unlike a lot of men, he hadn't changed styles. He'd made sure to choose a model that was identical to the original Shelly, except twenty years younger. She even came programmed with all the memories of Sean's real mother.

So what was the problem?

"It's all right, dear." Shelly patted his hand. "He's just venting. He's sixteen. That's what they do."

He looked over at her, found himself captured once again by the woman he'd married. Gone were the gray hairs and sagging boobs. Tired eyes sparkled again, and youthful skin showed not a trace of wrinkles or laugh lines. Most importantly, gone were the annoying habits she'd developed over the years – the nagging, the complaining, the demanding.

And splurging on the increased sex drive option had definitely been worth the price.

"I'm getting tired of it, Shell." He shook his head. "His mouth, his attitude. And he's been slacking off at school, too."

Shelly patted her lips with her napkin and took a sip of wine. "Well, maybe it's time to upgrade," she said in a soft voice. "I could stop at the dealership and pick up a catalog tomorrow."

He sighed again. "I don't know. It's like admitting I failed to bring my son up right."

She got up and came around behind him, wrapped her arms around his chest. The feel of her young breasts, the smell of her fresh-washed hair, all of it combined to make him want to forget dinner and carry her upstairs.

"It's not an admission of failure, Sid. It's no different than sending a child to a private school, or putting him in rehab. It's something you do now so that later on his life is better. You're helping him to make something of himself."

He closed his eyes and thought about it. It would be nice to be able to brag about Sean the way Bob Harrison was always talking about his daughter. He'd replaced her two years ago, and she'd been on Dean's List ever since. Did all her chores, too, without a single complaint.

Sudden noise erupted as Sean turned his stereo on, filling the house with raucous music.

Sid knew when to admit defeat.

"Pick the catalog up. We'll look at it when I get home from work tomorrow."

26. 'CRUSH' BY JODY NEIL RUTH

She looks like she is praying; her knees, naked, hands clasped, head down. The thin trickles of blood creeping down her shaking arms encourage any religious expectations.

Her body trembles as she lowers her palms to her forehead, teeth pulled back from painted lips as tears and spittle hit the floor below.

Her body convulses as she tries to contain her rage; hands snapping open to reveal the wounds her own nails have inflicted on her palms.

Music plays loudly from the boom box on her dresser, drowning out her sorrow as she puts her bloodied palms to her face and drags them down; the blood stains giving her a macabre make-over.

Thin hands encase her mouth, her primal scream filling her cupped palms as the heavy metal music builds to a crescendo, until both it and she collapse; the girl smashing her fists upon the floor, lithe body stretching out in the low lamplight.

She unclenches her fists as heavy breaths expand her bony ribs. She stares at the floor. The carpet is black and burgundy, and she can feel her mood slipping into the fibers beneath her. Rising to her knees she forces herself to relax.

Staring pitifully at her feeble palm-wounds, she sighs and tilts her head back to look into the dark corners of her room. Posters decorate her walls; various metal groups glowering down at her, as a guitar-heavy band thrashes emotion from the stereo system and into the room.

She can see her head and shoulders in the dresser mirror. Her eyes are eaten by a layer of black liner, the same color washing her lips. The black smudges into the blood on her face and she giggles at the sight of herself; a somber extra from a horror-rife music video.

Smiling at herself she slowly raises her arms above her head and sways in time with the new song beginning to play. Her naked body is paler than ever in the low lighting, and her nipples harden at the sight.

The girl writhes as her hands criss-and-cross before her face, raven-strands of hair falling around her shoulders, beautiful green-and-black eyes peeking through the gaps in her hair.

And then those eyes trace the photographs surrounding her mirror. Small and large, some cut down in size, some cut into shape around a forever deleted person; but all featuring a man in various poses, mostly with his arm around the girl in the mirror. They smile together in every photograph.

She stops swinging, arms falling to her sides as she stares at one such picture; the man dressed in a suit, side-profile, a small smile on his lips, a glass of wine in hand. The girl gets to her feet, pulling the photo from the mirror frame, holding it close to her face.

She holds it to the light from the stand next to her bed, her head tilting as she brings it for closer love and scrutiny.

"Such a handsome man that evening," she says, her eyes stare beyond the picture. She can see him as he enters this very room, carrying her through the door and gently laying her on the bed as he removes her clothes, and then his. Their love-making had been intense and passionate; his mouth never leaving hers unless it was to explore her body with his tongue.

She shivers at the thought, biting her lip hard.

And then her eyes narrow, the photograph shaking in her hand as her body vibrates to a different memory.

"And then you screwed her that same night!" she spits, a trace of blood from her lip landing on the man's image. "And you were sleeping with that slut all along."

The picture in her hand crumples under the return of her rage, and she throws it into her opened-door wardrobe where it bounces off a small black chest. Her anger pauses as she stares at it, her mind going over the memories inside.

She gives in to the box, pulling it from its resting place. The contents roll and tumble inside as she turns it over in her hands. The box was a gift from him. He had asked her to hide their love inside so others could not see.

She runs a black fingernail along the velvet trim surrounding the container, opening the lid as she sits on the edge of her bed.

She can smell the flavored lubricants before she sees them as the box cracks open. Two small bottles nestled between various adult DVDs and sex toys. Her mind wanders again as she reminisces of the two of them naked on her bed, experimenting with the contents of the box as the films lit up the room with their flickering images.

Trembling, she can feel the touch of his hand against her cheek, his stubble bringing a rash to her face, as it would in other tender places. Her fingers flitter through the contents of the box, pausing upon each object, a faint smile decorating her beauty as memories arouse themselves.

But the girl cannot forget the pain which followed, slamming the lid shut again and casting it back into the deep recesses of the wardrobe. Her fists ball and she pounds them on her thin white thighs, a cry rattling her throat, threatening to escape from behind her teeth.

Her fingernails scrape against her skull and she pulls her hands through her hair, tugging at the black locks as she stumbles blindly towards the dresser.

She stops herself and gazes into the mirror; the dried blood on her face shining black in the gloom. The sight of her own sadness halts her, her buttocks slumping onto the stool beneath them.

Gently she pushes her damp hair from her face, smiling apologetically at her mirror-self in an attempt to soothe the troubled visage. Breathing normally, she pushes the pain and anguish ignited by betrayal back down her chest. The hollow feeling remains in her stomach, a black pit of despair she must try and ignore for now.

"Am I not beautiful to you?" she asks the man in the many photos. "What does the slut have that I don't?" Her bottom lip protrudes in a manner which takes years off her, and even she can't help but break into a smile.

Her eyes lock with her reflection, her shoulders stiffen and she straightens her back. Snatching a make-up wipe she applies it to her face, scrubbing blood and make-up from her skin as harshly and as quickly as she can.

A brush plays her hair into a smoother state. A contrasting-white headband pulls her fringe away from her face, and a fresh application of blusher, lipstick and eye shadow enhance her natural beauty once more.

"You said you liked my schoolgirl outfit," she said, leaning forward to kiss one of the pictures, fresh lipstick smearing upon it. "Well I think it's time we got it out once more."

The box is retrieved from the wardrobe and reopened, the contents strewn across her unmade bed. Her thin fingers flitter between the memories and treasures as she searches.

She finds what she is looking for, pulling out a pair of black stockings and a suspender belt from within the jumble. She puts the belt on with slow, deliberate expertise; pretending her reflection is that of her lover. Dancing again, this time for him, she slowly flicks her hips in time to the rhythm, her mind turning back to sensual thoughts.

She opens the drawers of the dresser, withdrawing a pair of knickers which she turns over in her hands. Her eyes flicker back to the photographs, before she puts the underwear back where she found it with a smile. She won't be needing those today.

She dances both for the pictures and again for the girl in the mirror, swaying to the sounds of the darker beats that have replaced the sounds of guitars and drums. It suits her mood; black and sensual, giving her body more momentum.

Dancing towards the wardrobe, she takes a short pleated skirt from a hanger, twirling it around her head before stepping into it. A black bra followed by a thin white blouse. The mirror-girl reveals she has achieved her desired effect, and she continues to gyrate, a small moan escaping her red lips. Losing herself in the sounds, time becomes a stranger to her as the bass rumbles and a haunting man's voice sings about his soul's need for someone.

She stops to pick up a pair of heels from under her bed, turning them over in her hand before deciding on a lower-heeled pair to complete her look. She studies herself in the dresser, lifting up on tiptoes to examine her outfit. A small nod of her head and she returns to her stool to apply the finishing touches to her make-up.

The vision of beauty stands again, straightening her blouse, erasing any blemishes of make-up she finds. A fitted blazer, complete with school badge is lifted from the back of a chair in a corner and the outfit is complete. She looks immaculate.

A twirl in the mirror, and the music descends deeper, her feelings and soul continuing to drown in its grasp. She shakes her head, her hair flailing around her face, and she dances for her man now; trying to entice him out of the worn pictures around her mirror.

Sadness comes when he does not.

She speaks to him as she opens a drawer.

"No more of that slut," she says, and a razor blade emerges in her withdrawn hand. She holds it a breath from her face, a blazing green eye dangerously close as the dim lighting flashes against the blade.

"And if you won't have me, then you won't have either of us," she sighs, drawing the razor down a picture of her and her man, cutting him through his face.

Wrapping it in tissue the weapon is tucked into a small pocket of her skirt as she sits at the dresser.

Rubbing her hands up her thighs she parts them, and her lips, slightly.

"But who could turn down such a perfect little creature such as I?" she asks her other self, the pictures framing her face, laughing until it becomes a high-pitched squeal.

And then sadness again.

"Except you come and go as you please," her voice purrs, the anger now controlled. "The slut and I have to share you… but you are my man." A hand thumps the dresser, knocking bottles and items of decoration over, a couple of photographs falling from their places.

"But not anymore!" she hisses, containing the wildness in her eyes instead of releasing it through her body. "Not anymore," she whispers.

Standing, she smooths any wrinkles from her outfit. Turning the music off, she takes a final look in her mirror, her transformation complete. The quietness of the room allows her to hear a car crunch upon the gravel driveway and she rushes to the window.

"My man," she smiles.

A knock at the door startles her, and it opens slowly.

"Ah good," says the attractive middle-aged woman as she steps into the room. "I'm glad you are ready. Your father has just pulled up. You don't want to be late for school, now do you, dear?"

"No mother," she says, her smile still in place; one hand slowly pulling the front of her skirt lower to hide her stocking-tops.

The woman closes the door.

The girl stares at it, her other hand tracing the outline of the razor blade in her pocket.

"No, we wouldn't want that now, would we?" she smiles.

"You slut."

27. PROMISES, PROMISES BY SHENOA CARROLL-BRADD

Sarah hummed to herself as she stood at the sink of her family's cozy farmhouse. The old architecture let in drafts when it snowed, but right now, in the soft days of early spring, it was just right. Her husband, Nathaniel, had left after dawn to work the fields, and their two daughters, Annabelle and Katie, played upstairs. She kept one ear turned to the ceiling to monitor them as she washed the breakfast dishes.

Something thumped the floorboards overhead, and their sweet voices went quiet.

Soapy fingers tightening around the dish in her hand, Sarah froze and strained to hear. Her breath staled in her throat.

Then came a giggle from above, and their happy sounds resumed.

Sarah let out the depleted breath and plunged her hands up to the elbows in the soapy water. As she lifted the big serving plate for a rinse after scrubbing off specks of dried gravy, Sarah realized that, while she could still hear the girls playing, something wasn't right. Only one voice spoke upstairs, and it was going too fast for normal conversation, too guttural to be understood.

Oh, no.

"Mom!" Annabelle shrieked. "She's doing it again!"

Sarah spun away from the sink and dashed toward the sound. The soapy dish slipped from her hands to shatter on the floor, but Sarah didn't stop. She leapt the stairs two at a time and pushed past her youngest daughter, who cowered by the door of the room the girls shared. The roof peaked sharply, drawing her eye directly to the tortured form in the center of the room.

Her eldest stood on pointe between their narrow beds, contorted, back arched so far that her straw blond hair swept the bare boards. Her arms hung straight down, as did her head as she continued to mumble a harsh, dead language. Her eyes, while open, did not seem to register the familiar surroundings. They shot back and forth and stared past her family, like the girl was speed reading upside down and miles away.

Sarah darted to the far wall, where a quilt normally hung between the windows, and found the hook empty. Without hesitation she scooped up the fallen blanket from its crumpled pile on the floor and cast it over her child like a hopeful net on an empty sea, letting the thousand hand-stitched crosses land face down on the girl.

Katie's chanting cut off mid-syllable. Her arms flew up, rigid as posts, but they weren't long enough yet to dislodge the blanket. She collapsed, thrashing beneath the quilt in a violent, whole-body tantrum that rattled the floorboards.

Sarah fought every maternal instinct that shouted at her to go to her daughter's side, to hold her, and soothe the tremors.

Not yet.

Not yet.

She traced the silver-pink scars along her forearm from when she'd first learned that lesson.

When the small figure beneath the blanket finally stilled, Sarah crept over to peel the cloth back from her daughter's reddened face.

Katie blinked and sleepily rubbed her eyes, brow furrowing as she looked up at her concerned mother, and then down at the blanket covering her. "Oh, no. Did I do it again?" Katie started to cry. "I'm sorry, Mama. I don't know what's wrong with me. I said my prayers like always, I promise."

Sarah scooped her daughter up and cooed, avoiding the blistered patches on the child's face and arms where the quilt's crosses had singed her. "It's okay, my darlin'. It's all right." She locked eyes with Annabelle, who watched, big-eyed from her place by the door. "No one's blaming you, baby. Come on, let's all go downstairs for some ice cream."

Everyone was quiet as they moved into the kitchen and accepted their treats. Katie sniffled as she ate her ice cream, but Annabelle just sat there at the table, hands loose in her lap.

Sarah looked at the shattered dish by her feet and sighed. "Anna-baby, come help me clear this mess."

Annabelle obeyed without making eye contact, kneeling on the floor to gingerly gather broken china pieces.

Sarah angled her head, trying to see her youngest daughter's face. "Babydoll, why didn't you help your sister? You were right there."

Anna kept cleaning, holding her hands awkwardly, like she was trying to make a game of it.

"You know it only gets worse the longer it goes on. We gotta catch the fits early. Your sister needed your help, and I need you to look out for each other. I can't always come running in time. What if I'd tripped on the stairs and broken my ankle?"

No response, though Annabelle now sniffled, too.

"Promise me you'll help your sister out next time."

Her littlest kept her head bowed to the broken dish.

Fighting a fear that crawled up from her gut, Sarah grabbed her daughter's wrists and turned them, exposing her blistered palms to the light. "Oh, baby, no," she moaned.

Annabelle looked up at last, eyes big and starting to well. "I tried to grab the blanket, but I couldn't hold on. Does this mean I have what Katie's got?"

"It don't mean nothin', darlin'. All it means is I need to speak with your Daddy soon as he gets home."

***

When Nathaniel came in for supper, Sarah cornered him in the kitchen, hands balled into fists. "You said you would only promise him one!" she hissed.

Her husband deflated, bowing beneath the truth of their circumstances. "And I did, at first. But then the right field failed." He glanced around the kitchen before lowering his scratchy voice. "I had no choice. It was give them both to him, or watch 'em starve."

"We could have done something. We could have figured it out, if you'd just come to me–" She shook her head, nails biting into her palms as she resisted the urge to slap him. "What will you do if, after all we've given, the other fields fail, too?"

He didn't meet her eye.

"Who will you offer, then?"

"I did it for the family." Nathaniel pushed away from her. "It's all I ever do. I'll explain it to them when they're older. They'll understand." He finally met her eyes, his own desperate and sad, wanting to believe his words as much as she. "They'll see why I did it. They're good girls."

"And until then? It's killing me to watch him take over one child – now both?"

He shrugged, turning away, defeat in his every gesture. "I'll think of something. I'm the man of this house. It's my job to provide and protect. I'll...think of something. Until then, you'd better start on a second quilt." He rubbed the back of his neck, making a sound like wood on sandpaper. "Our girls are growing fast. They're going to need another security blanket."

28. ALL THINGS CONSIDERED BY JEFF MCFARLAND

The French have a phrase specifically for the idea. You know the one I'm talking about, at one point or another we've all felt that glitch in the Matrix – "whoa, déjà vu, man." That's all well and good, but what I wanna know is, what the hell do you call it when you've got a thought that sticks to you like gum on the bottom of a shoe? Nothing downright scary, just an idea that won't leave you be. Something that worms its way into your brain and just sort of sits there, lying underneath all your day-to-day nonsense, ready to spring as soon as you make the mistake of relaxing. That whole did I leave the stove on feeling... do they have a word for that? I mean, the French have one for all the witty crap you should have said during an argument too, so they've gotta have one for not being able to remember if you left the garage door up or not.

I've noticed that you tend to have these thoughts way more often if you live alone. It happens to me all the time, and I'll usually chalk it up to my shitty memory. Yeah, sure, I probably left the light on in the kitchen. Whoops, did I forget to lock the front door again? I don't remember leaving the TV on before I left... Obviously, I have a hard time remembering little stuff on my own, never mind when I stumble home drunk or ready to pass out. Oh, and did you ever notice that these thoughts usually pop into your head when you're about a half second from falling asleep? You're lying there, not quite awake, but not gone either, and suddenly you wonder how confident you are that your house won't burn down in the middle of the night. You'll get up to check, every fucking time. Hell, I still do. I know good and goddamn well that stove is off, but some part of me just won't take my own word for it.

Somewhat related, is there a phrase for when you see something that drops a ball of lead in your gut? Like someone just dumped a bucketful of dread down your back? "Oh shit" is the first phrase that comes to my mind, but I suppose it's personal preference. Some people call it the creeps or the heebie-jeebies, but none of those really have the zing that comes with a different language, you know? The thing is, I'm not talking about day-to-day stuff like almost getting t-boned in the intersection or having your cat jump out at you from the dark. That shit just makes your heart pound. I'm talking about the stuff that makes you straight up uneasy, makes you run up the basement steps every time you grab the laundry. Besides, isn't a word like "creepy" pretty relative? Some people get the creeps when they see a spider skitter across the floor, but I know a girl that squeals when she sees one like it's a fucking puppy. Despite my forgetfulness, I do have one routine I try to stick to: Every morning when I get out of the shower, I leave the curtain open. I do forget from time to time, but I do my best to remember though, because it lets the tub dry out a bit, and it gives me somewhere to spew later if the toilet's too small a target.

When I came home last night, I was so tired that I could have started pissing on the closed toilet seat and wouldn't have realized it until it started dripping onto my shoes. As I lifted the seat up, the first thing I noticed when I unzipped my pants was the draft coming from the open window. A chill up my spine wouldn't do my aim any favors while trying to take a leak, so I went over to the window to close it, and that's when I first got that feeling.

Did I leave the window open? It gets pretty toasty in that bathroom, especially considering I take my showers hotter than the Devil's rectum, so it was possible I had opened it. Still, I didn't think I would have left it that way. Winter is creeping up in this neck of the woods, and I'm not fond of the idea of my toilet water turning to ice. I stood there and kicked myself for not remembering something so simple. Between the state of my vision and the dark of the room, everything seemed blurry. Why would I have left the window open? Looking back, that was red flag number one. I started to close the window and stared out at my backyard for a moment, zoning out and watching the snowfall in the glow of the light in the alley. I just forgot, that's all. I forget all the time! I went to turn away from the window, and I noticed something else. It was dark out there, that light in the alley doesn't do much, but you could see them in the fresh snow. Just barely. They were mixed in with the paw prints and the occasional rabbit tracks.

Footprints. Barefooted, human footprints. They trailed from the alleyway and led right up to my window.

I felt my eyes that had been heavy a minute ago open wide. A pounding swelled in my temples. Now, I struggled to remember: did I close the shower curtain that morning? I turned to look at the curtain, and suddenly, my vision had become crystal clear. The closed curtain was fluttering silently in the window's breeze. I started to inch the window the rest of the way shut, and it squealed in the sill. The shrill sound bounced off the walls and made me wince. The curtain still fluttered. I held my breath, and with a ginger touch, slid the window all the way shut.

The curtain continued to move.

I stood there for a long time debating, weighing my options. Every Alfred Hitchcock, John Carpenter, and Wes Craven movie flashed through my mind. I thought about grabbing my phone and hauling ass out of there. I thought about grabbing a pair of shears from the counter and re-enacting the scene from Psycho. I thought of a million things I could have done, but instead of doing any of them, without me realizing it, my hand slowly began to inch toward the curtain. It was happening before I could stop myself. I can't explain why. My heart hammered in my chest, in my ears, shit, I'm pretty sure even my fingers were pulsing, but that was probably just my hand shaking. When my fingertips were only inches from the fabric, my lizard brain wrestled for control: What are you doing, you fucking idiot?! Get out of there! Have you learned fucking nothing from the movies?! I stopped. Just for a moment. The curtain had stopped moving.

"Fuck this," I muttered to myself. I grabbed a fistful of the curtain, and threw it to the side.

Nothing. There was nothing.

I let out a huge sigh of relief and felt my body relax. Just as I did, I heard a crash from the kitchen.

Despite my initial stupidity, I promise you, no matter how tired or potentially drunk I might have been, I've never moved that fast in my life. "Oh shit" was definitely the proper phrase then. As soon as I hit my front yard, I had 911 on the line. A few officers had been on patrol in the area, so they showed up pretty quickly, grinning at my slurred and panicked report of someone in either my bathtub or my kitchen. After a lot of yelling and pleading, I convinced them to search my house top to bottom. Every closet, crawlspace, and corner had a flashlight shone at it. Do I need to tell you that they didn't find anything? When I brought them to my backyard, someone or something had trudged through the footprints and erased any sign of them being there. The snow was already starting to replace what had been moved. The cops decided they had humored me enough, and told me to go sleep it off. They left me with a shit-eating grin and a pat on the back. They thought I was just another drunk.

Hey, one last thing about these heebie-jeebies or whatever – there's no way you can know how you'll react to them. Some people just freeze up. They can't move or say a damn word, they just stand there looking like a deer in headlights. Something in the 'flight' part of their 'fight or flight' response is busted. Those people are always the first to go in a horror flick. Other people try to fight the feeling away. They curse and spit and puff their chest out, hoping they can be scarier than whatever it is that's about to wreck their day. And then there's people, smart people, who get the fuck out. No questions asked, no "Hello? Is someone there?" No reaching for the curtain, they're fucking gone, man. I wanted to be one of the smart people, to get the fuck out of there, but I couldn't afford a motel room. My family lives in another town, and I'm falling a little short on the whole "friends" bit. Besides, whoever was in my kitchen had clearly booked it when the police showed up, so I settled for locking literally every way into the house and being scared shitless. I gave the house another looking over, found even more nothing, and decided on a drink to calm my nerves. When I reached into the fridge for the last beer, my hands were still shaking. I stopped for a second, and just stared into the mostly empty refrigerator.

I was struggling to remember. I could have sworn there had been two beers left...

29. IT'S IN HER SMILE by Stacey Longo

Jessica had the most beautiful smile he'd ever seen. Not a wide, teeth-and-crinkled-laugh-lines type of smile. No, hers was subtler: closed, purple lips, tugging up just slightly at the corners. A smile that said I know where I'm headed, and I don't need you to get there. Callum was intrigued at the first sight of her: it was an instinctive reaction, a snake uncoiling in the core of his being that suddenly woke up starving, wanting to consume this woman. He felt a cool sweat break out in his palms.

Callum didn't fall for women easily. Sometimes, after a long shift on the ambulance, he'd stop by the Auburn Mall for Chinese and watch the couples strolling by. He'd stare at them, studying them with the curiosity of a scientist observing strange animal behavior. Sometimes the couples would be holding hands, and Callum would watch dumbly. Was that what love was like? To willingly want to be in physical contact with another person? Callum couldn't stand being touched. Even as a kid, when his mother would kiss him goodbye and gently push him toward the school bus, the first thing Callum would do was wipe her kiss off his cheek where the dampness of her lips still burned. He'd shudder as he watched the couples in the mall walk with arms wrapped around waists, hips touching. Is that what love did? Make you not hate the things that normally made your skin crawl?

He didn't get it. Couldn't wrap his mind around the idea of sharing space, or kisses, or intimate touches with another person. It was why he liked being a paramedic. Gloves were worn at all times; even CPR required a plastic shield to avoid lip-to-lip contact these days. He was cold, clinical, and by the book. His patients didn't like him much, but his supervisors loved him. And without a woman in his life, he never objected to picking up extra shifts or staying way past his out time.

Until Jessica.

It was a 9-1-1 call that brought them together. Callum and his partner that night—Rautio, a good enough guy, though he insisted on hooking up his iPhone to the radio and playing 'N Sync between calls—were first on the scene. Jessica's mother had been hysterical, but had no wounds or immediate symptoms presenting, so she wasn't the patient. While Rautio tried to calm her down and make some sense of her words, Callum had called out, trying to determine if there was anyone else in the house. He moved swiftly from room to room, until he found a door ajar at the end of the hall, the scent of patchouli incense still burning; beckoning. Callum had laid a gloved hand on the doorframe and peeked in.

He saw her immediately: her coy smile, a mystery waiting to be solved. Her neck, long and pale and delicate. Her silky back hair pulled behind her ear and over her shoulder in a loose braid that matched the braid of the rope around her neck.

The cold, logical part of Callum's brain knew she was gone: she was motionless. Lividity had painted both those beautiful amethyst lips and her delicate, puffy hands. The puddle beneath her from her bladder letting go was cool to his Latexed touch. He stared at her for a moment, reaching out to slowly trace a gloved line down her arm, across her hip, cupping her shapely calf. She was dazzling. In that moment, his heart squeezed out an odd, arrhythmic beat.

But he had a job to do. He shouted for Rautio, and the two of them cut her down, Callum cradling her body against his as Raut loosened the grip of the rope. Callum laid her down on the hardwood floor (away from the puddle of urine; couldn't have this ethereal woman soiled by such piffle) and began compressions. He wanted to be the one to do this. Needed to be the one, to work on her until the M.E. could arrive and call it.

He alternated between pushing on her chest and leaning in to breathe against her teasing plump lips. She made no movement, offered no resistance, and Callum felt encouraged. He moved in closer, searching her drooped lids and flaccid cheeks for a sign that he was going too far, but Jessica was silent. He tossed a glance behind him, just to make sure the scene was safe, no peering eyes from partner or parent—and kissed her, letting the plastic mouth guard slip, so that flesh met unprotected flesh. Callum sighed.

Jessica's lips were cold and soft, sliding back until he could feel the hardness of her teeth against his skin. Exquisite. He pulled back, his head spinning, his stomach flip-flopping with excitement and amazement and awe. He wanted to tap-dance and cry and shout nonsensical nothings and hug her close, never letting go. Never. An old Disney song sprang up in laughable falsetto from the filing cabinet of his brain where such trivialities was stored: "So this is love, da-da-da-dee . . ." He giggled. Yes. So this was love. He got it. He finally got what the fuss was about. He leaned in again to steal a second kiss. Could he—should he dare to—try and slip her the—

"What're you doing, man? Christ!" Rautio pushed him aside roughly, taking over the compressions. "You need serious help."

It was the first time Callum had been in love. But it was not the first time he'd heard that.

30. FOOTSTEPS ON THE STAIRS BY MICHELE TALLARITA

Roy installed the security cameras because he kept hearing footsteps in the middle of the night. No, not just the normal noises a house makes. Footsteps, damn it.

His wife thought he was nuts.

Confirming her suspicions, the video footage showed nothing. Just his house, still and quiet.

So why could he still hear footsteps?

It started around three in the morning, every night. First, there was a soft clicking sound. Roy could swear it was the sound of the front door opening.

"Then why doesn't your fancy camera show the front door opening?" his wife demanded, and okay, she had a point. The camera had yet to capture the front door opening.

But anyway, the clicking sound. That was how it started. Then came the footsteps.

First, they were in the living room, back and forth, back and forth. They were spaced far apart, several minutes between each, but moved steadily across the room, then back again, heavily, like the thing had a hard time moving.

"Maybe your evil spirit needs to lose some weight," his wife joked.

But this wasn't a goddamn joke. Roy's heart would race as he lay as still as he could, listening. Thump. Thump. Thump.

It would pace the living room for about an hour. Then, at four, it would take its first step up the stairs. Thump!

Roy would sit bolt upright and shake his wife awake.

"There's nothing there, Roy. You've checked. You've watched your videos. Go back to sleep."

Of course she thought that. It never happened when she was awake.

Was he crazy?

So he stopped waking her up, just to see what would happen. The night after that, he let it climb all the way up the stairs. Thump. It was in the hallway. Thump. It was coming toward them.

"What do you want?" Roy whispered.

Nothing. No response. The footsteps stopped.

The next morning, Roy studied the footage and found nothing. Okay, he had a new idea. Maybe the thing couldn't be seen, but heard.

He dug his old tape recorder out of the closet and kept it under his pillow the next night. At four, he breathed heavily as the thing moved up the stairs.

Thump.

"What do you want?" Roy whispered, turning on his tape recorder.

The footsteps stopped. Roy waited ten minutes. Still, the footsteps didn't return. Shaking, sweating, he crept into the bathroom. He was tired. He was old. He played the tape at full volume, pressing the speaker to his ear.

And there was a whisper! Indiscernible, yes—but he swore he could hear it!

"You crazy old man," his wife said, scraping his uneaten breakfast into the garbage. "It's just the tape recorder making a noise. You bought it for Jim thirty years ago, for goodness sake."

Okay, okay. So he had to let the thing into the bedroom, had to let it get close enough that he could record it properly and prove it was real. Which it was.

At this point, his wife was threatening to send him to the doctors.

Thump. It was on the stairs.

Thump. In the hallway.

Roy lay stiff in bed. He hadn't felt this alert in years, like his every sense was sharpened to a point. God, he felt 22 again.

Thump.

It was just outside the door. Roy turned on the tape recorder.

A figure moved into the doorframe, just a shadow, one hand outstretched. Roy's heart boomed in his chest. It turned its head abruptly and locked eyes with him.

Thump.

"KATHY!" Roy shouted.

He shook his wife's shoulder, but she didn't rouse. The thing vanished. Roy forgot about the thing. Kathy wasn't waking up.

She'd died, died in her sleep.

Three days later, they buried her. Roy was shocked, numb, unable to cry. He thought of the thing standing in the doorframe. He'd thought…he'd thought for a split second it had looked like his wife: same face, same hair. But that was impossible.

How could the thing have been his wife the whole time?

He visited her tombstone, a rock in her family plot, next to her mother's. God, her mother. She'd hated Roy. Fifty years ago, she'd forbidden him to marry Kathy, but they'd eloped anyway. Kathy's mother had disowned her, passing away a few years later without making amends.

Kathy's mother.

Roy dug out the tape recorder again. Cringing, he played back the night of Kathy's death. Amidst his own cries, he heard the whisper again, louder this time.

"She's mine. She's mine. She's mine. She's mine."

31. THE YARD BY ROB E. BOLEY

At the edge of Old Man Henderson's long driveway, Kenny Davis pulled the black stocking mask over his face. He felt tougher but his gut still quivered. The picture window at the front of the farmhouse glowed in the distant darkness like the flat screen t.v. at the old closed-down Wing Palace. The house was maybe fifty yards away—close enough that he could've pegged it easily with a football.

His two best buddies, Kyle and Jason, put on their masks too. Jason had drawn a garish silver smiley face on his, while Kyle's featured abstract shapes. Jason flicked his cigarette butt into the yard. Kenny retrieved it, his nerves so tense that the ground seemed to tremble at his touch. He pocketed the filter and flipped Jason the bird.

"What?" Jason said.

"Littering isn't cool, man," Kyle said.

"Neither's leaving evidence," Kenny said. "C'mon, home invasion. Just like in the movies."

Gravel crunched under their boots as they walked the long driveway. They'd hiked all the way here from town and Kenny's left heel throbbed from his thrift store boots. They were two sizes too big, but that was the point. Couldn't have the police looking for someone wearing his size 10's. The wind rustled grass and jostled trees. Dead leaves scurried in the darkness. A half moon skulked crooked in the sky behind a thicket of clouds.

That picture window's curtains were spread wide, displaying the tops of two old recliners facing the front yard and a smattering of framed pictures hung askew on the wall.

"Gear up," Kenny whispered.

That was what Coach Henry always said before a game. The three boys jogged past the house and Kenny noticed that the grass was a ragged mess—patchy and worn out. Odd, considering Henderson was notorious for his lawn care. Any time you passed by this house, you'd likely see him pushing a mower, edging, or spreading feeder.

The boys ran to the shed on the property's north side. Kenny pulled gloves and a crowbar out of Kyle's backpack. He pried the lock off the door while Jason provided light with his phone.

"Got a signal?" Kenny said.

Jason shook his head.

"Good. Neither will he."

The boys had known better than to bring their own weapons. They'd leave nothing behind that could be traced back to them. Leave no trace—just like back in the Scouts. He longed for those simpler times—sitting around a campfire, sneaking smokes, and telling urban legends about Meadowboro's more infamous disasters or mutilated deer corpses or missing persons.

The door creaked open. Predictably, Jason picked a sledgehammer—as big and blunt as he was. Kyle grabbed an axe. Kenny, a pitchfork.

"Dammit." Jason pointed at a bin of dog food. "You said he didn't have a dog."

"If he did, it'd be barking already," Kenny said. "Chill."

"His dog probably died like a decade ago," Kyle said. "Old people never throw shit out. My mammaw has cans of Spaghetti-O's from the 70's."

They laughed, followed by deep silence.

"We're not just scaring him, are we?" Jason said.

Kyle and Kenny exchanged looks.

"We'll do whatever's necessary," Kenny said. "This old fuck is the last hold out. If he doesn't sell this property, the new development doesn't happen. That means no construction. No new jobs. All our folks stay unemployed. Ain't like he hasn't been offered good money. I don't know about you guys, but I can't keep coming home from school and finding Dad deep into a case of beer."

Kyle nodded. "My folks fight every night. Sometimes Dad hits Mom. Other times he leaves. Don't know which is worse."

"Whatever my ma's been doing to pay the bills ain't legal," Jason says. "She cries herself to sleep each night."

"We're doing this for them," Kenny says. "Hell, for the whole town."

He was only a few months away from graduating. He couldn't abandon his family and go to college—not with the way things were now. But the thought of spending his best years here in Meadowboro taking care of them—tending to their needs and not his own—filled him with dread. Sometimes he felt like this whole town was smothering him—crushing him under the weight of its expectations and misery. Lord knows the sleepy lil' town had seen its share of sadness.

They walked back to the house, stopping to cut the phone line. In the front yard, Jason gasped and threw himself on the grass. Henderson sat in one of the recliners in the window.

"Get up, asshole," Kenny said. "He can't see us. It's dark as hell out here, and he's got the lights on. His window is all glare. He's probably watching t.v."

Sure enough, the old man stared vaguely at the window—or more likely at whatever was below it. He wore a faded button-up and munched on a bowl of popcorn.

Kyle waved his hand. The old man gazed—oblivious.

"Creepy," Kyle said.

"'Bout to get creepier," Jason said, stepping toward the house and slinging the sledge over his shoulder.

Floodlights flashed on.

Henderson didn't react except to stuff another handful of popcorn into his wrinkled face. Kyle pivoted toward the road, but Kenny grabbed his backpack. Jason reared back his sledge— poised to break the window.

The ground trembled.

Jason slipped downward—as if the earth sucked him in down to his shins. A jagged column of the soil in front of him rose, jerking him forward face-first. His knees bent the wrong direction with a jagged crack.

That horrid noise echoed in Kenny's gut. His bladder released. Hot wetness seeped into his crotch. Still grabbing Kyle's backpack, he ran back toward the road—away from the crunching noises and Jason's terrible screams.

The yard swelled in grassy green waves and propelled him back backward. Kyle gasped, and suddenly Kenny was holding onto a tattered scrap of bloody backpack. Chewing noises crunched around him. The ground trembled in synch with his friends' screaming. He cut left toward the driveway. Except the ground yawned and swallowed him whole. Black soil surrounded him. Rocky teeth bit into his neck. He knew he was going to die.

He was wrong.

Darkness.

He awoke to the smell of dirt—buried neck-deep in the ground and completely helpless. The gashes on his neck stung. The earth smelled like blood, grass, sweat, and dog food. Henderson stood over him, shaking his head.

"We didn't mean—" Kenny said.

"No, I reckon you didn't. Why're you here, boy?"

"To scare you away, so the new mall could be built."

"You thought everything would be better if I was gone, right? You thought the town would be better off because you don't understand why I'm here. I'm taking care of the Yard. It chose me when I was about your age. Now it's chosen you. It marked you."

He crouched and pointed at Kenny's wounds. His hands smelled like butter and icy hot cream. Moonlight illuminated scars on the old man's neck.

"I'm too old to handle the yard alone," Henderson said. "You're young and strong. You'll do just fine. It needs you to tend to it. Otherwise, whatever's down there will rise up. It's happened before. You know the stories—fires, massacres, accidents— decades of tragedies. This town needs us, boy."

The dirt surrounding him snuggled and purred. Dread twisted in his belly. Rocky teeth grinded against his hands. He kneaded the Yard, and it needed him.

You're new. I can tell. Mind if I walk with you?

I saw my child today. He was resting in a nest of ashes beneath the looming white willow tree. His little body was just as I remembered it in the hospital. He was stillborn. The nurse, Helena I think her name was, held him out to my wife Susan at arm's length, not allowing the baby to touch her ample, heaving bosom which was barely contained in her blood stained scrubs. She didn't so much as hand the child over to my wife and drop it into her arms. My wife sobbed and cradled our dead child. I couldn't understand her grief. We had known the baby was dead for some time. She carried the fetus full term and delivered it; a dead mass of formed matter drenched in foaming afterbirth. His skin was purple.

I pushed my wife out of the hospital an hour later and I deposited her in a taxi cab. The driver, named Juan or something, kept looking in the rearview window with an annoyed look on his face. My wife was making a lot of noise, with the crying and all. I didn't feel much like shushing her just to make the driver happy. I didn't feel like saying much at all.

We never named the child. Thinking back on our reasoning, maybe it was just a way to dehumanize the whole experience, making it hurt less. I don't think it worked.

I see my wife from time to time. She crawls, her arms jut out from the shoulders at an odd angle. Her ass is held way up in the air. She moves like a spider. I don't think she recognizes me at all, or at least doesn't let on that she does. I tried talking to her once, but she just passed me by. The land expands here. It's hard to explain, but it does. There is plenty of room and the people don't congregate much, at least not intentionally, but I run across her quite a lot. It's as if we're connected by an invisible tether where she is crawling and I stand still. She can move all she wants, but the tether holds her to me, twisting around me until I am bound completely. She passes, relentless in her movement, right on by me. It's like we never met.

I don't like the white willow tree. Whenever I draw near the draping branches turn toward me, creating a canopy inches over my head. Sometimes I think about reaching up and touching the hovering, leafless mass, but I stay my hand. Nobody talks to me here. I have no guide. At least I don't think that I do. I can't remember too much about how I came to this place, but I have a feeling that I didn't end up here on my own accord. I was put here by somebody. I must have been.

I tried to pick up my child but his hand snapped off in my grip. He was alive, must have been. His chest was rising and falling in shuddering rhythm. At least he can breathe here, although his eyes are still closed. I felt bad about breaking his hand off, but it didn't seem to hurt him any. I thought about telling him that I was his father, but ended up saying nothing. Before I left I pushed ashes over his body with my foot, burying him. I don't know why I did that.

I left the willow; I don't like to stay there for long. I walked along a long sloping trail that had been well trodden by countless others before me. That was when the man came for me. He always does, eventually. I don't know who he is or where he comes from, but he seems to have taken a liking to me. He crawls too. He moves faster than I do, but it's not as though I try and outrun him or anything. He bites me. He goes for my arms, sinking his teeth into my triceps. It's useless to try and shake him off. He hangs on me, entwining my body with both his arms and legs. He doesn't bite me for long. I only have to carry him a mile or two. The last couple times he's bitten me, he's been able to take off bits of flesh. It's not like it hurts or anything – I just don't like how my arm looks with all the holes in it. It doesn't seem natural to me. I wish I knew who he was.

That was around the time I found you walking. I knew you were a new one and I have a pretty good idea as to where you're going. Mind if I walk with you?

The path is going to spread out here and I like to stay to the middle. I suggest you set your feet carefully here. There is nowhere else to walk except on top of people. I mentioned before that the others don't congregate on purpose, but there is a drawing to this place. I feel it myself. My feet bring me here constantly. I never stay long. Others never leave. The path stops abruptly and the people begin, lying prone and bunching up together so tightly that it seems like an endless living carpet of torsos stitched together by arms and legs. You can step on them. They don't seem to mind. Sometimes I stumble and my foot goes through a person's face. The skulls are fragile. I'll pause to look down upon whom I've trodden (call it morbid curiosity) until I feel hands groping up my legs. If you stay in one place too long you're apt to be pulled down. If you look carefully, you can see others who have been pulled down struggle to get free, but I've never seen anyone reemerge after they've been taken down. Sooner or later they will turn their gaze up to the being in the sky and be lost.

He's above us. An angel of black. A figure of perfect beauty, hovering mindlessly over all who dwell here. I've only looked upon him once before. His tremendous wings spread out so wide that they touch from one end of the sky to the other. He created such a longing within me that I raised my hands up to him, my heart breaking that I could not reach to touch him. I don't feel much of anything anymore, but he made me feel something, even if it was just desire for contact. Everyone else here seems to have lost themselves in that desire. I was able to tear my gaze away and now I don't look up at the sky anymore. I don't want to end up like these others. My reasoning might not make much sense. It's not like I have anything to lose by lying down and forgetting myself completely under the angel's apathetic gaze. I have nothing left to give. I don't think the angel had anything left to give, either.

It's like when we came here, wherever this is, we lost everything along the way. Here we dwell in the separation. I think we missed the message.

Well, it looks like you've decided to take a peek above and will be staying here awhile. I thought you might be one of those types. You didn't have anything to say. I'm going on now, but I'll be seeing you. The invisible tether binds us all together and we never stay apart for long. Goodbye.

33. EYE OF THE BEHOLDER BY J. T. SEATE

There are tales of primitive cultures refusing to let their pictures be taken in the belief that the camera would steal their souls. Perhaps the phenomena I experienced in a musty antique shop held something akin to this superstition.

The wooden box stood on a primitive tripod. The old-time camera dated back to the Civil War, the kind where the photographer threw a black canvas drape over his head to shield out unwanted light. I pictured Mathew Brady standing beneath the covering that once protected the chemically coated glass plates. An exterior flash of gunpowder might have gone off to illuminate a portrait setting. This box had small, gilded engravings placed along the edges of its panels creating a decorative touch, almost like a small coffin. What made this particular camera unique was that it was supposedly haunted.

I'd heard of the box from a friend who worked for a photography magazine. Since I write about the supernatural and occult, I tracked down its current owner and offered a handsome payment for a look-see. It was said that when you covered yourself with the canvas and pressed your eye against the peephole, the lens reflected things that could not exist, things that hadn't been photographed for one-hundred and fifty years.

"Do you really believe this simple device to be dangerous?" I asked its owner.

"Not physically, perhaps. I looked through the camera only once to see if what I'd been told held any truth and I've chosen not to look again. I was further tempted to destroy it, but that would mean I believed it held magic that could contaminate others. Instead of such an unalterable act, I've chosen to keep it in my collection of antiques. Here I can protect others from its effect."

"Then why offer me a viewing?"

He cleared his throat preparing to justify exceptions. "Of course, there are times when someone such as yourself comes along and is willing to make a generous contribution for the preservation of antiques and to satisfy one's curiosity. If you'd rather not—"

I held up my hand to stop his ingenuous words. I hadn't come all this way to back out.

"All right then. After you're under the hood, remove the metal cap covering the brass lens and simultaneously push the button on the side of the box. This will trigger a timing device for ten seconds of exposure. When the ticker stops, promptly recover the lens."

"What does exposure time matter since a glass plate is no longer being exposed?"

"Regardless of what you see, you want to cover the lens when the ticking stops. Please follow that instruction."

Even if a plate had been in place, there was nothing in front of the camera to take a picture of, no composition, just a black backdrop without embellishment. I crawled beneath the ancient shroud and placed one eye against the peephole. I removed the cap and pressed the button.

What appeared to be a family of five came into focus as I twisted the lens. Appearing before me was an adult male and female, two young girls, and an even younger little boy. They were dressed in formal wear of the day, circa mid-1800s. At first, I thought the owner had somehow placed an old slide into the box, but that theory died when each one of the people in the image moved slightly. Their positioning seemed odd as well. All of them were leaning into the back of the large couch upon which they were perched rather than sitting in a traditional pose. My thumb and forefinger rubbed the bridge of my nose hoping to clear my vision and my head. My eye continued to strain for details as the ticking mechanism continued its countdown. Just as it stopped, the family, all of them, closed their eyes.

"Cover the lens," I heard the camera's owner say, but I ignored him, caught up in the unreality of what I was seeing as the scene became more than a scattering of light across my retina. Another second or two went by before I felt the shop owner's hand remove the cap from mine and the image went dark, but not before I realized the tragedy of the scene. The people before the camera had not only become very still; I understood to my horror that they were, in fact, dead.

A coldness made me cringe. I was familiar with the custom begun in the mid-nineteenth century of taking photos of corpses as if they were still alive, to preserve images of the deceased. They were called mourning pictures. As grisly as it sounds, burial was often delayed for days or weeks waiting for the photographer to arrive. Had influenza taken this family, or some other scourge that swept over battlefields, towns, and villages during those times? I remained under the hood a few seconds longer as the covered lens could not remove the image planted indelibly in my brain.

The box's owner pulled me out. He didn't ask me what I saw or what I thought. He merely thanked me for my contribution and escorted me to the door. My mouth felt as dry as the wood that filled the shop. Strangely, I did not ask him what he or others had seen, for I felt I knew. Whether it was the photo I saw or something equally impossible, there would prove to be unsavory ramifications.

I now know it was not merely a haunted antique that had given the wooden box its reputation. It was the haunting that followed a viewing. The scene had passed from the device through the lens of my eye, and into my consciousness—an indelible print of this family posing for the camera, postmortem. But there was more. The image of the dead did not remain frozen in time as if viewed on printed paper.

The camera was certainly haunted, but now, so was I. Whenever I looked into the viewfinder on any photographic device, be it digital or otherwise, the corpses were there and evolving, cadaverous flesh decaying before my eyes into a mass of putrefaction like modern time-lapse photography. Five sets of sunken, caved-in sockets with eyelids peeled away, retaining the ability to stare into my soul, especially those belonging to the little boy. Horrible.

What could create such hallucinations, if that is what they were? Even worse was the concept of the people in the scene being animated by some power that lay beyond death and the grave? I considered telling my photographer friend about my experience, but he would just talk about stock overlays, inverted shadings, and pixel differentials. What was the point? I knew what my indulgent mind told me I'd seen, and without the benefit of a surface on which to print the image. Both reality and rationality failed to explain it. "What you see is what you get," like the old song that goes, Just one look, that's all it took, yeah, just one look....

It can be a revelation—what a man can learn about himself when he is forced to look into the depths of his soul. I had clearly stumbled onto a haunted relic, something involving a time-warp. Either that, or I was going mad. I wasn't even sure of my feelings; whether it was panic or a deep pulsating…thrill. What I saw within the magic box my mind would not let go of. The scene was impossible to dismiss and began to leak into my dreams and fantasies.

I decided that the old photo was a glimpse of inevitability; lenses lined up to expose the reality of the human condition—the reality of the grave, the completion of a cycle no less terrifying than when Edgar Allen Poe wrote of it nearly two hundred years ago—life, death, decay. The wooden box may be a coffin of sorts for the dead that passed through its lens, and just as likely for those foolish enough to peer at its captured images. Not knowing how all-encompassing this power might be, I deemed it equally unwise to be the subject of any electrical device. What irony if it caused my own…well…no more Skype, and no Selfies for damn sure.

Most would say this haunting was just the funny monkey in my brain rattling around, looking for new bizarre twists for my authorial endeavors, but I know what I saw…and still see. That would be logical to the outside world, but I thought of a way to see if it was more than my fantasies going rogue. I purchased an old camera, a boxy little Kodak. I looked in its viewfinder just once. Need I tell you what was there?

I have a neighbor I don't like. He's an asshole, his wife is a snob, and his kids are brats. I don't even like their dog. I told him I wanted to try out my retro camera on his lovely family. How could he refuse? I knew my neighbor would do no less than get them all to smile at a chance for a free family portrait. I was, of course, only interested in seeing if anything unusual developed. Without looking into the camera, I pushed the shutter release and took the picture. Nothing happened right away. I told the pater familius I would show him the artistry old cameras could produce when the shot was developed. I had no film in the Kodak, of course.

When I got home and dared to look into the viewfinder again, all I saw was the 1800's family of five still decaying away, little left of them now but grinning skulls perched upon stiff-collared clothes. I wondered if the pictured dead would eventually turn to dust and blow away, but that could take years and I was currently more interested in what, if anything, might result from pointing the camera at the family next door.

Within a week, my neighbor, his wife and children, became ill. The kids stayed home from school and the parents, home from work. It apparently all happened too fast to consult a doctor. When another alarmed neighbor checked on them, they were all dead in their beds, a rare case of isolated influenza.

What to do when you have quite possibly given someone a death sentence? Look once again into the viewfinder, of course, but I refuse to take the blame. Who could have guessed…? What has changed in my life is that I no longer see the 19th century dead family in their Sunday finest through the looking glass. I now see the dead family down the street on their modern sofa, decaying ever so gradually. Whenever I look into a lens, a viewfinder, or bring up a photo on my cell phone, I see their tongues swelling…forcing their jaws apart as skin sinks onto bone, and lips peel away from dead teeth, rotting away in familial horror.

Just one look is all it took.

34. THE HATE ENGINE by Shaun Avery

The atmosphere was tense, the faces of his colleagues grim, when Mike entered the squad room.

He stood at the door, trying to assess the situation, and finally he looked to his partner, Dave.

"What's up?" he asked.

Dave looked over at him. "We've got Wayne Jarvis in the cells again."

Mike sighed. "So what else is new?"

His fellow detectives shared a look.

"What?" Mike placed his hands on his hips, resting his left against his service pistol. "What is it?"

"It's just..." Dave paused. "The guy, he's... different this time."

"Yeah?" Mike took a seat at his desk – the Captain always gave him a hard time about how messy it was, but Mike's impressive case clearance rate kept the guy from taking any further action. "How?"

"It's hard to describe, Mike," Dave said. "For one thing, he handed himself in tonight."

"Wow," Mike said. "That is strange." Then, his eyes falling to the photograph on his desk, the one thing that always rose above the mess, he said, "I suppose he's been asking to see me."

Dave nodded.

Well, Mike thought, at least some things never change.

He made the usual trek back towards the cells, shoes clicking in the silence of the hallway, until he stood before Cell 46.

"Hello, Wayne," he said.

Mike placed his hands against the bars of the cell as he spoke.

And now that he was closer, he saw instantly what Dave had been talking about.

The first thing that struck him as unusual was that Jarvis seemed to be sober.

More, he wasn't frothing at the mouth and calling Mike an increasingly colorful number of names for stealing his girlfriend.

Instead, he sat meekly on the cell mattress and looked up and said, "Hi, Mike."

Mike was more unsettled by this seeming change in personality than he cared to show. So he remained stony-faced as he said, "I heard you wanted to see me."

"That's right."

"Why?" Mike took his hands off the bars, placed them back onto his hips. "You want to apologize for all the crank calls? All the threats?" His voice grew lower as his anger rose. "You know, you're lucky. If it wasn't for Jessica still caring about what happens to you, though God only knows why, we'd have pressed charges and locked you up for good long ago."

At this Jarvis hung his head in what looked like shame and mumbled something.

"What was that?" Mike asked.

Jarvis looked up.

"A different me," he said.

"Yeah?" Mike smirked, unable to help himself. "So how come you ended up in here tonight?"

"I begged them to lock me up," Jarvis said. "Told the man on the front desk I would kill myself if they didn't."

"And would you have?"

Jarvis made no reply.

"Just like I thought," Mike said. "You haven't changed at all. You're still spineless."

And he turned and walked off, not yet knowing how wrong he was.

Hate, hate, hate – it needed more hate!

It had ate some before – sucked it straight out of the man who had called it here. But that had only been enough to propel it out of the house and into the street. Now it needed more, much more.

So it walked through the town, and though the night was busy no one saw it. It was good at that, at hiding. It was only ever seen when it wanted to be seen.

It sniffed the air.

Felt hate somewhere.

And moved towards it.

Mike sat down at his desk, shaking his head.

Dave looked over at him. "What'd the guy say?"

"Nothing that made any sense."

Dave smiled. "So that hasn't changed, either."

Mike returned the smile, enjoying the easy rhythm they had fallen into after so many years working together.

There had only been one bone of contention between them in that time, and as unbelievable as it was, it had been over the guy currently being held in Cell 46. Dave, an old-school family man when he wasn't chasing down crooks, had not approved of Mike sleeping with Jessica before she had officially called it off with Jarvis. They had never argued about this disapproval, had not let it come between them on either a personal or work level. But Mike had always known that it was there.

"Well," Dave said, "he's been quiet so far. Let's hope –"

But before he could finish his sentence, the squad room burst into activity.

A squadron of patrolmen marched a dozen naked men through the room in handcuffs, leading them towards the cells. The men squirmed within their grasp, but not to get away, Mike noticed. No, instead the naked men were trying to grab at each other.

And all of them had erections.

"Hey," Dave said, watching the procession go by. "Isn't that – ?"

"Yeah," Mike said. "The GWAF boys. The self-proclaimed God's Warriors Against Fairies."

"Hey, you," Dave said to one of the patrolmen, an eager young guy called Keane.

Desperate to impress, Keane came straight over, saying, "Sir?"

"What are you bringing those guys in for?" Dave asked. "The usual?"

"The usual," Mike knew, included intimidation of minorities, domestic abuse and puking and peeing all over the street whilst under the influence. But this time Keane surprised them, saying, "No, sir. Public lewdness."

"Tell it like it was, Keane," shouted a patrolman called Buckley from the hallway. "They were having a goddamn fucking orgy in the middle of the street."

"An orgy?" Mike looked to Keane. "You mean they raped someone?"

"No, sir," Keane said. "They were having an orgy with each other."

"An orgy?"

Mike stood in the hallway looking at the GWAF boys.

He could see where they had got their name.

Even with erections they didn't have much to write home about.

The thought made him flash back to this morning with Jessica. She always liked to wait up for him, no matter how late he got back from work. And she would never let him turn to drink to wind down from a shift. No, she always used her hands and mouth for that. And he never tired of it.

"Yeah," said the man in charge of the cells tonight, a thirty-year veteran named Briggs. "Had to give them all their own cells." He shook his head in disbelief. "Guys just wouldn't stop trying to fuck each other."

"That's what happens," Jarvis said from his cell behind them, "when something takes away all your hate."

Mike was rapidly losing patience with his onetime love rival. "What are you talking about?"

Jarvis gestured to one of the GWAF boys, now frantically masturbating in the corner of his cell.

"All that gay-hating garbage," he said. "They must have hated themselves so much, for what they were hiding. But now that the hate's gone..."

Mike looked to Briggs. "Give me five minutes here, would you?"

Briggs nodded, then headed back to the front desk.

Mike looked to Jarvis, tapping his fingers against the butt of his gun.

"Okay, friend," he said. "I'd like you to start making sense now."

"Sense?" Jarvis shook his head. "I wouldn't know much about that. Not since you two..."

Mike waited, expecting another one of the man's rants.

But instead Jarvis looked at him and said, "You took her from me, man."

Mike had once thought this, too, had once felt guilty. But that was before really talking to Jessica, really getting into her past. Now he told Jarvis, "No, man. She told me what you were like – about the control, the putdowns." He came closer to the bars, trying to push his way as far as possible into Jarvis's personal space. "You lost her all by yourself."

"Yes, well." Jarvis smiled. "That's one way of looking at it, I suppose. But one thing's for sure: the hate was killing me. That's why I... did what I did."

"You kill someone, Wayne?" Mike asked. "That why you came here tonight?"

Then a thought suddenly hit him.

"You wouldn't," he said.

He looked at Jarvis.

"You wouldn't have the balls."

Jarvis said nothing.

Keeping his eyes on the prisoner, Mike slid a hand into his pocket and pulled out his phone.

Called Jessica.

It rang.

And rang.

No answer.

He slowly placed the phone back in his pocket.

"If you've done something to her..." Mike said.

Then he was running.

Back through the station and past his messy desk and towards his car.

Calling her again.

Still nothing.

He threw himself into his car.

And drove.

It felt good.

The more hate it ate, the more hate it could generate.

And re-distribute. Soon it would roll through this town, turning petty grievances between neighbors into full-scale wars.

But first...

A car sped by, and it could smell that the man driving was almost bursting with potential hate.

It followed.

A smile on its face.

"Blood," Jarvis was mumbling to himself in his cell. "Needed blood to make it work, the incantation." He rocked back and forth on the mattress, arms wrapped around his knees. "And the way our lives were going, it was either her or me."

And...

Mike pushed open the door.

"The hate was killing me. That's why I was getting drunk every night, getting in trouble, ending up in here each morning. But now I don't hate anyone anymore. I have no hate left in me."

He smelled the blood.

"The Hate Engine took it all from me."

He found her body, cradled her in his arms, wept into her hair.

"I thought my hate would be enough for it. I thought it would go back where it came from when it had drained all that from me."

He stormed back out to his car, gun in hand.

"I didn't know how greedy it was. And now it's free."

He didn't know that something was following him as he drove erratically back towards the station.

"I've probably killed the whole town – but who cares? I'm free of my hate, and that's all that matters."

And he lay down on the bed and closed his eyes.

"Mike!"

He paused at the doorway, gun by his side, Jessica's blood still on him.

The rest of the detectives looked around each other.

It was like a replay of earlier tonight, when he'd first come in. Only this time he knew what was going on. He knew that Wayne fucking Jarvis, woman-killer, had to die.

"What's going on?" Dave said.

Mike saw his hand creeping towards his own pistol.

"He killed her," Mike said. "He killed Jessica, Dave."

Then Mike heard a creak behind him, as if someone had come to stand there.

But he saw nothing.

He felt something, though.

He felt his anger rising.

"Out of my way, guys," he said. "I've got someone to kill."

The detectives did not comply.

They all went for their own weapons.

But Mike, his pistol already drawn, was quicker.

He killed the other men in the room. Only Dave he hit to wound, and then came to stand over him.

And heard that creak again.

Was something following him?

No.

That was crazy.

But the thought persisted.

And something seemed to be stoking his anger again as he looked down at his former partner.

"Never did approve of me and her, did you, Dave?" he said.

Dave spat blood.

"Well that's fine," Mike said. "You got your wish now."

And he shot Dave in the face.

Back in the cells the GWAF boys were cowering in the corners. But not from him. They seemed to be looking at something behind him. Something that he could not see.

But that didn't matter.

He only had eyes for Jarvis.

He stood in front of the prisoner.

"You bastard," Mike said. "How could you do that to her?"

"It was her or me," Jarvis said, eyes still closed. "My hate would have killed me. I chose to kill her instead."

"Yeah," Mike said, lifting his gun. "And now I'm choosing to kill you."

Mike heard the creak again.

And it seemed that Jarvis did, too.

"Are you?" he said. "Or is something else choosing for you?"

He opened his eyes.

And in the brief second before the bullet entered his forehead and propelled his brains out onto the wall, he saw The Hate Engine standing behind Mike, smiling.

35. WHERE SHADOWS COME TO STARE BY

MICHAEL SCHOMAKER

"I did it," the boy said calmly. "I killed them all; Mom, Dad, Bella. The boy looked to the ground showing contrived remorse, and twisted his wrists in a pair of police handcuffs. They were very loose around his wrists.

"You know son, I only put those on to keep you safe," the detective said as he closed the door to the conference room behind him.

"It's ok, I understand." The boy would not meet the detective's eyes.

"So your name is Riley right?" the detective asked. The boy bounced his head while staring at his hands.

"Well my name is detective Fitz – you can call me Tom. I'd like to talk to you a little bit about what happened tonight if that's ok?"

Riley again bounced his head slowly to acknowledge and continued to turn his hands in the chrome handcuffs. They reminded him of his neighbor's old pet Rottweiler champ. His collar was made from a shiny chain. Riley remembered the sound of the clanging chain-links as the dog ran up and down the fence barking, always barking. Champ was dead now, Riley thought to himself, then aloud, "just like Mom, Dad, and Bella."

Tom was unnerved by the unprovoked statement. And did the boy just smirk? Tom thought to himself. "What's just like them, pal?"

Riley answered quietly, "Nothing." A cold chill ran through Tom's body that shook his to his core. In 33 years of law enforcement he had never seen anything so disturbing.

Tom pulled a handkerchief from his pocket and offered it to the boy. "You've got some… dirt on your face." The dirt was dried blood. Riley took the kerchief and wiped at the boy's face. This simple action reminded him of watching his own son twenty years ago, at the age of ten. After every little league game his son would be covered in sweat and infield dust, and Tom would wipe the dirt from his face. He had never missed a game.

"So would you like to tell me what happened tonight, son?" Riley finally looked up and met Tom's gaze for the first time. "What happened in that house tonight, buddy?" Tom leaned toward the boy in anticipation; the silence in the room lay thick with tension.

"It's a little bright in here," said the boy.

Tom noticed Riley squinting and shading his eyes. It was 4:00 in the morning, Tom thought to himself. "Sure pal." Tom got up to adjust the lights in the room with the dimmable light switch. As he turned his back and slid the dimmer switch Riley began to speak.

"We don't really like bright light."

"Well, I can understand that." Tom stopped in mid-sentence. "We?"

Riley, if it was still Riley, took on a completely different persona as the dark and shadows dressed him. Tom would have never thought it possible; he was a veteran police detective and in pretty good shape – how could he feel downright scared of a ten year old boy? "What did you mean when you said we, Riley? Was there someone else in your house with you tonight?"

Tom could not shake the boy's stare. It seemed as if it tracked his every move, and noticed every twitch of his facial muscles.

"I meant me and Nuknuk." Even his voice had changed as if mottled with years of knowledge above his actual age.

"Who is Nuknuk?" Tom asked.

"Mom calls him my imaginary friend, but she knows now that he's real."

"So you and this Nuknuk did this to your family?" Tom asked. "Where is Nuknuk now?" The next word uttered by Riley all but stopped Tom's beating heart.

"He's here, with us."

Tom subconsciously scanned the room with his peripheral. His skin broke into both goosebumps and cold sweat simultaneously. "There is no one in here but us, pal. Look around," Tom replied nervously.

Riley did not answer but leaked that smirk again as he looked toward the floor.

"So Riley," the detective began, forcing composer and an authoritative voice, "did you use a weapon to do this? Something like a knife or maybe an axe?"

Riley shook his head side to side.

"Now you expect me to believe a ten year old boy – with his bare hands and the help up an imaginary friend – dismembered, and disemboweled a grown man, an adult woman, and a three year old toddler?" Tom gasped the last word and tried to reclaim it back into his mouth. His thoughts turned again to his son. Riley was just a boy, certainly a boy with some mental dysfunction, but a boy none the less.

As Tom wrestled with what to do next, the dim overhead light seemed to fade a bit more, and a hot breeze slid across the nape of Tom's neck. He turned his head with a crack. The room was almost completely black behind him. Tom immediately turned his head back to Riley. The boy was holding his small hands up to the only wash of light in the room. His handcuffs inexplicably laid on the steel table, still locked. Riley held his hands to the light in a messianic pose. Then in a voice that could not be mistaken for a ten year old boy, Riley said, "I used these."

Tom noticed his blood covered hands and even bits and pieces of what looked like flesh and small hairs beneath the boy's fingernails.

"And I never said he was imaginary."

Tom's eyes froze as wide as they could be stretched. The small amount of light that shone across the face of the boy slowly faded to nothing. A place where shadows come to stare.

36. NOCTURNAL USHER BY JOHANNES PINTER

Are you lying comfortably? Want an extra pillow? Here, take this. It's important that it feels good for you.

I usually don't say it's fun that people found their way here, because it's not funny that they had to look me up to begin with. There's more people every passing month, and that's sad. But on the other hand: that my calendar fills up suggests that people understand that the puzzle won't be complete until all the pieces are in place, right? There is hope for humanity after all.

Now. Let's get all the boring facts out of the way. I see that you have signed the certificate that your presence here is voluntary, and what transpires here is at your own risk. As you received information about earlier, we will keep going all night, for at least eight hours, starting now. It's because we need a good margin to be sure we'll reach the deeper sleep cycles. The longer you sleep, the shallower the sleep becomes, and it will gradually lead to longer periods of REM sleep.

Excuse me?

Well, during the deep sleep stage the dreaming occurs in isolated, static tableaus. While during REM sleep the dreams have a more narrative flow. And it is these "stories" that are our goals during this session. If one would compare sleeping with a fishing ground, it is in the REM sleep that we will catch the biggest and most interesting fish.

So. What is the reason you came here? Wait, let me guess. You feel a stress that never really seems to leave you? Or ... you wish you had the ability to fantasize more, as you did when you were a child? Or perhaps there is a darkness inside of you that frightens you, that you want to get rid of?

You don't know? Then I will reveal something to you - all options are equally right! It's like this; you see, every person hosts a darkness that needs to come out. When they were kids, they had the monster under the bed. No matter how horrible it was, it was still somewhat safe, because it had substance and could be dealt with. Defeated. Mom could come in and check that it was not there. Maybe speak a rhyme that made it go away, and then they would sleep safely.

As an adult, with all the adult knowledge and the rational adult thinking, the monsters are phased out. But the darkness remains. And it needs an outlet. Otherwise, you start to feel bad. The risk is that your darkness comes out in ways that are far worse than your childhood monsters under the bed. And that's where I come in.

I dream your nightmares.

Deep in there, you have that darkness that needs to come out. You must find a way to drill deep, drain your subconscious so to speak. Together with me you will dream.

However, I must raise a warning finger; it will be unsettling. It will be harsh and frightening. Obscene and grotesque. Sometimes even shocking.

It will be like when you were a little kid and swam too far out from the shore, and felt something slimy touch your leg down in the darkness of the water. Like when you went out on the bog outside of Ramsele alone and tread wrongly, finding yourself suddenly thigh-deep in mud, and your squirming only made you sink deeper, and no one heard your cries. Or that time when you drove past that accident and saw the woman in the car with her hands still on the steering wheel, and her head on the road in front of the car.

However. You will discover – as all who visited me have done - that in the darkness there is something comforting and liberating and sometimes even beautiful. When you wake up afterwards, you will feel better than you've done in a long time. Along the way you might not feel that way, but when you leave me afterwards, you will be glad you chose to come here.

The practicalities? How will we dream the same nightmares? It's not that peculiar really. You and I will for a moment share the same dark place in the universe. That room will be filled with images. Call it suggestion. Call it magic. Either way, I will trigger the nightmares you thought you would never experience again. And it will make you a more complete and satisfied person.

That should be all, I think. If you'll lie comfortably, just close your eyes and relax, and we'll get started. You can hold my hand if you want, some feel safer that way in the beginning.

Are you ready? Then, let's go.

37. THE PREACHER BY K. TRAP JONES

I thought God had prepared me for any occasion, but I was wrong. My mind was clear and the vengeance bleeding through my veins was free of vile and corruption. The church lay in ruins; the pews are scattered about the barren terrain, but yet I see beauty in the destruction surrounding me. Devastation overshadows the once peaceful tranquility of the small town. Even within bloodshed, God displayed his art. I do not question his whereabouts during our time of need, as I know what we endured was just another part of his master plan. It served as a test for humanity; one I intended to pass.

We honestly had no chance. Bred through bloodlust, the demons of Hell rose from the trenches and scoured the land. The touch of evil caressed every living person and animal leaving behind a wake of the dead. My small church resides in South Georgia, just across the Florida line. Like watching a hurricane approach, the media animated the demon outbreak.

There was no more fear; there was no more doubt. Time was not our ally. The splitting bark of the trees echoed around us as the others gripped their weapons. The demons were unlike anything in the scriptures. Beastlike and frail, they climbed upon one another in order to advance. The trees were engulfed with them. It was a steamroller of death as high as I could see. Sporadic gunfire snapped me back to reality as I found myself being the only one standing outside. I became a victim to fear as I stumbled through the doors, sealing them tight.

The others fled to the cellar. Alone in the sanctuary, I stared at a statue of the Lord hanging above the pulpit. The walls began to bend and splinter. The plywood used to block the windows was torn away as the stain glass imploded. Carrying a bible and a staff, I stood and watched as the front doors buckled under the pressure. They filtered into the church like a stream running down a mountain.

Anger rose within me as my blood boiled with the sight of evil inside the walls. A smirk stretched across my face as my knuckles cracked holding the staff. Toleration was no longer within the array of emotions. With insanity reaching the apex, I slammed my fist deep into the floor of the church. A shockwave created a radius of wind gust that pushed back the surrounding demons. The walls shook terribly as the demons were sent funneling out the door and windows.

My muscles felt powerful, hidden beneath the cloth. Every inch of my being felt alive with vengeance, eager to disrupt the tides of war. They swarmed around, but dared not touch me. I became blood drunk with anger and did not stop the swing of the staff until every single demon was gone from the church.

Drenched in demon blood, damnation greeted my sheltered eyes as I walked outside. Demon troops riding large hounds were numerous with the burning landscape. Massive ogres were vomiting fire on anything not already scorched. The ground shook as two of the giant beasts were being guided by the demons saddled upon their shoulders. Their lips were blistered from the acid dripping down their necks. Rusty chains formed a rein, lifting the top portions of the mouths. As they neared, I lunged forward and swiped the staff across a monstrous shin. The skin separated and swayed the giant creatures. Pulling at the reins, the demon tried to control it, and as the ogre leaned down, I skewered the demon and tossed him aside. The crucifix at the end of the staff cut through the neck of the ogre. The acid blood caught fire, ignited by the torch each of them held.

The beast became enraged as its skin melted. Deranged and uncontrollable, one ogre attacked the other. The molten blood coated its comrade, who stomped its way through the army.

The demons converged upon me, eager to rip the flesh from my bones. Rotating the staff, I was able to keep them at radius, until the paws of the hounds scraped the dirt, clouding the air. The pearly white teeth were similar elephant tusks, dripping with the drool of hunger. A demented handler of a man held them at bay with charred chains wrapped around each of his forearms. He was as tall as one of the pine trees and just as sturdy. My robe wore heavy from the blood. I could smell the burnt cloth, but my heart rate remained steady. I wasn't about to surrender; I wasn't about to give up my parish.

As the chains unraveled and the hounds howled with eagerness, I jumped back and crested up to the roof of the church. The wind carried me until I found my footing on the tiled foundation. The large hounds barely needed to jump to reach the top. Their mouth snapped and growled as their claws removed the tiles like the shuffling of a card deck. I climbed to the peak of the roof and slid down the other side where a waiting hound pounced with an open mouth.

Leading with the staff, I continued to slide down and allowed the crucifix to dagger deep into the throat. Its eyes rattled with confusion as the tongue licked my hands still holding the end of the weapon. With my foot placed against the face, I felt the crucifix tearing through the inner flesh.

The other hound came sniffing around the other side as I tried desperately to retrieve the staff, but it became lodged as it passed the spine. I slipped down the tile as the dead hound slumped to the ground.

Looking to the skies, I whispered a prayer to the winds. No sooner than I was done, a lone lightning bolt split the clouds and ignited the staff. The bolt twisted around the staff, engulfing it and burning my palms. The electric tendrils penetrated the dead lips of the hound, illuminating the mouth as it siphoned deep into the beast. When it reached the crucifix, the hound exploded in a bright, bloody mess of smoking fur. The staff glowed with vengeance as I stood upon the church. As the other hound leapt towards me, another bolt shot from the end, splitting the beast in two.

My head was full of confidence, but it did not last long. Without much hesitation, I jumped down and spliced my way through a large portion of the demon army. Saturated in blood, my energy level lessened with every attack. My breathing became erratic as the strength in my weapon weakened. I continued until the weight of the staff became unbearable. My arms burned, but still I carved my way through. The demons were hesitant to attack and gathered around me as a loud horn sounded. Dropping to my knees, I had nothing left to give.

Through the haze, I saw a large man approaching. Due to his immense size I could not see his chest or head. The smoke danced around him and siphoned in and out of his armor. The skulls of giant goats adorned his knees and the teeth of hounds forged his boots. Behind him he dragged a large axe, the weight of which bore a gaping trench. The last thing I remembered was the boot swinging my way.

When I awoke, I was only able to rotate my neck. My staff was splintered into four pieces, stabbed into each of my limbs. Kneeling down, his horned helmet blistered the smoke. His eyes were as red as lava. His elongated beard was tethered with human skulls. My lungs convulsed as he placed the sharpened blade onto my chest. The weight of the metal threatened to crush my bones. The whistling sound of the blade as it spliced the air caused an unnerving fear. I pondered death and sought comfort in the afterlife. I wasn't ready to leave the world, but understood if my time was up.

There was a brief moment of reflection as I remained helpless between the heavy boots, awaiting the blade that would split me in half. That was when I felt it; a glimmer of hope. It was the smallest of sensations, one I had felt many times within my life and always took it for granted; a raindrop.

The clouds casted a shadow upon the land as thunder growled from above. Turning my neck, I was able to see the demons scattering as the rain grew heavier. Each drop was burning their hardened skin. The rain fell hard, prompting one of the boots to be lifted. I took a deep breath with every tremor of the ground as he walked away.

With intense pain, I slid both of my arms up from the splintered wood. Sitting upright with the rain pelting me, I watched as the demon army funneled down into a trench, disappearing from the land.

Everything I saw weighed heavy upon my mind. I doubted it all and trusted nothing. Even though I looked to the clouds for answers, I received none. The sun seemed unwilling to highlight the dead land. Hell had spilled from the core and scouted us for our weaknesses. They butchered our lands and pillaged our cities, but they did not cease the human civilization.

The Devil has his army and God has his.

The war is not over; it has barely begun.

38. THE DOLL COLLECTION BY DOUG ROBBINS

A spacious front and back yard, kind neighbors and a tire swing... I thought that was the neatest house ever. It was located in Savannah Georgia. The place belonged to my grandmother. She lived there all alone. Grandpa died eight years ago and she never found anyone else. "I'm too old for that sort of foolishness," she would say.

Mom tried fixing her up with a couple of old guys she worked with, but grandma always declined. As a kid, I would spend every summer with her, from six years old to thirteen. This particular story I tell is set in that final year. It was the summer before grandma passed away, and the cause was said to be a heart attack.

Grandma had this collection of dolls. She kept them in a China case, under lock and key. All the dolls were female with green eyes, and each was dressed in black. The only thing about them that differed was the colors of their hair. There was an assortment of red, black, brown and blonde. Everything else was the same, even down to the shoes, which were basic black.

This room was down the hall from the playroom; this was the place I spent most of my time. The playroom was a real paradise as far as I was concerned. Grandma updated it from year to year, depending on the state of my current fancy.

The only thing that remained the same were my video games, a Gamer Guy. I used to want one for myself, but mom and dad never got me one. Grandma bought me one and kept it at her house, so I could play it in her playroom. After she died, I kept it. The Universal Movie Monsters posters, Dracula, Frankenstein, Wolf Man, I left those.

I arrived at Granny's in June. She wore her gray hair in a stylish ponytail. She also wore an Atlanta Braves sweatshirt which was rolled up at the sleeves. Only a southerner could dress in long sleeves during June.

"Hello, baby," she said, before kissing my cheek, her warm smile illuminating my heart. "We're gonna have a lot of fun this summer."

"Every summer is fun here," I admitted. "I enjoy the autonomy away from mom and dad. I mean love them, but you know."

"A kid, or in your case, a teen, has to assert his independence. Am I right?" she asked.

"Right," I replied, winking.

She winked back. "Elise is visiting her Aunt and Uncle this summer. She's coming over later to see my doll collection." Elise's Aunt and Uncle were Grandma's neighbors.

"Why?" I asked.

"She's really into dolls," Grandma answered.

"Since when? Last time I talked her, she was into bug collecting," I snorted.

"Now she's into dolls," Grandma shrugged.

A couple hours later, Elise arrived. It had been two years since I had seen her. I expected to be greeted by a gawky, glasses-wearing girl, but what I beheld was a brunette goddess. She had freckles like back then, but they rested on smooth white skin, under eyes bluer than Christmas Elvis could sing about.

Her brown hair shimmered in the sun. Perhaps she still had that tomboy thing about her. She was wearing blue jeans ripped at the knee and a ball cap worn backwards.

She hugged me. The bubble gum she chewed smelled strong of what I would describe as classic bubble gum scent. It was pink and it tasted how you would expect the color pink to taste, if one could smell a color. "It's been a long time," Elise announced.

"Huh? Oh, yeah, sure." My reply was very uncool, unsure of itself.

Of course my body reacted in a teenage way. I slouched. She sat on the sofa next to me, her gaze fell upon the television. "What were you watching?"

"Some zombie movie," I stated, becoming acutely aware of how suddenly my voice sounded a couple of octaves lower. In my own insecure mind, I figured she noticed and wanted to laugh at this hormonal fool, attempting to woo her with a fake deep voice.

She never laughed. Grandma walked into the play room. "Well, hello, Elise."

"What's up Miss Rose?" she said.

"Not much, dear. You ready?" Grandma asked, her voice hinted at a slight tone of impatience.

"Sure. Lead the way," stated Elise.

Elise followed grandma as they left the playroom. About twenty minutes later, Elise came back in and sat down on the sofa next to me.

"Your grandma has a cool doll collection," Elise admitted.

"I guess," I kind of shrugged.

"Let me guess, you're not into dolls. Right?" she questioned.

"Not really," I replied, sincere.

"Dolls are cute. They can be friends, you know."

"I always thought dolls were sort of creepy," I confessed.

"A lot of people have phobias about dolls," she started.

A few minutes later, I heard giggles coming from the other room. "Did you hear that?" I asked.

"You mean giggling?" Elise asked.

We put our controllers down and went to investigate it. The doll room had wooden floors. It was the only house like that. The wallpaper was yellow; a nice literary allusion made by grandmother. She specifically had told the painters to make this room as yellow as sunshine. They listened.

Elise and I stepped up to the purple case and gazed at the dolls through the looking glass. Perfectly still, that was how they remained. Those eyes stared back at us, seeing nothing, or so I thought. Elise and I looked at each other and shrugged it off. As we were walking away, we both heard a voice say, "Die." Elise went home after that.

At dinner that night, I asked grandma if she had any weird experiences with the dolls. "None that you would believe," Granny replied.

"Try me," I challenged her.

"For starters," Grandma answered, hesitating for a moment. "The dolls are alive."

"What?" I asked, incredulous.

Grandma nodded. "They have their own souls."

"How is that even possible?" I asked.

"After your grandfather died I sank into a horrible depression. I thought about suicide a couple times. Never went through with it obviously, but, thought about it. I met a gypsy named Beth and she gave me this potion to feed the dolls. Well, it brought them to life. Beth claimed it would allow my husband to haunt the dolls. He never came through, but it brought something much darker."

I dropped my fork. "Are you serious? What's inside those dolls?"

"Something so evil, you couldn't possibly imagine," Grandma's voice was a whisper.

"Like demons?" I squeaked out.

"Yes. I've tried to have the dolls blessed, but to no effect. So now I keep them locked in the case. But something has been stirring them up," Grandma confessed.

"W-What?" I stammered out.

''I don't know,'' Grandma answered. "Just don't ever unlock my case."

We both heard a terrible roar like a lion, followed by an awful crash. In the doll room our fears were confirmed. The wood was splintered and shattered glass littered the floor. The dolls themselves were nowhere to be found. We prayed that the dolls had gone.

Had trouble sleeping that night. A strange dream plagued me. Grandma sat next to me watching static on the television, as though I wasn't there. All of a sudden she begins to scream. I looked and saw my grandmother's face melt.

When I awoke in the middle of the night, I smelled smoke. Staggering through halls of my grandma's house, I saw smoke pouring from under the door. I hurried down the stairs and grabbed the fire extinguisher. I tore open my grandmother's bedroom door and the smoke rushed at me. I coughed and waved my hand, cutting through the dense, black smoke. The bed was an inferno.

I put out the flames and discovered my grandmother's charred, burned corpse, looking up at me, but never seeing. In blood, I saw a disturbing message scribed on the wall. "Dolls."

I fled in horror from that room of incinerating death, out to the middle of the road, where I watched the blaze engulf the house, and with it I prayed, those terrible dolls.

39. DADDY'S GIRL BY NACHING T. KASSA

Cold, not unlike the chill of death, crept into Mona Lumina's bones as she sat upon the stone floor. She pushed the feeling from her mind, readjusted her nightgown so that it covered her knees, and refocused on the candle before her. The single, red taper stood fixed to the concrete floor, its flame leaping up under her attention, reminding her of the moments that had just passed.

A dream she couldn't remember had torn her from slumber. All that had remained of it was a feeling of urgency and the thought that she must conceal herself or face her own demise. The cacophony of shattering glass which followed supported her thought and she acted on it, descending into the basement before she could be discovered.

She'd removed the bulb from the overhead light after taking the candle from the storage cupboard. Lighting it, she now sat listening.

The ceiling above her groaned in protest as heavy footsteps crossed it. The man they belonged to would probably search each floor of the refurbished Victorian house before resorting to the basement. If he did, she would have time. Time to save herself. She continued to stare at the flame.

Blackness covered the area outside the candle's light like a shroud. If Mona had looked up, her eyes wouldn't have penetrated it. She knew this, just as she knew what lay waiting in the dark. Her power allowed such inner sight.

As the light danced before her eyes, images intruded themselves upon her mind. She concentrated on them.

Long and wicked, a blade glinted in the candlelight. She couldn't see the one wielding it, but she felt his excitement reaching for her like the perverse tendrils of some Lovecraftian creature. His desire—no—his need to kill swept over her like a tsunami. He moved quickly across the floor, shadows flickering over his face.

Mona's breath caught in her throat when she looked into his gray eyes. Those orbs resembled her own, as did the dark, chestnut hair and high cheekbones. She stared into the gender-swapped mirror of his face and shook her head.

He'd always hated her, this one with whom she'd share the womb. She couldn't say why.

Unvoiced, the question hung between them and, just as the answer seemed to gain clarity, blood exploded before her eyes. It splattered over the both of them, warm and crimson. She opened her mouth to scream.

With an abruptness that nearly sent her reeling, the vision ended. Far off in the silence of the house, more floorboards creaked as her would-be murderer continued his hunt.

Mona covered her mouth with her hands as her heart thudded in her breast. A scream would've revealed her location. She released a pent-up breath, resolving to control herself in the moments to come.

Like a moth, she returned to the flame.

Less vision than actual memories, images of another man filled her mind. Tall, with black hair and kind eyes, he towered above her. She smiled up at him as he lifted her into his arms, and giggled when he tickled her.

A lump formed in her throat as the memories continued. She saw him handing her the keys to a car, his smile at her graduation, the tears he shed at her mother's funeral.

Unlike the wielder of the knife, the only emotion she read from this man was love. Even when she didn't return it, when she rebelled against him, it was there.

It was still there when he found himself arrested for murder.

She had been away at college when it happened. The news broke in all of the newspapers before she actually heard it. Not exactly the ideal way to learn your father was a hitman for the Mob.

She'd never gone to visit him, not even on the eve of his execution. When the Prison Chaplain had given her the letter, she hadn't dared read it. When she finally did, she found no apology within the few scrawled lines. All that she found was a promise.

Mona planned to hold him to it.

She turned her head away from the candle and the man she had envisioned suddenly appeared at her right hand. Clothed in prison-issued orange, he sat cross-legged, a hand on each knee. Dark eyes, filmed white by death, seemed to stare through her.

"Daddy," she whispered.

He smiled at her.

Mona strained her ears, listening for the footsteps that were sure to come. When she heard nothing, a knot formed in the pit of her stomach. Perhaps her twin had already arrived.

"I need you, Daddy," she breathed.

The smile faded from her father's face. He nodded.

Another memory came unbidden into her mind. Ten years old, she stood at her father's side while her brother rode his bicycle down the driveway of their modest home. For several weeks she'd been tortured by a question; a query that she didn't really want an answer to. It spilled out as she watched her twin.

"Do you love Horatio more than you love me, Daddy?"

"I love you both the same, Desdemona."

"But what if you had to choose? Which one would it be?"

"I wouldn't choose."

"What if Horatio wanted to hurt me? Who would you choose then?"

His face took on a strange cast. At the age of ten, she couldn't recognize the emotion.

"I would always protect you, Mona. Protect you from everything and everyone who wanted to hurt you."

"Even Horatio?"

His eyes turned toward the boy and, this time, an emotion she did recognize passed over him. He seemed worried. "I would protect Horatio too. Even if it meant protecting him from himself. But, Horatio would never hurt you."

"He has bad feelings about me sometimes."

"How do you know that? You can't read minds."

Mona had fallen silent. At that time, her power wasn't strong. It wouldn't fully mature until after college. In hindsight, she realized that she should've been grateful.

The memory slipped away, leaving her in the basement again. She glanced to the right. The specter remained seated on the floor, waiting. Something had changed in the subterranean room however, and it seemed wrong. She peered about and when the voice called to her from the shadowy depths of the room, she jumped.

"I was wondering how you did that," the voice said.

Mona froze as her brother materialized before her. How long he had waited unseen she couldn't say.

"My talent came later than yours. If I'd known that staring into a candle flame could summon the dead, I would've come for you long ago. I had to do it the hard way."

Mona stared at him struggling to speak. "Why, Horatio? Why do you hate me so?"

"I don't hate you."

She searched his eyes. The feelings she sensed betrayed no falsehood. She looked deeper.

His body seemed to tremble under her psychic examination and a wave of his true intention overwhelmed her. As in the vision, she felt the almost predatory need for the kill.

"It's nothing personal, Mona. It's just that…well…I've never killed a woman before. I thought you should be the first."

The knife suddenly appeared in his hand and he stepped forward.

"Go, Horatio," Mona cried. "Please, I don't want to hurt you."

A sneer spread over his face as he eyed the man beside her. "You gonna sick Dad on me?"

"Yes."

Her twin shook his head. "You picked the wrong version."

Like water from the Red Sea, the darkness behind Horatio parted and out stepped a younger version of her father. Dressed in a dark suit, hair slicked back, he stared at her with his cold, dead orbs. Mona had never seen this aspect of her father. She averted her eyes.

"Do you know how he killed his targets?" Horatio asked.

She shook her head.

"He used piano wire. Then, he cut the bodies up in the bathtub. I think he used the wire because he's like me. He likes the intimacy."

Mona stifled a sob. The older ghost beside her lowered its head, eyes on the floor.

"My Dad wouldn't mind killing you," Horatio continued. "But, I think yours would have a little trouble killing me."

"I guess we'll have to see what happens."

Horatio's eyes glimmered. "You're going to put up a fight? This is better than I could've hoped."

Mona nodded to the spirit at her side. It rose to its feet, stepped over the candle, and advanced toward Horatio.

Before Mona's father could reach his son, the ghost of his younger self intercepted him. The two phantoms locked arms, each struggling against the other.

Horatio strode past them, knife tucked against his arm ready to slash, his body blocking her route to the stairs.

Mona scrambled to her feet. Before he could reach her she blew out the candle, plunging the room into darkness.

Rushing across the room on silent feet she sought escape. Though her eyes saw darkness, her mind saw the room fully lit. To her left, the manifestations of her father continued their battle. Neither gave her a second look. Horatio appeared blinded but had parked himself on the first step of the basement stairs directly opposite her. There would be no getting past him.

It was then that the unthinkable happened.

The ghost under her control fell to his knees before Horatio's wraith. Her older father held up his hands to the younger as though in supplication. The act gained no mercy.

Mona watched as Horatio's creature unhinged its jaw and its mouth fell wide. It leaped upon Mona's phantom, consuming it.

She wanted to shriek. Mona covered her mouth with one hand as the sound rose in her throat.

Having won the fray, the younger version of her father began to glow. Sickly, white light filled the room.

"Looks like you've lost, Mona. You're not Daddy's girl anymore."

Horatio advanced and the ghost followed.

She saw the glint of the knife but made no sound as it flashed toward her.

The last thing she'd do was give him satisfaction.

Blood erupted over the both of them. Warm and sticky, it filled the air in a torrent. Mona gasped unable to breathe.

Her brother's eyes widened and he screamed as his arm fell away. The knife fell from his detached fingers, clattering on the floor.

The ghost of age tore at him.

Mona screamed and turned away. Blood soaked her nightgown and hair as she cowered against the wall. She covered her ears, shutting out the wet sounds of tearing flesh and splintering bone.

When it was over, a voice sounded in her mind.

"Desdemona."

She turned. The younger version of her father faded away before her eyes, leaving the elder one in its place.

"Oh, Daddy," she whispered.

Holding out a hand, he smiled at her.

When she reached out to touch it, he vanished into the night.

40. THE CLOWNING BY KEN MACGREGOR

Jaxon barely made it. Not bothering with the overhead, he aimed by streetlight and somehow got it all in. The last few drops were immediately followed by a full-body shudder.

Through the windowpane, he heard a faint jingle-slap, jingle-slap. Shaking himself off and snapping his pajamas back into place, he leaned over to look. In the street, a single clown with bright orange hair and yellow-and-green silk was taking street-eating steps along the dotted white line. Tiny bells on its ankles caught the streetlight.

"Go back to the circus, nutjob."

The clown froze mid-step and cocked its head toward Jaxon's building. The painted smile on its face drooped at the corners until it resembled a hobo's frown. Jaxon held his breath. That's impossible. His pulse throbbed in his neck. After at least a minute, the clown waddled away. Jaxon exhaled in a rush and washed his hands.

The next day, brushing his teeth, he kept throwing glances out the bathroom window. Outside, sunshine glinted off the previous night's discarded beer bottles. People in suits drank coffee from paper cups and bustled past homeless people they didn't seem to see.

Jaxon's T-shirt stretched tight across his barrel chest and thick upper arms. In the mirror, he clenched his jaw and flexed his biceps. He gave his reflection a superhero grin that only lasted an instant. In his prime, he could bench 420 but he was years past that. That bastard Gravity had sucked much of his bulk down to pool around his waist.

Outside, a woman stood alone at the bus stop. He saw her every day he went in to the shop, but didn't know her name. She was pretty, in a stark, angular way. Watching her from the corner of his eye, he imagined that, under her suit, her breasts and hips formed sharp, dangerous geometric patterns.

She nodded to him as they got on the bus. Usually, only seven or eight seats would be free. Today, it was almost empty.

As the bus eased past a miniscule public park, he saw a clown trying to grab a woman. She fended it off with her laptop, swinging the thing like a board. Jaxon turned his head, but the combatants had slipped out of sight.

He turned to the man in the seat behind him.

"Did you see that?"

The guy looked up from his smartphone and shook his head.

"Mugging?"

He shook his own head.

"Maybe. It was weird."

Seven hours of tire rotations, inflations and repairs later, Jaxon rode the bus home. This time, only one other passenger was present. The man was so pale he was almost white. His lips were swollen and very red, and he was wearing shoes that looked five sizes too big. Jaxon took a seat near the back door and kept an eye on him. The man with boats on his feet didn't move. It wasn't clear if he was breathing.

Once home, Jaxon threw the bolt on his apartment door. He took a box from the freezer, peeled back one corner and slid it into the oven at 350. He showered, getting most of the grease and dirt off and sat down to eat. His cuticles were still black; they always were.

Halfway through his meal, tires screamed and brakes squealed outside, followed by the jarring crunch of metal and shattering glass. He rushed to the window. A Toyota Prius was wrapped around a lamppost. Smoke poured from the crumpled hood. A young man with a bloodied face struggled through the open door onto his hands and knees. He scrambled to his feet, looking back, but fell.

From the car, a plump, white-gloved hand shot out and grabbed the man by his ankle. Puffy, polka dotted sleeves emerged, followed by a neon green afro. Lastly, two enormous feet flopped out and braced themselves on the asphalt. The clown pulled the young man backward, lifted him off the ground and threw its head back. The clown's mouth opened, unhinging like a python's and from it burst forth a loud, goofy laugh.

The clutched man kicked and flailed, but the clown ignored the blows. It put one fat hand in its pocket and a stream of liquid shot from the daisy on its lapel, hitting the guy in the face. He went limp. The clown dropped him and walked away.

Jingle-slap.

After several seconds, the man shuddered. Jaxon watched from the second floor window, breathing fast. The man's hair grew long, kinky and pink. His shoes expanded to size fifty. His face went white and his red lips blossomed into a smile that grew from ear to ear. Multicolored silks replaced the man's clothes and his nose blew up like a tiny red balloon. Enormous, cartoonish eyes bulged from his head. The new clown stood and cracked the vertebrae in its neck.

Nearby, the door to a bar opened and four college kids staggered into the night. The clown jingle-slapped toward them with surprising speed.

One of the four pointed and laughed. The others took a step back, doe-eyed.

Spinning away, Jaxon slammed his back to the wall and squeezed his eyes shut.

"Shit."

After a moment, he shook himself and looked around the kitchen.

Grabbing three refillable water bottles from the cupboard, Jaxon filled them all from the tap. He snagged two boxes of protein bars and tossed them in a gym bag with the water. A change of clothes was next. He thrust himself into his leather jacket. From behind the door, he grabbed one of the crutches that was still leaning in the corner from a sprained ankle last fall. If there were psycho clowns out there, he wanted a weapon.

As he reached for the knob, someone knocked. Jaxon froze, clutching the crutch. He waited, hoping they would go away. They didn't. Knock-knock.

"Let me in, man. There's a clown after me."

"Damn it," Jaxon said. He pulled open the door. Three clowns stood in the hall, grinning.

"Surprise."

One reached for him, but he ducked and swung the crutch. It hit the closest clown in the head with a satisfying crunch. Its painted eyebrows crawled like caterpillars to the top of its head.

"Oop," it said, and dropped to its knees.

Shoving the top of the crutch into its throat, he backed one of the other clowns into the hall. It made exaggerated choking noises as its arms pinwheeled, and its eyes bulged. The white greasepaint turned purple. The clown stopped choking, tilted its head and grinned at him.

Jaxon's eyes got wide.

"Uh oh."

Someone hit him hard in the side with a football tackle and he lost his footing. He teetered at the top of the stairs.

Damn. He had forgotten about the third clown. The bastard popped up next to him, green afro filling the air above its head. Spinning around, it dropped its polka dotted pants and thrust its buttocks toward him, bumping him and sending him down the 23 steps to the first floor.

The clowns fell over each other coming down the stairs like a nightmarish comedy routine.

He stood shakily and lunged away from them, hitting the glass door and going through it. A transparent dagger sank deep in one thigh.

When Jaxon hit the street, he grabbed his leg around the wound and screamed.

There were clowns everywhere. Bulbous, red noses all swiveled toward him and the night air swelled with jingling bells and slapping feet.

The crutch and gym bag were still inside. Jaxon pushed himself up on his hands and tried to stand, but his leg shot waves of fire to his brain. Resting his forehead on the sidewalk, he fought against the pain to stay conscious. When he looked up, he was surrounded.

With one fat hand, a clown hauled Jaxon to his feet. A stream shot from its flower and hit Jaxon right in the mouth.

Sputtering, he fell.

Moments later, where Jaxon had fallen, a clown got to its gigantic feet, favoring its one good leg. It looked around and saw nothing but clowns. It absently pulled the glass out of its leg and tossed it aside.

Reaching up, it squeezed its nose, producing a discordant honk. All around, clowns honked their noses.

The sound spread out, like ripples in a pond. Hundreds of honks. Thousands. Millions of honks.

Billions.

41. THE PHANTOM PARK BY CHARLES D. BENNETT

A wavering. A pulsing of shadow. A strobing of darkness briefly manifested itself outside the front bay window of Jim Miller's home. He observed the phenomenon for the space of several minutes before it quickly moved off, merging with the murky shadows beyond the street lamps. Mr. Miller had been, unsuccessfully, trying to watch a movie and drink one entire cup of coffee without it going cold. But the phone kept ringing with friends on the other end, wanting to drag him out on some sort of deliberate freak-out or other. All of these requests were met with a firm, "No." Then, of course, there was his mysterious shadow dancer. The latter had disturbed Jim's super-liminal/subliminal senses however, and he found concentrating on his wonderfully weird movie impossible.

"Something's out there," he said to himself. "It's possibly something I may not want to know about but, none-the-less, it's something I cannot resist."

Sighing, Jim decided that a late night walk was in order. 'The night air will do me good,' he thought. He stopped the movie and clicked off the TV, got up, closed the blinds, located his backpack, then adjourned to the kitchen where he placed within it a few items he required for long distance wandering: a small sack of trail mix, an orange, a half pint flask of whiskey and a small flashlight.

A glance at the wall clock said it was 2 A.M. Sunday morning.

Presently there came a knock at the door.

Jim knew the porch light wasn't on and wondered why the doorbell wasn't used, as it would have been hard to miss its sickly orange glow. Following that train of thought he knew it had to be a stranger calling, as all of his crazy friends loved to ring it multiple times in an annoying manner.

There came a second knock, harder, louder.

"Yeah, yeah, I coming!" he said, irritated, as he made his way towards the door.

Just as he was reaching to unbolt the lock there came a third knock, or rather, a hammering that shook the door in its frame. He paused, eyed the table next to the door and retrieved the Taser from its drawer. He tried the Taser to see if it still held a charge. "ZAP!" it said, as blue fire jumped between its prongs. Jim looked through the peep-hole and saw nothing but a dark, empty front porch.

"Hooligan pranksters," he thought.

Jim switched on the porch light and opened the door just far enough to stick his ruddy face through while keeping his right hand, which still firmly gripped the Taser, out of sight.

There were two kids, both boys wearing hoodies and dirty jeans, staring at him. Their pale blank faces held eyes that had a mydriasis quality about them. The coal-black soulless orbs, like a great swath of a starless and bible-black night, pierced his will and sent cold frosty blades down his spine.

"What do you two little shits want?" Jim asked in his best deep, authoritative voice.

"We have lost our way while Trick-or-Treating and would like to come in and use your phone to call our parents," said the taller, older of the two.

"Sorry. I'm not in the habit of letting strange children in my home after 2 A.M. in the morning, or any other time for that matter," Jim replied, noticing that they had no sacks of treats on their persons, and that his hand felt sweaty on the Taser.

"However," Jim continued, "If you give me your names and parents phone number, I'll be happy to call them for you."

"This night wounds time," said the shorter, younger kid wearing the Miami Heat hoodie. His voice sounded distorted.

Jim's eyes cast down at him. "Pardon?" he said, wrinkling his nose.

"We cannot come in without your permission," said the taller one. "LET. US. IN." The words were full of anger, and his voice sounded far older than the ten or twelve years of his apparent age.

Jim slammed the door, bolting and locking it as he did so. He backed off to the middle of the living room, looked at his sweaty and shaking hand holding the Taser and thought about calling the cops-then thought better of it.

"What the hell would I tell them?" he grunted.

Jim waited thirty minutes or there abouts for another banging at the door but there was nothing forthcoming, nor were any strange intruders present when Jim opened the door a second time.

"You're losing it man! Go for your walk, the fresh night air will do you good," he said out loud. Jim shrugged then put on a light jacket, shouldered his backpack and was out the door.

He went down the sidewalk and out to the street, he walked to the corner and took a right up 7th Avenue. He walked perhaps ten blocks before turning down an alley that ran parallel to some railroad tracks. He paused and lit a cigarette, there was a huge tomcat in the alley licking its asshole; he kicked gravel at it. "Vile beast!" Jim hissed. The feline hissed back then ran off. Jim chuckled, flicked his cigarette butt at the beast and continued on up the alley. He thought he heard the gigglings of children and rustlings coming from the brush on the other side of the tracks. His hand found its way into his jacket pocket where he firmly gripped the Taser. He walked on as the night and the shadows stalked him.

After a little better than half a mile, Jim came up behind a large business building---some sort of data processing center from the looks of it---it's windows were dark but he could see several picnic tables there; he was due for a rest and the tables looked inviting. Jim unsoldered his backpack, sat, and took a load off. There were four picnic tables placed at odd angles, a well-used gas grill off to his left, and several trash receptacles dotted about. Jim fished his flashlight out and shone it around, the grass was well kept, lush, and there was a hand crafted wooden sign affixed to the wall of the building that read: 'PHANTOM PARK.'

Jim raised his flask of whiskey in salute to the sign, took a long pull off it, winced, then lit another cigarette and let his mind wander.

They came out of the shadows all around him, the black eyed kids, giggling and chanting: "You'll never get out! You'll never get out! You'll never get out!"

Jim was on his feet in an instant, pulling the Taser from his pocket as he did so. They encircled him, staying out of reach, and chanting all the while. Jim became nauseated, and the whiskey drilled his stomach, as his surroundings began to whirl.

One of the little shits broke off from the main group and came sauntering up to him, it was the tall kid that knocked on his door earlier.

"We've been sent to collect you," said the pale face with rotten breath and the dead, black eyes.

"Is that right?" Jim replied, then, rushing forward: "TRY THIS FREAK!" he screamed, jamming the Taser's prongs into the kid's neck and pulling the trigger.

"HA, HA, HA, THAT TICKLES!" boomed a chorus of evil voices, and all the kids began disappearing in wisps of smoke.

Jim felt the ground beneath his feet begin moving and he struggled to keep his balance. Pale bluish-grey arms with little hands that had grips like vices, burst forth from the lush grass and began to pull him under. Fingernails, sharp as razors, cut into his flesh, shredding his blood soaked jeans as he became insane with fear.

"OH NO FUCKING WAY!" he screamed, as he punched and Taser'd.

"H-E-L-P! OH DEAR GOD, SOMEBODY, PLEASE, HELP ME!" His screams fell on darkness and the Taser zaps echoed metallically down the alley, as the big tom cat arched its back and hissed at the scene from its hidden perch in a nearby pine tree.

Jim's final thoughts were absolute horror, knowing nobody had heard his desperate cries for help, as he gagged on the dirt entering his airway.

***

The following afternoon, at lunch break, the employees found a ten foot circle of dead grass with a blood stained Taser in the middle. The police were called, and put the device in an evidence bag, but could offer no clues as to what had happened.

218

42. DREAMS OF GENERATIONS BY ROBERT HOLT

I fear the dream nearly as much as I fear the reality of the dream, and by reality I mean what the dream means in the real world, not that the dream is real. I know it is just a dream. I have psychoanalyzed it with a hundred friends of varying professions over a hundred beers in a hundred different bars. It is a dream and only a dream, but it brings with it a darker awareness of reality that has haunted me through my entire life.

When I was seven, I hated bed time. It wasn't because I feared the monster in my closet or the alligator under my bed; it was because I feared the dream. I feared how it made me feel. I feared how it made me think. I feared what it meant about the real world. I have grown older, and the sting of the dream has faded, but I still wake up screaming every time the dream invades my slumber.

The dream first came when I was seven. My great maternal grandmother was on her deathbed, and her daughter, my grandmother, was in a hospital battling cancer. It was a hospital that she would never leave. The end wasn't far away for either of them, and at the age of seven, such things meant very little. They held less weight in my mind than the G.I. Joe cartoon I watched with my morning cereal.

My parents tried to explain to me that my great grandmother wouldn't be around much longer, and I remember thinking that this was good news because it meant we wouldn't have to visit her at the nursing home anymore. My older brothers were disturbed by my lack of interest in our dying matriarch and put it upon themselves to explain the severity of the situation. They explained her impending death as best they could through their own adolescent understandings.

It was the night that Nana passed that the dream came to me. I am seven in the dream, even to this day. And I am running through a field of tall grass with sun beams kissing off of the grain stalks as they tickle my ankles. My mother is behind me, young and thin in a way that I never remember her, as she looked in old photographs from before I was born. She is carrying a picnic basket.

I turn to her and hurry her on, but she stops and waits for her own mother, a woman impossibly tall and thin, then proceeds with helping her up the small embankment that my seven year old legs had ascended without noticing. We reach the top and settle down at an old wooden picnic table. The basket is opened and the sun beats down as plates and sandwiches and potato salad are passed around with a feeling that everything in the world is right.

A single cloud in the sky begins to darken. There is talk of heading back to the car, but this thought is scoffed away by the older women, and we are soon laughing and singing anew. It is then that a thunderous crash echoes through the sky as a flash of lightning hits my Great Grandmother, knocking her to the grass where she lay blackened and dead.

I scream out only to be hushed by my Mother, and my Grandma takes me by my hands.

"Robbie, it's okay. These things just happen," she says. "Nana was old, and it was her time to go."

The instant the words leave her mouth a second bolt of lightning blasts through my Grandma's head, ripping her hands from mine.

I scream out, and my mother takes my face and buries it into her. "It's okay," she says, "it's okay."

"Why?" I ask her. "Why is this happening?"

"This is all a part of life. Death is just the last step. This is simply how it ends."

"I don't want it to happen to you. I don't ever want it to happen to you."

"When it does, you'll need to move on." I sit up, and she brushes a tear away. "Be brave for me."

I nod, and she hands me a cookie from the basket. I grasp it and as I'm taking my first bite, lighting strikes my mother, and she falls to the grass beside me. As I look down at her I take another bite, and then realize that I feel nothing whatsoever.

That is when I wake up screaming.

"Fuck! Something just bit me!" Sarah squirmed underneath Aaron on the red blanket they'd laid on the grass.

"Just relax Sarah, I'm sure it wasn't something horrible," he said as he continued to kiss the tender skin of her neck. "Just relax and I'll make you forget all about it."

Sarah knew him well enough by now to know he'd winked when he'd said it. Aaron was certainly a charmer and there was no way he'd miss a chance to get into her pants. "Seriously dude, it hurts. Get off. Now!"

Aaron continued to kiss her neck, running his tongue up the length of it and using his lips to draw her ear into his mouth. He sucked for the briefest of moments until he felt her shiver before letting his mouth fall back to the spot just above her collarbone. His hands traced a number of paths over her clothes, venturing closer to the lower hem of her powder blue t-shirt.

Suddenly Sarah's body jerked; the length of it jumping off the ground in chaotic movements. A seizure. Aaron had no idea how to help and wished he'd paid better attention to her lessons on what he should do if her epilepsy flared while they were out.

Rolling to the side, he brought himself up to his knees, taking her right hand in his and patting her shoulder awkwardly. As he stared into her face, tears of helplessness welled in his eyes. He could see the angry red rash creeping over the landscape of her skin, but he was at a loss at what to do.

Grabbing his phone, he called 911 and was connected in short order.

"Fire, Police or Ambulance?"

"Ambulance. My girlfriend is having a seizure or something and I need help!"

"Calm down, help is on the way. Tell me where you are." The calm demeanor of the operator had no effect on Aaron.

"You have to come quick. She has epilepsy."

"I need to know where you are sir. Can you tell me?"

"Granger's Park. Behind the Snack Shack. Hurry! Please!"

"I have a unit on their way to you now. Can you tell me your name please?"

"Aaron. Aaron Samuels."

"Thank you Aaron. What is your girlfriend's name?"

"Sarah Codger."

"Do you know if Sarah takes any medications for her epilepsy?"

"I have no idea. Can't you just come and make her better?" At this point Aaron was crying, the words coming out in huge slobbering gulps.

"Aaron, I'm going to need you to calm down. Can you do that for me?"

Aaron took a deep breath, trying to steady his nerves and compose himself. Within a minute he'd calmed down a small amount as he continued to stare at Sarah flopping around on the ground. Shakily he answered, "I think I'm okay now."

"Good Aaron. Is Sarah still seizing?"

"Yes."

"How long has it been going on?"

"Maybe 3 or 4 minutes?" He heard the pause on the other end and said, "That's bad isn't it? You've got to get here faster! Sarah can't die!"

"Aaron, calm down. No one is going to die today. Can you do me a favor?"

"What is it?"

"I need you to put the phone down and place something like a belt or some sort of stiff fabric between her teeth so she doesn't bite down on her tongue. Can you do that for me?"

"Ummmm, yeah, I think so." Aaron activated the speakerphone before placing it down on the blanket beside him. Unbuckling his belt, he drew it through the loops until he held it in his hands. "Okay, I've got my belt off and I'm going to try and get it between her teeth. She's foaming at the mouth a bit, is that okay?"

"Aaron, that's normal during a seizure. I just need you to concentrate on getting that belt between her teeth, okay?"

It took Aaron more than a few seconds to get the belt worked into place, the whole time worrying he was hurting her. "Okay, it's in."

"Okay good, now I need you to hold her head somewhat still. Can you do that?"

Aaron repositioned himself at the top of Sarah's head and bent over her, placing his forearms on either side of her ears and tried to keep it stationary. "She's moving around a lot still."

"That's okay. Her seizure will be over soon. You're doing an excellent job, Aaron."

The next few minutes passed as the operator talked to Aaron, trying to keep him calm throughout the ordeal. Aaron did his best to follow the instructions of the voice on the other end of the phone, but he found his resolve slowly melting away. He wanted this all to be over, and he wanted Sarah to wake up.

"Wait! I think it's stopping. She's stopped shaking!"

"That's good news Aaron. When she wakes up, she might be groggy or confused. I will need you to keep her from getting up. Can you do that Aaron?"

"Yes. I think so." Part of him was relieved, the other part still scared shitless. "Sarah, everything's going to okay. Help is on the way."

"That's good thinking Aaron, keep talking to her."

"Ummm, I think there's something wrong…"

"What do you mean Aaron? What's wrong?"

"Are they coming soon?"

"They should be there soon Aaron, just hang in there."

"I can hear screaming."

"Screaming?"

"Yeah, it's close too. This is really beginning to freak me out."

The line fell silent for a moment and the eerie sounds of screaming in the distance came through the operator's receiver. The switchboard lines at dispatch lit up almost instantaneously and all she could do was stare at her computer screen as the cacophony of calls echoed through the room.

"Aaron, are you still there?"

The last thing she heard before the line went dead was his scream, terrified and full of panic.

It hurt. It hurt like hell.

And it was a hurt that would not go away as Karen had discovered in the hours since the blister of pain had burst in her head.

"God!" she moaned as she dropped the book she was having no luck reading and slammed her fists to the sides of her head. She held them tight to her temples; pressing hard against the migraine from hell. But the pain persisted, a blinding, pulsating raw rub that raged inside her skull.

Karen and headaches were not strangers. Too much coffee? Too much red meat? Bills? A full moon? She would get one at the drop of a hat. But this was more than the 'take two aspirin and call me in the morning' type of skull bucking. This felt like something much deeper. Something more deadly.

Her hands fell from her head and she buried her face in them, rocking back and forth as a low sob escaped her.

Karen left the living room couch and went to the kitchen. She turned on the tap and watched, glassy eyed, as water bubbled into the glass. Karen turned off the faucet and turned to the kitchen table where a lot of bottles from a lot of drug stores stood at attention. Karen picked one up as the pain continued to stab.

Take two tablets every six hours. Karen had taken two an hour ago and the pain was still buffeting her brain. She picked up another bottle of extra strength something. Take two every four hours. Do not mix with other medication.

Death by overdose couldn't be any worse than this, winced Karen as she pried open the child proof cap and downed two. Gulping convulsively as a particularly sharp throbbing rocked her world. Karen's grip on the glass turned to steel; shattering it in a shower of glass that, luckily, did not draw blood.

Karen made a half-hearted swipe at the shards before grabbing up a dish towel and moving, very slowly and painfully, to the bathroom where she soaked it in cold water. A hot compress had not worked three hours ago. A cold one at the base of her neck might work now.

She sat down on the toilet, her head pitched forward. After a moment there was a slight, pleasurable numbness beneath the towel. This was promising. A razor blade slice across the inside of her skull, followed by thudding thunder, dashed her hopes.

Karen rose, staggered, and saved a nasty fall by grabbing onto the edge of the sink. It was the worst yet; a crushing beastly bite, like a demented earwig chowing down on her brain.

What had she done to deserve this?

Karen regained her balance, took a deep breath and walked back through the hallway. She passed the bedroom door where Phil lay, sawing wood like a lumberjack laying waste to a rainforest.

A neck massage and a reminder that it was probably PMS. That was Phil's answer for everything. I love you Phil but if this were truly PMS...

I'd run to the kitchen! I'd come back with a carving knife! I'd castrate you in your sleep, force feed you your balls and bury the bloody blade in your skull!

And there wouldn't be a jury in the world that would convict me. Karen sighed, smiled and blew her dozing hulk a kiss. I love you Phil. Pleasant dreams.

Karen moved gingerly on her brain wracked journey. She was dreading the next stop. She took a deep breath and looked into her daughter Cheryl's room. The pink ruffled curtains. Wall decorations that ran the gamut from Big Bird to Mötley Crüe. And finally her Teddy Bear, Biff, tucked into the corner of the always well-made bed. It was too much.

Karen broke into an uncontrollable wave of sobs. The roaring fire in her head magnified as the tears came. Part of the anguish was the pain. Part of it was the realization that, in the sense that a mother loves a daughter, little Cheryl was gone forever.

She turned away and returned to the living room where the memory of her daughter faded as the punching against the inside of her head increased. She paced. She sat. She smashed her head against a wall. To no avail…

The sound of a car moving slowly down the street interrupted her agony. Karen went to the window and peered out the corner of a shade as something big and black on wheels pulled to the curb. A door on the driver's side opened and a demon with greasy long hair, dressed in leather and chains, got out. It lurched to the passenger side of the car and, with an appendage seeming more claw than hand, snatched the door open, reached in and dragged Cheryl, her clothes torn to rags, out roughly to the pavement.

Karen's eyes grew wide. She bit her finger to stifle a scream. The pain in her head mushroomed. She blinked out the atrocity in front of her…

And opened her eyes to that nice young boy Jim opening the car door and helping her fully clothed daughter from a sensible American compact. Karen glanced instinctively at the clock on the mantle. Curfew was 11:00 p.m. The clock said 10:45.

The pain in her head dropped a perceptible notch.

Karen moved back into the shadows as Jim walked her daughter to the porch. Her pain suddenly returned as she blinked back into the nightmare of the demon pawing at Cheryl's breasts while savagely kissing her mouth. Then with a flash she blinked back to the reality of Jim giving her daughter a peck on the cheek.

Karen's pain went flat-line.

She forced a smile as she started back into the bedroom. It was better to not get caught being a parent.... as she then heard the blasphemy coming innocently from Cheryl's mouth.

"Next Friday? Yeah. That would be neat."

The pain inside Karen's head jumped up and bit her one more time. It was a reminder...

That it would be back.

The couple's red station wagon wound its way up the serpentine road, shadowed by ancient oaks arching protectively against the fading sunlight. Margot shivered, silently cursing her husband for dragging her out into the middle of nowhere. Jeff looked ahead, stoic despite his wife's rebuke of what he felt was a valiant attempt to repair their marriage.

"It'll be great, Margot. Just what we need."

"Okay."

"Aw, Come on, this will be really good for us. Just try to keep an open mind. Please?"

"Fine. I will try to keep an open mind."

They continued along the little muddy road, which was shrinking by the second. Jeff worried it was too much for the old wagon to handle but the car roared back to its full glory for the final stretch up the mountain. A small trail, just wide enough for the vehicle to fit, led to the cabin. They pulled up and could see the warm glow of the fire place.

"Look! The owners got everything ready, honey. I told you this would be great!" Jeff grabbed a few bags and practically skipped to the cabin's front door.

Margot got out of the car, did a little stretch, then looked around at the new habitat. Her annoyance and anger started to melt enough that she could acknowledge how beautiful the place was. Not a soul around for miles, trees and woods surrounded them.

Maybe this will be good for us. Maybe we can work through it.

The couple stepped through the front door of their temporary mountaintop abode. Margot grasped Jeff's hand as she took in the fresh bouquet of roses on the table, the fire roaring, a bottle of chilled champagne. It was beautiful and perfect. She suddenly felt like a newlywed again, her cheeks blushed with the realization, not unnoticed by Jeff, who grinned at his victory.

"I told you, my dear. It's perfect!"

"Jeff, thank you. Sincerely, I love this place."

After a glass of champagne, Margot unpacked while Jeff finished unloading the car. They settled in front of the fire, exhausted from the six hour trip, munching on sandwiches and finishing the champagne. Both had such a serene sense of peace. Margot admitted she couldn't quite remember why they had ever fought in the first place. Jeff cooed in her ear, his breath warm and soft. They fell off the couch in a love fueled pile, putting their first honeymoon recreations to shame. Margot drifted off to sleep wrapped in Jeff's arms, wondering how it was she could feel this amazing. As he pulled her closer and took a breath of her hair, his eyes fell upon a small door above them. Curiosity overtook his thoughts, why was there a door with no obvious way to get to it? He shivered.

Both felt apprehensive at the sudden euphoria that had overtaken them upon arriving and both had tried, and failed, to mention the shared experience. It just felt so good, any words against it would melt away before they could be released by wary lips.

In the wee hours of the morning, Margot sleepily meandered towards the bathroom, careful in the unfamiliar cabin. A nightlight provided a muted illumination of the space for which she was grateful. After a brief examination of the area for uninvited guests (it was the woods after all), she sat down. The shock of cold from the toilet seat, though not unexpected, elicited a squeal and brought her hands to her face, as she feared she had awakened Jeff. Bladder relieved, Margot glanced up with a start. The door handle moved, I just saw it move.

"Jeff?"

No response.

You're being silly, stop it. She splashed her face with cold water, smoothed her long dark hair back from her face and peeked in the mirror. Behind her the shower curtain gently stirred. Margot shrieked and ran out.

"Jeff! Jeff, honey, Jeff, WAKE UP! Someone's in the shower!"

Jeff opened his eyes slowly, rubbing them as he tried to understand Margot. A beat later, he was on his feet, running towards the bathroom, Margot in tow. He charged the shower without a thought, stubbing his knuckles on the tiles in the process.

"Shit! Margot, there's no one here."

"I saw it move, Jeff."

Jeff inspected the area. Above the shower curtain was a vent, currently shooting out hot air.

"It was the heater. See, the vent up here? That's what did it."

Margot, not totally convinced but not wanting to argue, sighed. "You're right, you're right. I guess it's just being in a new environment. Want some coffee? I certainly can't go back to sleep." She giggled and slapped Jeff's ass on her way to the kitchen.

With coffee helping to fully revive their brains, Margot began to feel rather silly. She confessed with a giggle. Jeff wrapped his arms around her, flashing his infamous grin. They got dressed, had breakfast and left to explore the woods behind the cabin. A light snow had fallen over night, giving the woods a bright, inviting facade. They'd been walking for about an hour when Jeff turned towards his wife, a scowl forming on his face. Margot's face had hardened too and as her eyes met his, and the anger that had threatened to take over during the journey here returned with a vengeance. They locked eyes for what felt like a life time. Then Jeff shook his head.

"What the hell just happened?" He looked dazed.

"Don't yell at me. You know what you did!" She looked like a rabid animal.

"Margot, no. No, I don't know." Jeff was frantic in his sincerity. He reached towards his wife, searching for some sign of warmth.

Margot softened, grabbed his hand, her face confused. "Something is off. It's like I'm going through puberty again or something, one minute all is wonderful, the next I'm just filled with a fury I can't explain. Does that make any sense?"

"I think so. Probably because we're tired. It was a long drive yesterday and we were up pretty early today. Why don't we just head back and relax. We have plenty of time to explore. Besides I don't like the look of that sky, I think it's going to snow again." At his last word, a gust of wind picked up Margot's hair, wrapping it around her neck. She nodded in agreement and they trekked back to the cabin.

Upon arriving, they found the fireplace had been started, wood replenished. The previous night had been colder than expected, so the owners were being overly attentive, that's all. The pleasant feelings of their first night returned. Jeff made some hot chocolate while Margot set up mugs. She strolled towards the small sofa in front of the fire and noticed a pile of small books on the second shelf of the side table. Opening one up, she understood at once that they were guest books.

"Hey Jeff, look at these. They go back years!" Jeff brought the mugs over, now filled, handed one to his wife, and smiled. Her enthusiasm reminded him of why he fell in love with her so many years ago. "Here, look at this one." Margot handed over the book. He started to read the entries, most of which were versions of 'What a lovely cabin! Perfect for a romantic getaway.' and 'We celebrated our 10th anniversary here and will be sure to return for our 20th!'. After a few pages, one entry caught Jeff's eye.

"November 13, 1994
We've been here for three days. The first night was lovely. Arriving to a roaring fire and champagne and roses, well that was just perfect! But last night the little door near the ceiling started jiggling. There was no wind and we heard no other sounds. We felt overwhelmed with a sense of dread. And my wife swears someone is living in the bathroom. That is why we are departing early. God Bless."

They opened another one, then another. All contained similar entries.

"May 20, 1982
Had a great vacation here! Although the attic door kept opening by itself when there was no wind. Hope the face I saw was nothing. :) The Johnsons"

"October 10-16, 2003

Our oldest daughter decided to leave during a teenage fit on our third day here. She insisted the attic door moved on its own. We had a lovely time once she left. Hoping to return next year. The Roberts Family"

Margot grabbed his hand, then giggled. "You know we're being ridiculous. A couple of weird feelings and we're acting like teenagers." Jeff laughed in agreement and got up to stoke the fire. Something shifted, the sound reached Margot and Jeff at the same time. They whipped their heads up towards the little door. It was rattling. A tapping at the window whipped their gaze downward. The wind was howling. Snow had begun and a small skeletal branch was rapping on the pane of glass. The two burst out into laughter. "Just the wind, sweetie." Jeff had a grin so wide you could see his fillings and all Margot wanted to do was smack him. With a smile, she picked up the guest books again. "Now that we've got that out of our system, let's see if any other loonies stayed here."

Several entries mentioned strange activity in the attic, like one that strongly suggested that it's best "not to disturb him...sounds like he has claws". Others detailed theories about raccoons living up there but upon checking, no sign of anything was found. Aside from the near universal uneasiness about the little attic door, the entries all had something else in common. No one had ever met the owners. All communications were through phone calls to a third party, and that changed throughout the years apparently. And once technology advanced, no more calls, just texts and emails. It didn't seem weird to either Jeff or Margot, until they realized there was a path dug out in the snow outside. And no footprints or tire tracks were visible anywhere.

Jeff went to shower while Margot prepared dinner. He had gone out in the storm to gather more wood (actually, he went to look for any sign of people but found none), causing a chill he couldn't shake. Hopefully the hot water will do the trick. He turned the water on. Giving it a chance to warm up he went to the mirror to do a quick trim of his beard. Fog started to cloud the surface and

Jeff wiped his hand to clear a space. Snipping a stray hair, he swore he saw the shower curtain move. He checked the vent but there was no air coming out. Chuckling, he resumed his grooming. Another snip, another wipe of the mirror, another snip, one more wipe. Back to the mirror for a final look, and he became aware that a feeling of danger had begun to seep in.

Margot thought she'd heard Jeff say something, but he didn't respond to her calls. She went back to cooking, a feeling of anger started to surround her, making her swipe at her shoulders as if to squash a mosquito. She swung around only to see the little door near the ceiling slightly ajar. A gust of wind threw fat flakes against the windows and the lights flickered. Wanting to make sure she finished cooking before they lost power, the door left her mind.

Jeff dried off as fast as he could. The atmosphere inside the bathroom had become heavy, wet, dank. He wondered if the odor was mold. He realized no, it was closer to the smell of death. He tossed on fresh clothes and rushed to the kitchen. Margot was on the floor, the kitchen knife grasped tightly in her hand. The lights were flickering rapidly, one by one the cabinet doors started flapping like birds in a frenzy. His head began to swim, his legs felt like jelly.

Jeff woke up in bed. The snow had stopped falling, casting an eerie blue hue over everything. He got out of bed and started to walk. He felt like he was floating. His head was fuzzy and as he tried to think of his last memory, he saw Margot standing at the window. She was naked, her dark hair cascading down her back. Jeff called to her but she didn't move. He reached for her but could not seem to touch her. It was then that he noticed how filthy the cabin looked. The walls, the furniture, the paintings on the wall, the mirrors, all dusty and covered in a moss like substance. The air became thick and his nose was overwhelmed with the smell of rot. He called out to Margot again, a feeling of desperation washing over him. Slowly, Margot started to turn around. Jeff started to retreat from the scene, setting one foot behind the other, feeling first for any obstacles. Dread started to rise up like a rubber ball in his throat. He couldn't breathe. Margot's hair covered the space where her face should be and he tried to scream. But nothing came out. He screamed again. Silence. She was getting closer. Jeff searched her form anxiously for something familiar. A fury took him over and he grabbed her in a bear hug. His triumph disappeared as quickly as she did. Hugging himself, he was finally able to scream.

"Jeff? Jeff, wake up, baby. It's a dream, honey it's a just a dream." She was cradling a sleeping, shrieking Jeff, rocking him. But he wasn't waking.

After twenty minutes, Margot was beside herself. Jeff had a pulse, though faint. He had always been in good health. None of this made sense. She had a vague memory of collapsing in the kitchen, but nothing else until she awoke to her husband's terrified wails. Once she had gotten his screams to subside to a quiet whimper, she tried to find help. Her cell phone was dead, so was Jeff's though she swore they had just charged them. The landline was also dead and the power was out. The snow had stopped but not before at least a foot had fallen. She considered driving them both of out there, but realized there was no way the old station wagon would make it through the snow.

She thought back to the drive up, had she seen any neighbors, any other houses? Yes. There had been one a few miles down the road. The wind picked up again, blowing the snow hard enough for a white out. Margot went back to Jeff.

Jeff's eyes were open now and he was rocking himself on the bed while muttering incoherently. Margot ran to him and his eyes got wide. The mutterings increased in speed and volume, though she couldn't understand a word. She threw her arms around him, pleading with him to tell her what's wrong. Jeff shrugged off her arms and stared at her, his eyes somehow getting even wider.

Margot felt like he was boring a hole into her heart as he fell over on the bed. She lightly touched his arm, he was ice cold and unresponsive. Shaking her head, feeling dizzy and confused, Margot wandered over to the window and gazed upon the winter landscape, collapsing into a pile of tears. Her vision grew foggy but she thought something had changed outside. She stood up, wiped her eyes, and yes! Something had changed. There was a fresh pile of wood on the back porch. That hadn't been there a moment ago. Feeling a sense of relief, she ran out the front door, hoping to catch the owners for help. But, once again, no sign of life. No footprints in the snow, no tracks on the unplowed road. Just a freshly shoveled path in the back and a new cord of wood. A gust of wind shut the door on Margot's shocked face.

Not knowing what else to do, she prepared to walk to the house that she believed to be down the road. Glancing at her red leather boots, she silently apologized to them for the damage that was about to occur, and set out for help.

It was 9 a.m. when she left. By eleven, she realized there was no house. In the two hours she had been trudging down the mountain, she hadn't seen a single sign of another person. The temperature was below freezing and Margot couldn't feel her fingers and toes. Every time the wind blew, the powdery snow stung her face like needles. A new sense of urgency rushed her frozen body back to the cabin.

It was one by the time she arrived. As Margot approached the door she noticed the lights were on and the fire was roaring. It had been mere embers when she left. She threw the door open, excited that Jeff was okay and that soon warmth would defrost the ice from her limbs and face. But there was no sign of him. She searched the entire cabin, all three bedrooms, the bath, kitchen, everywhere. No footprints outside, no sign inside. All their belongings were still there. But there was a steaming cup of hot chocolate waiting on the coffee table in front of the fire.

She sat down, picked up the mug and took a sip. Her nose wrinkled as the steam rose, filling her sinuses, and thawing her face. As the warmth spread to her belly, a slight breeze brushed her cheek. Margot touched her face, stood up and looked around. The little attic door was open. She questioned herself, was it open when she left? Was it open when she came back? She couldn't remember. Looking around she found a wooden ladder behind a wolf tapestry on the wall. Margot grabbed her flashlight and started to climb, praying Jeff was up there.

As she ascended the ladder, glimpses of the various guest book entries flashed in mind. "Hope the face I saw was nothing...", "best not to disturb him, sounds like he has claws." Shaking her head, she continued to the top and opened the trap door.

The door opened easily. The air was heavy and reeked of mold and must. There was a faint light at the other end, where the far door was open. She shined the light but the space seemed empty. As she was about to climb back down, a sliver of movement caught her eye. It was in a corner where the ceiling angled downward to meet the wall. As she moved closer, she shined the light to see, but never seemed to be close enough. She kept moving closer, sure there was something lurking in that dark corner. Closer, closer, closer still...shined her light and nothing.

She whirled around and her neck caught on something, stopping her in her tracks. Reaching up and gasping for breath, she tried to pull herself away from whatever held her. Her hands failed to connect with anything, but she couldn't breathe. Her eyes bulged from her head and her neck was collapsing, as the air was unable to reach her lungs. She grabbed at her face, scratching herself in her panic. But it was no use. Margot knew this, and with a final burst of adrenaline she ran towards the open attic door and threw herself down. Her final sight as she fell was what she thought was a shadowed face gazing down from the darkness above. She was dead before she hit the floor.

Both the attic and trap door closed, simultaneously, with a satisfied thump. Blood pooled around Margot's twisted body, morosely highlighting the red of her favorite leather boots.

Jeff stumbled out of the master bedroom, half in a trance, feeling like he'd just been sleeping in ice. He looked at the roaring fire and the mug of hot chocolate, still steaming. Tottering like a drunk toddler, he made his way towards the fire, steadying himself as needed along the way. When he reached the couch in front of the fire place, Jeff crumpled. Leaning his head back, a sigh left his mouth without permission. Quick flashes of his nightmare passed before his open eyes, transparent and gossamer. Head still back, he looked towards the odd little door near the ceiling. It looked different. Like someone had applied a fresh coat of paint. His mind wandered back in time. Back to when he had decided to take Margot on a surprise vacation to help take their minds off of the stress. He remembered the picture of the cabin randomly popping up when he was searching for vacation ideas, and he knew it was perfect.

One of the guest books fell onto the hardwood floor, startling Jeff out his fog. The book was open. Jeff felt some trepidation picking up the book, but was unsure why. He read the entries on the pages where the book had opened.

"January 9-13, 1974
I enjoyed your cabin so much that I don't want to leave! My wife went home early, not sure why. She never said. It's for the best. I've never felt so great and at complete ease. This place fills me with the most pleasant sense of warmth, no matter how bad my mood. I've read some of the previous entries and don't worry. The attic door only opens when there's hunger. Once it's filled, the whole property just glows! Sorry my offer to buy was rejected, but I will return. That's a promise! M&J McAster (I guess just J McAster now.) See you next year!"

Hey, where is Margot? Jeff realized he couldn't remember the last time he saw her, with the exception of his nightmare. He called for her to no avail. A search turned up no evidence. No sign of her anywhere. Even her stuff was gone. It was as if she was never there. The car was still in front of the house. There were no footprints or tracks of any kind, just unblemished snow. He sat back down and drank the now cold hot chocolate. The fire roared, the place was glowing with warmth. If he was supposed to feel upset or distraught, it wasn't happening.

Jeff's face went blank and he sighed. Then he looked up and said to no one in particular, "I guess you're not hungry anymore." Smiling, he opened a bottle of wine, picked up his phone and checked his email. There was a new one, from the cabin owners.

"Dear Mr. McAster, Of course we accept your offer. You'll find everything you need, if not just think of it. Warmest Regards, The Owners".

46. SOME THINGS YOU JUST CAN'T PREP FOR
BY WINIFRED BURNISTON

Trisha and Marci leaned against the wall next to the restaurant's kitchen entrance smoking a cigarette as "The Green Love Mobile" screeched into its regular parking spot. The driver slid out with liquid ease, sauntering towards the ladies with a bow-legged, tight-jeaned, cowboy strut.

Trisha exhaled a plume of smoke. "That man's nothing but a wolf. One hundred percent lady-killer, from the top of his Elvis hairdo to the tips of his spit-shined shit-kickers." She winked at Marci and turned her attention back to the one hundred seventy pounds of testosterone headed in their direction.

Marci leaned in and whispered, "Lady-killer or not, you have to admit Steve is good-looking. Trouble is, he knows it, and gets more women than he can shake a dick at. He claims those tally marks on his car door are for all the tail he's gotten. It boggles the mind."

They couldn't help smirking when he reached them. Tipping an imaginary hat in their direction and drawling out a "Lay-dees", he slunk through the door. As soon as the screen snapped shut behind him, they burst into a brief fit of laughter.

"What a piece of work!"

"Yup," Marci agreed. "By the way, I wouldn't exactly call him a wolf. My mother always reserved that term for a higher class of skirt-chaser, such as my father. It was his greatest gift and biggest downfall." She paused for a second, considering the fellow who had just passed. "That boy," she continued, "is a smarmy asshole."

"Amen to that!" Trisha replied with a snort. Crushing out the cigarette stub with the back of her shoe, she opened the door. "Breaks over. We'd better get back before the boss catches us." Stopping to fling her pack of cigarettes into the cubbyhole with her bag and jacket, she headed back to her station.

The night was fairly typical. Food flew out of the kitchen at an incredible pace. Steve flirted with every female working and dining that evening. Trisha decided to keep her own tally for a while. Steve had slid his hands over no less than twenty tits and ass before the evening rush ended her count.

Halfway through the night, she went into the walk-in to get some prepped vegetables. Reaching up to get them, two hands suddenly appeared on the shelf on either side of her head. The full weight of another body pressed against hers, pinning her to the shelving. Warm breath traced down her neck and Steve's voice asked, "Anything I can do for you?"

She went rigid and couldn't seem to move. Thoughts raced across her mind. Can anyone hear me yell from inside here? Is this how he gets all those marks on his goddamned car? She wanted him to stop touching her, but her entire body was betraying her at the moment. She felt like a deer blinking stupidly at oncoming headlights.

"Yeah," hissed Marci, appearing in the doorway. "Get the hell off her, you piece of shit!"

"Don't get your panties all in a knot, Marci." Steve pushed himself back and turned around. "Just having fun, teasing her a little. No harm done." He swaggered out the door, heading back to the kitchen. Turning back for a second, he added, "Looks like you could use a little fun yourself. Give a holler if you ever change your mind."

Marci ignored him and asked Trisha, "You okay?"

"Yeah, I'm fine. He's a misogynistic prick, but I'm okay."

"Well, if he tries any of that shit on either of us again, his ass is mine."

The rest of the shift went without further incident. Steve gave both girls a wide berth, which suited them both just fine. When things slowed down about a half an hour before closing, Trisha was chosen to go home early. Normally, she would have balked at losing the money. Tonight, she was glad she could skip the after hour clean up with Steve. She waved a guilty good-bye to Marci, who had to stay. Marci waved her off, grinning. "Don't worry, I can take care of myself," she pointed at Steve's back and fired her finger like a gun. "And him," she added as Trisha left.

About halfway home, Trisha decided to call her friend Beth so they could meet for a late drink. She was still a little rattled from earlier. It really bothered her how she'd just shut down instead of defending herself. Groping around inside her purse for her cell phone, she couldn't find it. She pulled the car over and dumped the contents out onto the passenger seat. No phone anywhere.

Shit, it must have fallen out in my cubbyhole. This wasn't the first time she'd left the damned thing at work. Turning the car around, she headed back to get it.

The front parking lot was empty and dark. She drove around to the side entrance, hoping someone was still there. The outside light was on. That was a good sign. Crap! Steve's car was still there, which wasn't. Further back in the parking lot was Marci's beat up pickup truck. Salvation! She wouldn't have to face him alone.

Pulling up beside the truck, she hustled up to the door before noticing the silence. No music blasting as it typically did during clean up. Opening the door, she was surprised to find the main lights were off, with only the emergency lights dimly illuminating the kitchen. This was odd. It was always the last thing done before leaving for the evening.

Heading for the main switch by the cash register, she'd just reached it when she heard a low moaning sound coming from behind her.

She froze.

Turning around slowly, she heard the sound again. It was coming from the walk-in. It began to add up. The lights off, only two cars left in the parking lot, and the incident earlier. Marci and Steve were in the walk-in and it sounded as though they were having sex. Had Marci decided to take him up on his offer? Had they been doing this for a while and that's why his behavior earlier upset Marci? Or worse, was she being raped?

Rushing over to the walk-in door, she didn't see the puddle. She slipped and slid on her ass right into the door. So much for stealth, she thought. There was a grunt from behind the door.

"Marci, are you in there?" Trisha got up and it suddenly registered that the puddle and what was now coating her was warm. And definitely thicker than water, her inner voice chimed in. Looking carefully, she saw it was blood. Whose blood, though?

"Jesus Christ, are you okay? There's blood all over the floor!" Trisha pulled a chef's knife from a nearby block and reached for the door handle. She was about to fling it open when Marci's voice called from within.

"Stay out there, Trisha. Don't come in here." Her voiced sounded odd, sort of muffled and tense.

"What the hell is going on? Is Steve in there with you? Or is he out here somewhere?" She whipped her head around, searching for movement in the kitchen's gloom, straining to hear any noise. The shadows danced, her blood thrummed in her ears, and the knife swayed a little as she tried to control her shaking. That was all.

Thumps, bangs, and moans came from behind the door, followed by Marci's voice. "Yeah, he's in here. You need to leave right now before this gets out of control!"

"No way! You leave her alone, asshole. I'm armed and coming in!"

"No!" Marci shouted, "Get the hell out of here! Run!"

Jerking the door open, the first thing she noticed was blood. Everywhere. The shelving inside was badly battered, food hanging and dripping from each. Hunched in the corner was some sort of seething beast, hovering over a crumbled body. The creature was breathing rapidly, its body convulsing under a tightly stretched kitchen uniform.

Speechless, her feet cemented to the floor, she was once again that helpless deer.

A deep rumbling sound burst forth—words from the beast, "You shouldn't have come in here." And this voice was all that remained of her friend Marci.

Rubbery legged and suddenly unable to breathe, she clutched a shelf to keep from hitting the floor. The beast turned around.

Eyes. Eyes and teeth. That's all the face seemed to contain. All the better to eat you with, floated through her head and she began to laugh uncontrollably. Laughing and laughing, until it became screams that seemed to go on forever. Tears flooded her vision as the creature slowly moved forward, its grin growing wider and wider until it was the only thing she could see.

The last thing Trisha heard was its rumbling voice say, "I told you he wasn't a wolf."

47. TRICK NOT TREAT BY APRIL BULLARD

"Trust me," winks Dave, "This is the Grand Master Halloween prank of all time!"

The Boones Ferry Marina kids from Mrs. Mather's sixth grade class gather in the north end shed. One girl and a redheaded boy with glasses sit in front of the monitor screen while Dave and Brad hover behind them. Dave gently squeezes Jenny's shoulders, taking the opportunity to smell her long, chocolate brown hair, and whispers in her ear, "And you have my front row seat."

"So, what's the big plan?" prompts Jenny, leaning her head back on Dave's athletic shoulders. She catches the twinkle in his deep blue eyes as he tries to peek down her sweater.

"Hey, it wasn't all Dave's idea! He's not the tech genius!" says Brad, patting Jason's back then tousling the red hair.

"Knock it off, Brad!" whines Jason, swatting the unwanted hand away before readjusting the glasses on his freckled nose. "Just don't chicken out with the robe job."

"Oh, baby, that's the best part!" drawls Brad, swaggering his tall, lanky frame to the black cloak hanging by the door. "It's not Halloween without the Grim Reaper!" He grabs the cloak and with a magnificent spin, the cape swooshes down from his shoulders and around his ankles. His hands flip the hood over his head. Cold, gray eyes gleam from the shadowed face inside. Brad raises his arms for a classic vampire pose.

The door bursts open, bashing his arm.

"We're all– hey!" Caitlyn squawks, lunging her twelve year old frame into the stopped door. Her blonde, pageboy cut swings under her chin, covering the dimples in her grinning, round cheeks.

The cloaked figure towers over the stocky tom-boy and growls, "Die, puny mortal!"

Caitlyn backhands the belly of the robed figure. He doubles over, anticipating a stronger blow, and she tugs the hood down over his face. "Get a grip, Brad!"

Caitlyn's pudgy, little brother, Donovan, charges into the cramped shed. "You should see the frog she's got like hangin' at the first covered moorage! It's like, right there, in front of yer face, and like hangin' by one toe, and like danglin' on like one thin line from like the biggest web, and like the dock light shines like right on it, and it's like hangin' upside down, and like just like the hangman card from like a tarot deck, and that like dead, bulging like gray eye, just like staring right at ya! Aw, man, it's beautiful! That guy's gonna like shit bricks!"

"Checklist!" commands Jason, tapping keys on his laptop. "Lights, check! Bilge pump triggers?"

"Check!" says Dave.

"Slip 42 radio?" Jason calls.

"Check!" answers Dave.

"Radio? What radio?" Brad's head pops out from the black hood, his dark bangs hanging over his flashing gray eyes.

"Slip 42! Don't you remember last summer? Tony, the guitar player's girlfriend?" Jenny explains, "The blonde that was all freaked because that boat radio would turn on by itself and blast that fire and brimstone preacher station at her every time she walked by?"

"Oh, man, you found a way to rig that up? This is gonna be good!" whispers Brad.

"Been testing it," brags Jason, "Made that grouchy lady that plays bass jump. Even made the old, tech guy that runs the security cameras trip up a bit."

"Shhh! Someone's coming!" warns Jenny, pointing at the monitor. Brad quietly shuts the door and douses the lights. The group huddles around the glowing screen. The screen is divided into thirty two squares. Two figures pass from the box in the center and one row up from the bottom of the screen to the next and the next. The marina kids freeze, hearing them talking as they stomp past the shed. They continue on to the noisy house at the very end of the marina dock.

"Hey, Jenny," asks Caitlyn, "Did you get the binoculars and the deck set up?"

"Oh, yeah," Jenny snickers back, "Already swiped some beers from the party house. You should see what old Ms. Norcross is wearing. You know, the one that plays the flute and the bongos? Think AARP hippie meets Vampyrella!"

Caitlyn rolls her hazel eyes. "I have got to see that! Last year she set her costume on fire and two of them ended up in the river! Let's go spy on them!"

"Not yet! Joke first, then we can party!" interrupts Jason. "Smoke bomb?"

"Check!" says Brad.

"Cloak and Scythe?" continues Jason.

"Double check!" grins Brad.

"So, what's the joke?" asks Jenny.

"Payback," replies Dave. "We're too old to trick or treat, and let's face it, we're out in the boonies here, limited pickings anyway. The grown-ups throw a huge, drinking party, but of course, we're too young for that. So, we are stuck babysitting," he glares at nine year old, Donovan, "with a couple corny, horror movies, a pile of popcorn and a couple candy-bars, while the grown-ups make noise like a wannabe rock band and get plastered."

"We decided Trick not Treat, this year," Jason chimes in, "As you know, Tony plays lead guitar for the band. And you also know, he lives in the sailboat at the south end of the marina, slip 125, to be exact. So, guitarzan Tony, with his long, gray hair, beer-belly and shorts, is always the last one to show up and always late. When he takes that long, quarter mile walk in the dark from his end of the marina to the party house at this end, we're going to shut the dock lights off behind him, run the bilge pumps as he walks by. At the first covered moorage the dock lights will go out as soon as he gets to them, things get darker and darker, then at the second covered moorage we blast the radio from slip 42. From then on, lights go out before he gets to them, all the way to this shed. Then–"

"Then," Brad butts in, "I'll set off the smoke bombs and step through as the Grim Reaper, swinging my sickle thingy at him! Should get a good scream or a stream out of him!"

Giggles and gasps fill the shed. "That's too cruel!" stammers Jenny. "Those covered moorages are filled with spider webs and bats! The raccoons scurry under the docks, too! It's creepy already!"

"All the better. Yea, though he walks through the valley, uh, the docks of death, he will fear all evils–" Brad is cut off as all the kids groan, smacking him if they can reach.

"Here he comes," cries Jason, hunching over his laptop.

"Where?" grunts Dave. They all rush to the monitor.

"Right there, see the mast rocking?" Brad points at the upper left corner of the screen. "He's climbing out of the boat."

"Close up on four screen view and here we go," Jason recites. "Uh, time, Dave? Recording for posterity and possibly YouTube, you know."

"Shit, I don't believe it! Damn it!" wails Dave, smacking his palm on his forehead.

"Dave just lost a bet, he needs a hug," teases Brad. He points at the time code in the upper right corner of the monitor. "21:17, that's 9:17, right? Jason just nailed the time Tony would leave, inside a five minute window!"

Dave fishes a fiver out of his wallet and pokes it into Jason's wiggling fingers. Jason's hand snaps shut like a trap and stuffs the bill into his jeans pocket without averting his eyes. "Here goes number one!"

The light behind the sailboat goes out. Tony's figure in the upper left screen twitches to look behind, shakes its head and walks on, carrying his guitar in his left hand and a beer in the other.

"Epic wicked!" whispers Brad, draping his cloak over the group. Dave and Donovan bat the cloak away. Caitlyn shoves Brad away with her shoulders.

"Knock it off, guys! Gotta concentrate. Bilge pump one!" orders Jason.

The figure on the screen jerks his head to the left and slows down. With a little shudder it walks on. Five steps past the next dock light, Jason taps his keyboard, and the light goes out. The figure slows down and turns its head to look behind.

"Next four screens," Jason taps again, "Just one more step and," he taps a key, "Bilge pump 2!" The figure of Tony jumps and snaps his head around to the right.

A huge, flapping shadow crosses the screen from one square through Tony's square and disappears. "What was that?" exclaims Donovan, finger on the monitor.

"Just a blue heron," Caitlyn answers, pulling her little brothers hand away from the screen. "But it flew right over him!"

"Check it out! He's getting up!" observes Dave.

"Scared him to his knees," grins Brad, "Perfect!"

"Ha! He dropped his beer!" bursts Donovan. "See, he's picking it up again!"

The shed nudges against the sock. "What's that?" Jenny twitches in her seat.

Jason checks his laptop, "Just a surge from a ship out in the main river channel. Big one, too. Let's see, the Golden Dolphin out of Singapore–"

"That'll make everything shift and creak the entire length of the marina," giggles Caitlyn, "Should make things extra creepy!"

"Come on, Tony," prompts Jason, "Just past the light and, bam!" Tony's figure stops, then slowly turns full circle, scanning for answers. Snickers fill the shed with all eyes on the monitor. The figure on the screen takes a swig of beer, shrugs its shoulders and walks on.

"Ooh, ooh, here he comes, right for the frog! See?" squeals Donovan. "He's gotta like walk right under it!" Caitlyn and Brad nod, grinning with glee.

"Close up, screen nine," Jason announces. The monitor displays Tony, full screen, squinting as he approaches. Suddenly, Tony's eyes open wide, his mouth distorting in disgust to the rollicking laughter of the kids in the shed. The screen goes dark.

"Hey! What gives?" wails Dave.

"Lights out! Next four screen view." trumpets Jason.

"Oh my god, he dropped his beer!" exclaims Caitlyn, pointing at the puddle on the dock as the figure quickens its pace in the covered moorage. Caitlyn and Donovan brush fingers with a low five.

The next few lights go out as soon as Tony's figure gets abreast of them. Giggles continue, watching the figure jerking its head side to side and wiping its forehead.

"Hey, what's he doing?" asks Jenny. Tony's image is staggering around the dock.

"Must be the surge," Jason pipes up. "Should be swinging all those yachts around, creaking up a storm!"

"Come on, Tony, don't stop now," Brad encourages the figure on the monitor. It begins walking again.

"And that's Bud's fishing boat, slip 66." Jason extinguishes another light.

Tony's figure progresses from square to square and screen to screen, visibly scared and jumpy, clumsily speed-walking with the guitar held over his right shoulder like a weapon.

"He's at slip 46, here comes the good one." Jason taunts grabbing the handheld marine radio, "Three, two, one, bingo!" He squeezes the button.

The figure trips, drops the guitar, and lands on its ass. It grabs its left arm as if stung by a wasp. Howls of laughter fill the shed.

"Take your station, Brad!" orders Jason. "Anyone want to hide outside to watch, go now. Be quiet! No talking!"

Brad grabs the scythe and follows Caitlyn and Donovan out the door. Dave gives Brad a "thumbs up" sign, shutting the door before returning to watch over Jenny's shoulder.

"Full screen, Tony's view," Jason whispers. Three faces smile in the dim blue glow.

The figure stumbles towards the party house clutching its left arm. A burst of flames then a wall of smoke blocks the dock. Tony's figure falls to its knees.

The hooded figure steps through the smoke brandishing the scythe that gleams in the moonlight.

Tony's figure raises its right arm then collapses before the Grim Reaper.

"Die, puny mort-" Brad stops short, poking the body with his scythe. "Aw fuck, guys! He's dead!"

48. MIDNIGHT DRIVE BY KELI HAINES

A brilliant game of lightning danced across the cloudy night's sky, and blinding bolts illuminated the wall of storm clouds binding overhead. As the trails of lightning connected heaven and earth, the echoing boom of thunder swept through the valley. Occasionally, a particularly bright bolt would illuminate the nearest peak of the mountain range. Its black spire jutted forth towards the sky as lightning struck again, and again.

Fog had settled on the lowlands at the forefront of the mountain's ascent. The valley coursed its way through the hills and buttes, following a river of mountain water, snaking its way downhill and southwards. The silver hood of the Ford F-150 shone briefly in the lightning flashes, its usual waxy finish overcome with the torrents of rain, spitting forth from the storm. The water beaded and rolled up the windshield, urged on by the gales of wind rolling off the mountains and into the lowlands. The trees blew violently, their leaves coursing through the air. Branches snapped off and flew across the road with startling speed.

It was all I could do to stay focused on the road. The high-beams seemed to make the storm look even fouler, and so I resorted to the standard and fog light combination. I tried to focus on following the yellow lines as my guide, but the massing water hid it from my sight. I kept an eye fixed upon the guard rail along the passenger side as a cautionary guideline. It was nerve-racking, to say the least. I glanced at the radio and back. Lime-green lights shone a quarter to three. It felt like it too, I felt my eyes had grown heavier.

I also noted the temperature had steadily declined in the midst of the storm. Despite the stinging sunburns on my arms, and neck from the morning activities, I had appeased my family with the heater. Coupled with the consistent 'hum' of the exhaust, and the rain pitter-pattering upon the windshield, I occasionally felt my head begin to nod, before I would jerk back awake. Of course, I knew the risk I was taking, but the truck was nearing half a tank, and I'd need to stop and fuel up soon.

I glanced over at my wife, Lori. Long, golden-blonde hair cascaded down upon most of her face, hiding her long, freckled nose from sight. In my mind's eye, I could see her brushing her silky hair over her ear. With her bright, green eyes, she would look at me, almost within me, and smile. Dimples would overtake her freckled cheeks with every smile she made. I glanced to the backseat, briefly at first, but again as the road straightened. There, between two car seats, lay a bulging purse filled with diapers and other necessities for the children. That purse alone depicted the change in our lives over the last few years. The days of long, sleepless nights and sporadic and spontaneous vacations were now behind us. Now, a diaper-filled purse sat in the closest proximity to us, while the beer-cooler lay forgotten in the attic, back at home. And I didn't have a pang of regret.

I glanced in the rear view mirror, catches glimpses of the children in the flashing lights of nature's fury. I couldn't help but smile. The eldest, Candice, was the spitting image of her mother, besides her hair. Candice's hair curled as if she had just had a perm; a trait from her dear father. She had just celebrated her third birthday earlier that day. She had worn herself out playing with her new bike, now tied down in the covered truck-bed, alongside the suitcases. Another flash of lightning and I saw my little man. Drool covered his chin as he snored softly. His long brown hair looked similar to my own, before my latest haircut. I think we both could agree on our dislike of haircuts.

I fixed my eyes anew upon the road. The high-beams of the truck almost made it more difficult to see, and I resorted to my previous lighting. The lightning flashed in a flurry, almost constantly, and thunder echoed concussively amongst the low-lands, reverberating through the valleys. The thickets of oak, pine, maple, and spruce flailed madly in the hurricane-like winds. My grip tightened on the steering wheel as the truck was ushered to and fro from the winds. The rain droplets were fat and heavy, I expected it would begin to hail, especially considering the temperature plummet. I hoped for the sake of my truck and windshield that it wouldn't.

My mind wandered to the banks alongside the road. As we began our ascent into the mountain, the road cut between rocky overhangs and cliffs, as well as steep, muddy, and tree covered slopes. I had heard of semi-trucks being swept off the road by a landslide. I also remembered Lori's fear of nighttime driving. She had once struck a deer on a late night commute from work in her Prius, and since then had been entirely fearful of nighttime driving. She also began to favor venison more often, and promoted my annual hunting trip in the prairies back home. I looked at her and smiled. Maybe it was the birth of the kids, but I also had become a far less reckless driver. And since I was unsure of how the beasts would behave during a storm of this caliber, I began to edge of the side of caution.

The road twisted its way up the steep mountainous slopes, and the engine began revving louder as the 'cruise-control' began to accelerate. I could almost feel the gasoline bill digging into my wallet. As we began the incline, the fog slowly dissipated, but the trees instead thickened alongside the road. It was such a dense forest, that my lights couldn't pierce the initial line of foliage.

Blinding high-beams greeted me as I rounded a corner. Nearly simultaneously, we both dimmed our lights. I found my eyes settle upon the white line upon the right of the road, in order to spare myself the blunt of the light. However, my attention was drawn back to the semi, as he flashed his lights twice, in a warning, or so I assumed. I slowed down in anticipation.

My eyes slowly became reacquainted with the darkness. I leaned forward slightly, and turned up the volume of the radio. The station was beginning to cut out, due to the elevation, but I could still hear well enough. The channel was occasionally cutting into some talk-show between two men, but I could hear enough of the song still to help keep me awake. 'Paradise City' by Guns 'N Roses was just beginning.

When the album came out, I had tracked it down to a questionable record store, on the far end of town with my dad. It wasn't so much of his interest in the music, rather than "Shutting me up about that damn record." I was fifteen at the time, and just beginning to take an interest in girls. And who else would be working at that very store? Lori. Not long after meeting her, I invited her to a concert. Our favorite song? Paradise City. I couldn't listen to the song and not think of home, of dad, of Lori. Now, it brought to mind green fields, meadows overgrown with trees, and my small canoe on the lake. The same vacationing spot we were heading to now.

I smiled, yet the grin instantly melted away. I realized that the talk show had replaced most of the audio of the song. Guitar riffs were interjected with some cynical conversation. The mutterings made me frown, as static rippled through the audio on occasions. I was able to make out a few of the twisted words. "…that sadistic, indulging fucking whore, couldn't keep her legs closed…"

The words grew darker. I reached for the dial for the volume, but something in my head, a voice, stopped me.

"You don't want to fall asleep, Trevor." The voice was smooth, and soft. It took me a minute to recognize it as Lori's. "Just listen, please."

I looked at Lori, jumped, and nearly swerved. Her eyes were wide open, and they had settled on mine, only they held no light. They were cold, and harsh. "Didn't I tell you about the time with the plumber? You didn't think they're really your kids, did you? Who the hell would love you?" My heart had plummeted as she spoke.

"Where were you when Candice broke her leg? Where were you when the heater gave out last winter? All you care about is your job, Trevor." She snarled my name, almost like a swear word.

"Lori…please…" I started, but she cut me off.

"You're nothing. You're not the man I fell in love with. My children hate you. Not your children. You're the reason that I cheat. Don't look at them!"

With tears in my eyes I had begun to twist in my chair, but her sharp voice cracked, and I stiffened. I blinked, hard, and when I opened my eyes, Lori's head was once more bobbing slightly against the windshield in her deep slumber. I tried to wipe my eyes clear, and began desperately counting the mile markers, trying to factor in my head where I was.

The radio was getting louder. "Kill them all. Sinners. Adulterous traitors. Faithless heathens. Kill them all." It began to chant, over and over.

I shut the radio off and ran my fingers through my hair. I wanted to scream, but dared not wake the kids. I needed to stop. I needed the voices to stop. I looked up and froze. A figure, clad in dark clothes stood in the middle of the highway. His finger was pointed towards the truck. The lights of the truck settled upon his face, and I gasped as I recognized myself. I could read his lips. My lips. I could hear the voice in my head. I could hear Lori's treacherous words time and again.

"Kill them all." I muttered. I pulled hard on the steering wheel. Tires squealed, Candice screamed, Lori snapped awake and looked deep into my eyes, terror etched upon her face. The front of the truck crashed into the guard rail. Metal crashed upon metal, and next thing I knew, we were rolling, and tumbling.

***

I awoke under the painful brightness of a fluorescent light, hanging directly overhead. I heard the beeping of medical equipment beside me, and terror wrenched at me. I wanted to tear the blankets off and find my family, but I found that I was handcuffed to the frame of the metal bed. Questions poured through my mind, but I couldn't focus on anything besides my panic. Where was Lori? What had happened? Was this for real?

I tried to yell, but only a groan came forth. I tried to roll, wiggle, sit up, but bound as I was, I couldn't move at all. A man suddenly appeared overhead. A bald man, with dozens of moles and freckles, and even more wrinkles in his skin. His brow was furrowed as he thrust his chart into someone else's hands. "Why is this man bound, doctor?"

"He's woken once before. He's deranged. I've heard him speak, and he confessed. That was no accident, officer. He looked me straight in the eyes, told me what he had done…and laughed. The kids died on impact. His wife bled out on the ambulance ride."

Somewhere, off in a distant room, between my sobs, I heard the faintest sounds of a television, and I could hear 'Paradise City'.

49. LITTLE FUGUE BY SYDNEY LEIGH

PROLOGUE
San Francisco, California — May, 2000

Mark grabbed his sport coat from the closet and shook his head at the bone and saddle-colored flute case gathering dust in the corner.

"I still don't get why we have this thing, Sarah. You haven't played it in the twelve years I've known you."

Sarah pushed a breath from the corner of her mouth and poured a cup of coffee. "I've told you a million times, Mark. I've had it since I was a kid."

"And?"

"And . . . I don't know, it just feels like something I should keep." She shrugged. "Who knows? Maybe Sadie will play it one day."

"Well, I doubt she'll just take it up on her own. Musical talent is only about fifty percent genetic, isn't it? I mean, it would be nice if she heard her mom playing and picked it up that way."

"I don't see you passing along any abilities to speak of, Mark. I mean, it would be nice for Sadie to see her father writing best-selling novels, but I suppose there's something to be said for writing the latest deodorant slogan, huh? Those things are pretty catchy."

"Jesus, Sarah. You really go for the throat sometimes." He shook his head and was quiet for a minute. "It's just so bizarre. I'm married to a prodigy I've never heard play a single note."

"Sorry to disappoint you."

"That's not what I meant, Sarah."

"Whatever. Just go." She waved him off with a flick of her hand.

"I'm sorry I upset you. Give Sadie a kiss for me, okay?" He turned back and briefly looked at his wife before walking out the door for the very last time.

Sadie sat up in her crib as the door closed and wept softly into the monitor. Sarah finished the last of her coffee and mustered a smile as she snuck into the nursery. Sadie smiled back, holding her arms out wide.

After dropping Sadie off at daycare, Sarah stopped for a bag of Decaf Noir, her favorite nighttime indulgence, before heading to work at The Slanted Door. As she exited the building, two small groups of people talking excitedly crossed her path and she stopped to let them pass.

Their conversations blended and hung in the air, causing Sarah to pause without knowing why. She stood, frozen in place, words echoing in and around her head like a foreign yet somehow familiar phrase from her youth. And instead of continuing on to the restaurant, she caught the nearest cable car and headed home.

Once back in the apartment, Sarah pulled the old Artley flute case out of the closet and wondered if the conversation she had with Mark that morning led to her sudden impulse to pick up her flute. She could not even remember playing it—ever—she just knew that as a child her parents had deemed her a prodigy, and in all the years since their deaths, the instrument just came with her wherever she went. Much like old photos, a quilt her grandmother had sewn by hand, and the china her parents received as a wedding gift, the flute just felt like something she should keep . . . even though she had no real idea if she could actually play it.

She lined up the joints of the body and foot and pushed them together, reassembling the instrument with ease. The headjoint slid on without any resistance, and she brought the mouthpiece to her lips like it was something she had done every day of her life for the last thirty-one years. Her fingers found the sterling silver pads, and with a steady, controlled breath, Sarah began to play.

The phone finally broke her from her trance—not the ringing, but the increasingly frantic voices leaving repeated messages.

"Sarah, this is Paulo. We were expecting you at work. Is everything okay? Cody had to fill in, and he's not happy. Give us a call and let us know what's going on."

"Mrs. Johns? It's Nancy from Bright Horizons. We were expecting you to pick Sadie up almost an hour ago. Please let us know if you'll be delayed further—the children from the afternoon session are arriving soon. We hope to see you shortly."

"Yes, hello—Mrs. Johns? This is Chief Wagner from the San Francisco Police Department's Southern Station. We have officers on their way to your house right now, but could you please contact me at the station immediately? It's important that we speak to you right away. Please call the following number as soon as possible . . ."

But Sarah never made it to pick Sadie up from Bright Horizons, nor did she ever report back to work. She didn't even return the call to Chief Wagner, who was phoning to inform her of her husband's death by gunshot during a robbery at the newsstand outside his office. She also missed the police car making its way to her apartment with blue lights flashing along the crowded city streets.

Sarah Johns took a cab to the Golden Gate Bridge, stepped out near the walkway looking toward the East Bay, and jumped over the orange steel railing into the cold water below.

Marin County, California — May, 2010

Sadie Johns wasn't like other girls.

After her mom and dad died, she moved across the bay to live with her grandparents, and that alone made her stand out from the other kids her age. While Sadie's classmates were dropped off at school by tan young mothers and fathers in shiny SUVs and sports cars, Sadie pulled up in a pale yellow Chevy Impala and kissed her Papa's pasty, wrinkled cheek before stepping out into a crowd of kids who pointed and laughed at her every morning without missing a beat.

"Sweet ride, Gramps!"

"Yeah, dope wheels, old man. Where'd you get that, the junkyard?"

Sadie couldn't believe the boys didn't get tired of this routine, or come up with anything new to say. To her they were carbon copies of one another, entirely unoriginal. But it was her part of the routine to keep quiet and fasten her eyes to the ground to avoid eye contact with them. She even bit her lip out of fear to keep from cracking a smile on the days her Papa pulled away and the car backfired, leaving a foul cloud of smoke to break up the crowd.

Sadie wore her long, auburn hair parted in the middle and pulled into two braids that rested on her shoulders. At twelve, most of the other girls had long since outgrown such a hairstyle, but Sadie had grown used to it and enjoyed the time she spent sitting at her grandmother's feet while she twisted three thick tresses of her hair and tied them together with tiny plaid bows. Sadie liked to find one-of-a-kind dresses and used clothes at the thrift store while Nana sized up trinkets, pillows, and antique jewelry every Sunday after church. The other girls donned all the latest fashions, wearing something new and cool each day, with expensive accessories and shoes to match, and teased Sadie at every turn.

"What kind of sweater is that, Sadie?" one of the Ward twins asked while they stood in line for lunch. A crowd of girls that followed the twins wherever they went formed a circle around them, spectators at a show about to get good.

Sadie shrugged.

"Is it Gucci?

She shrugged again. "Maybe."

"Oh, yeah. I'm so sure it's Gucci. Dumpster sales are always the hottest place to score Gucci and Prada sweaters." Brie stepped in front of Sadie and sized up her top. "What's the verdict, Lilith?"

Before Sadie could turn around, Lilith grabbed the tag from the back of her cardigan and inspected it, pulling the collar uncomfortably tight around Sadie's neck.

"Yup. It's Gucci . . . and I'm Lady Gaga." The girls erupted into laughter, and Brie poked a finger against the bridge of Sadie's thick black glasses.

"You're a loser and a liar, Sadie Johns. Four-eyes." The crowd swarmed around the two sisters and edged Sadie out of line. She went and sat by herself at a table against the wall and read from a book in her backpack.

Sadie was used to being treated this way, since she lived with her grandparents as far back as she could remember and had never known anything different. The girls had always been mean to her, and not just Brie and Lilith. But the boys were just as bad—even though by all accounts, Sadie was in fact a very pretty little girl.

Sadie did well in school despite not having any friends, but sometimes even her teachers seemed to single her out.

"Okay, class," Miss Knox said every morning. "Everyone take out your writing utensils and record your journal entry for the day."

And like clockwork, Miss Knox would make her way through the rows of desks with her eyes silently approving the other students until she stood, arms folded, above Sadie.

"How many times are we going to discuss this, Sadie Johns? You need to write in your journal every day—just like everyone else."

But I'm not like everyone else, Sadie wanted to say. Instead she just said, "Yes, Miss Knox," and picked up a pencil and traced letters in the air above the paper, leaving another blank page for her teacher to mark an F on at the end of each week.

I'm disappointed in you, Sadie, Miss Knox would write beneath the bold red letter. This was usually accompanied by a hand drawn sad face, or sometimes even stickers or stamps indicating a similar sentiment.

Sadie felt the other kids' eyes on her while Miss Knox scolded her each day, and this made it even worse. On Fridays, one of the teacher's pets was chosen to hand the journals back to the class, and without fail, Emma or McKenzie or Samantha or Ryan or whoever else Miss Knox picked—anyone but Sadie—would flip through the pages just to have a good laugh at Sadie's Journal of Disappointment.

"Way to go, Sadie," Thomas taunted, throwing the book on her desk with a disapproving shake of his head. A trickle of laughter spread across the classroom.

It seemed as though something similar always happened in each of her classes.

Sadie's grandparents played bridge at the Senior Center on Friday nights and Bingo at the church on Saturdays, so Sadie was used to keeping herself entertained. She had books, a computer with some games on it, puzzles, a bug catching kit, and a deck of cards. She didn't know why, but her Nana and Papa never let her play an instrument. She wasn't even allowed to have a phone or an iPod, and while the other kids attended music class at school, Sadie went to the library. She vividly remembered sitting at their old friend Mr. Hathaway's piano a few years back, when Papa suddenly scooped her up off the bench before she could even touch a key. Sadie had cried, and Papa knelt down.

"Pianos are for grownups, Sadie. You must never touch one."

"But why?"

"You just can't." His tone frightened her, but she hugged him and wept softly into his shoulder—mostly because she didn't understand. "Now be a good girl and mind your Papa." And she did. She always did. Her grandparents had been good to her, and even though she was isolated from other children her age—or perhaps because of that—she listened to them without fail.

Until now.

The basement had always been off limits.

"Papa's tools are down there, honey. It's too dangerous," Nana always said. "Besides, dear, cellars have mice in them—yuck!" and Nana would twitch her nose and Sadie would laugh and say Ewww!

But today, Sadie didn't care about Papa's dangerous tools, or mind Nana's warnings about the dirty mice burrowing in the walls below.

Today Sadie defied her grandparents' wishes for the first time and climbed down the stairs into the cool, dank basement.

The walls were lined with shelves stocked with knick knacks and vases and a few lamps, and there was even some old furniture covered up with plastic. Big machines making loud noises loomed in the dark, and Sadie saw her Papa's tool chest sitting atop a wooden counter with a little sitting stool tucked underneath.

There were boxes stacked in one corner of the basement, and as she wiped dust off the sides she noticed an **M** written in black marker on a few of them. Sadie knew by looking through one of those that the M stood for Mark because she recognized some pictures of her dad holding her as a baby. And then she saw a box with a very small S.

Sadie took down the box and unfolded the four flaps to peer inside. She dug around a bit, and under a handmade quilt found a long, off-white case with brown leather ends and a matching handle. She tried to return everything to the way she had found it and brought her new discovery upstairs.

Back in her room, Sadie carefully opened the case and marveled at the deep red velvet holding the shiny silver instrument in place. She traced a finger along the inside corners and felt a puckered flap lining the top. Sadie stuck her hand inside, and at the very bottom of the pocket found a small book with a pink satin cover and small silver locking clasp.

My Journal, it read on the slim spine of the book. Sadie immediately thought of Miss Knox and her stomach cramped a little. She was really starting to hate that woman—and it didn't help that all the kids used the journal as a way to tease her every day.

The pages were old and a little stiff, but despite the faded ink, Sadie could make out the inscription just fine:

This Book Belongs To . . .

Sarah

That was Sadie's mother's name.

Redwood City, California — September, 1970

Tuesday, September 22nd

Today was a good day!

For my 9th birthday, Mom and Dad got me this new journal and took me to a music teacher named Mr. Forsythe. He's kind of sad because his wife died but he was happy to have a new student and called me a prodigy. That means I'm really smart and really good at playing the recorder. Mr. Forsythe said it makes him smile to see a child my age be so good at music and he always has cookies at his house.

Tuesday, September 29th

Mr. Forsythe said I'm practicing a lot and if I keep up the good work he might give me a new recorder. But it's not really a recorder. He said it's a flute. A real flute! I think it makes him sad to think about because it was his wife's flute and she is dead. But if I finish my first music book and all my lessons he might give it to me!

Tuesday, October 6th

Mom and Dad said they were very proud of me for playing the recorder and going to my lessons. Tonight they took me out for ice cream even though I had cookies at Mr. Forsythe's house!

Tuesday, October 13th

I finished all my lessons at school during recess last week because I don't really like playing with Robert and Mary and Eleanor anyway. Today Eleanor called me stupid and said recorders are dumb. That's because she can't even play one! Mr. Forsythe said I was so good that he was going to give me the flute. I can't believe I'm going to have a real flute! My mom said it was okay and so I brought it home with me just to get used to it. I looked at my Learn As You Play book and was too afraid to take the flute out of the case because it's so nice I might break it.

Tuesday, October 20th

Mr. Forsythe cried a little when I played the flute today. He said I was a natural just like his Fern. She died but used to play the flute like me. He said she learned at the conservatory and that's the best school and I didn't even need to go there to learn! I don't think I play as good as her but still I am a prodigy, at least that's what he said.

Tuesday, October 27th

Mom and Dad were fighting all week and I was scared so I stayed in my room and practiced my flute. After my lesson tonight, Dad yelled that Mom doesn't pay enough attention to my dumb brother Roger and all she cares about is me being a prodigy. He said I'm not a prodigy, I just have no friends. That made me mad.

Thursday, October 29th

Yesterday we had to go to the hospital because my dad fell down the stairs and got hurt very bad and has all these funny things wrapped around him so he can't move anything except his eyes. He probably fell because he was so mad at my mom that he wasn't even looking where he was going.

Roger cried all night like a little baby and wouldn't even let go of Mom's hand so she had to stay with him in his bedroom until he fell asleep. I just played my flute and tried not to listen but he kept waking up and crying and it made me so mad!

P.S. Mom came in and made me stop playing because Roger has a fever and has to go to the doctor. Our neighbor Mrs. Jacobs came over to watch me while Mom took Roger to the doctor and said I should go to bed. But instead I hid under my covers and played my flute a little longer.

Friday, October 30th

Even Mrs. Jacobs is crying now. She stayed the night and in the morning I heard the phone ring and Mrs. Jacobs came into my room with a box of tissues and red eyes. She put her hand on mine and said "I'm so sorry dear" but I don't know what she's so sorry about. I asked when my mom was coming home but she just cried more and patted my hand.

Saturday, October 31st

It's Halloween and my mom is home but Mrs. Jacobs is still here and now they are both crying. Mom has her head on Mrs. Jacob's shoulder and keeps saying "No, no, no" and "I just don't believe it." I asked Mom if we were going trick or treating and she just cried and I asked Mrs. Jacobs if we were giving out candy and she said no and to just go play my flute.

P.S. Eleanor and Mary came to the door and rang the bell and knocked and I looked down at them out my window and said we weren't giving out candy. Eleanor yelled "Your family is crazy!" and said she would throw eggs on our house if we didn't give out candy like we were supposed to. She looked so stupid in her Raggedy Ann costume that I hope she chokes on a Baby Ruth and dies.

Tuesday, November 3rd

I didn't go to school yesterday or today because Roger's fever got so high that he burned up. Mrs. Jacobs said it was an infection. It's weird not to have a little brother anymore but my mom let Mrs. Jacobs take me to my music lesson because Dad is still in the hospital and I'm not sure why but I'm not allowed to see him.

Mr. Forsythe seemed very worried and was crying a lot today while I played and asked if I was sure I liked the flute. He asked if I would like to learn to play the piano but I said no. He said I was just like his Fern. I asked him how she died and he got real quiet and said he was going to get me some cookies but I heard him crying in the kitchen. He must be very sad about his wife.

P.S. Mrs. Jacobs didn't come to pick me up. She called Mr. Forsythe and said she had to go to visit her sister somewhere far away and so I'm still here.

Wednesday, November 4th

Mr. Forsythe took me to school today. I'm wearing the same clothes I wore yesterday! He didn't have any peanut butter so he made me a toasted cheese sandwich but I don't like those so I just ate the cookies and am writing in my journal at lunchtime. He even gave me money to buy milk. Mr. Forsythe is so nice.

P.S. The ambulance came today because Eleanor choked on her Sloppy Joe. The lunch lady kept hitting her on her back and squeezing her like she was giving her a hug from behind but Eleanor turned blue and fell. Then our principal Mrs. Olson came running in the cafeteria and fainted when she saw Eleanor on the floor. It was funny because I was playing my flute and Eleanor walked by and stuck her tongue out at me right before she and Mary sat at another table. So even though it wasn't a Baby Ruth, I'm glad Eleanor choked because she deserved it.

Thursday, November 5th

Mom talked to me last night but she didn't want to hear me play my flute. She just wanted to know why I wasn't sad about Roger or Eleanor or about Dad being in the hospital. I told her I wanted to know why SHE didn't want to hear me play my flute and she just cried and left the room. Grandma Rose and Uncle Michael came over to stay with us for a while and plan for Roger's funeral and everyone is so sad that no one has any time to hear me play my flute! It makes me so mad.

Uncle Michael told my mother it was important for me to see my dad and took me to see him at the hospital but my dad acted like he didn't even want to see me. I tried to show him how good I was on the flute and he slapped it out of my hand and it hit the floor. It didn't break, but I was very angry and my Uncle Michael asked my father what the h-e-double-hockey-sticks he was thinking. My dad cried and told my Uncle Michael to leave him alone and swore with a lot of other words. My uncle told me to stay in the hallway while he went back to talk to my dad. I heard my dad say there was something wrong with me and that ever since I started playing that (swear word) flute bad things were happening and I didn't care. He screamed that his baby was dead and he never even got to say goodbye. I thought I was his baby because that's what he used to call me. His baby girl.

Friday, November 6th

Uncle Michael said that Dad had an allergic reaction to medicine they gave him for pain. He also said that he didn't understand what was going on but he would get to the bottom of it. I guess my mom is in the middle of a nervous breakdown and if I was her I would be nervous too. My grandmother isn't much help so I'm not even sure what she's doing here. All she does is cry. My uncle said she's in shock because she lost her son and grandson in one week and that my mom is in shock too because she lost her son and her husband and I probably don't understand what that means and that's why I'm not acting sad. He thinks I am in shock too. I just want to play my flute and can't wait to go see Mr. Forsythe next week.

Sunday, November 8th

We had a "wake" for Dad and Roger today and tomorrow will be their funerals. I told my mom I thought it was funny that they are called wakes if Dad and Roger aren't ever going to wake up and she slapped me. She should never have done that. There's also a wake for Eleanor today but I'm not going because I don't care that she's dead. I'm glad she's dead and when I told Grandma Rose that she slapped me too. I think everyone around here must be going crazy because they all think they can slap me and get away with it.

Tuesday, November 10th

Even Mr. Forsythe must be going crazy. He said he knew about Roger and Dad and Eleanor and Grandma Rose (I forgot to say she had a heart attack at the funeral yesterday) and I asked him what did he mean he "knew." He said he would have to take the flute back because he knew what I was doing with it and I was really, really mad. I told him it was MY flute and picked it up and played it and he started to back away and did a backwards somersault down into his basement. He looked like a Gumby doll at the bottom of the stairs.

Mom will be coming to pick me up here soon and won't be happy when she sees me with Mr. Forsythe's blood all over my dress. He was calling to me from the bottom of the stairs so I went down to play him some more music and he tried to grab the flute out of my hands but missed and left a big red handprint on my sleeve. I sat on the steps and played him the song from Swan Lake and his eyes got all wide and he said "Fern" and blew out a big ugly breath and then got very still. I think he was surprised that I could play that song so well because he never heard me play it before. Maybe he was in shock.

P.S. Boy, was I right about Mom. She went crazy when she came to pick me up and saw me. She was too afraid to go see Mr. Forsythe's body so she called Uncle Michael and told me to stay where I was and she waited outside. I saw her pacing back and forth and crying and screaming and she even pulled some of her hair out. She sat down on the ground and kept turning back to look at me in the window like she was afraid. Imagine that?

So I crept out through the back door and hid behind a tree on the side of the house and started to play Little Fugue in G minor and she ran out into the street and got hit by a car that was going by really fast. Uncle Michael should be here any minute now and I hear lots of ambulances too.

Wednesday, November 11th

Uncle Michael smiled a lot at me today even though I know he is sad because when he got to Mr. Forsythe's and saw my mom covered up with a sheet on the road he started screaming and punched all the windows out of his car. Then he sat down and put his bloody hands on his face and cried so he was a real mess. The police came in and talked to me and they were really nice and said they liked my flute and thought I must be very smart to play an instrument at my age. I told them I was a prodigy and that made them smile. They asked me if I was going to be okay and I said of course I was. They told me I could call them if I ever needed anything so that was very nice.

Uncle Michael said he wanted to take me to someone to talk to about everything that happened and when I asked who it was Uncle Michael said it's a hypnotist. I said as long as I could play my flute and he said I could bring it with me so I said I will go. We are going to see the hypnotist now, so I will write when I get back.

EPILOGUE
Marin County, California — May, 2010

On Monday morning, Sadie kissed her Papa and stepped out of the Impala with a smile on her face. It didn't bother her one bit when the boys hurled their usual insults at her grandfather's car, or when Brie and Lilith rolled their eyes and pointed out her second-hand dress to their adoring fan club. And she even laughed out loud—perhaps for the first time in a long while—when her Papa's car backfired and left a rank cloud of exhaust smoke in the air.

She sat at her desk and continued to smile while Miss Knox wished the class a good morning and instructed the students to record the past weekend's events in their journals. She watched Miss Knox make her way around the rows of desks and plant herself, arms crossed, in front of Sadie.

"You know the drill, Sadie. You need to write in your journal—just like everybody else."

Sadie looked around the room at her classmates, who snickered and stuck up their middle fingers and shook their heads.

"Yes, Miss Knox," Sadie answered.

And today, Sadie picked up her pencil and began to write.

Monday, May 24th
Dear Journal,
Last night I played my new flute for the very first time. I think I'm a prodigy . . . Just like my Mom.

The brick walls kept them out, and even with no fire they wouldn't dare come down the chimney; the prey had learned something from children's tales, but so had the hunters. Outside under the blazing sun their howls, shrill and unnatural, mingled with gunfire and raucous laughter. Their prey trapped, the hunt had become a party.

She stepped away from the door, the crack too small to see outside anyway.

"Beth."

She turned at her husband's voice, traced up his work boots and denim overalls to his rugged, angular face, just visible in the darkness. Her heart broke at the despair in his amber eyes.

"They're going to get in."

She shook her head, an impotent denial of the inevitable. They'd taken the forest, she knew that. The game had fled or been slaughtered and devoured by the savages outside, no match for the trucks and ATVs and guns they'd taken to in modern day. Even rodents had gotten scarce, what trails there were crisscrossed and obscured by flat, wide tracks that stank of rubber and gasoline.

"No, baby, they're not. They're going to drink and fight and get tired and lazy, and we'll slip out when they don't expect it. This isn't a siege, it's—"

Creosote fell into the fireplace, dust rained from the rafters high above. The floor shuddered as massive diesel engines rumbled in the distance.

"They're going to get in."

Her heart raged against the truth in it. The last of their kind, at least this side of the Rocky Mountains, they were too big a prize to let get away. Homo sapiens sapiens didn't brook competition. They never had, even after their scientists had learned that their myths were wrong, that their respective species couldn't crossbreed. If anything it had emboldened them, given them an endgame.

Bullets pecked at the façade, a waste of ammo and effort. Someone whooped in drunken triumph. More laughter, more whoops and hollering. More pecks.

Hunting them below population viability, dooming their species, that hadn't satisfied them. No, their bloodlust demanded lives, pelts, taxidermied bodies posed as fearsome statues by cabin fireplaces.

Bragging rights. The scourge of the darkness under the pines, the masters of night, the lords of the moon; their hunters had reduced them not only to prey, but to bragging rights. God, how she hated them.

The house shuddered again.

The hatred bloomed in her breast, spread through her in shockwaves, and she grunted at the first twinge of the change. She crouched, breaths short and shallow. Coarse brown hair sprouted from her arms, claws from her fingertips.

Strong hands grabbed her head, pulled her upright. She snarled and tried to back away, but John pressed her against the wall and locked her eyes with his. "No, baby, you can't do this. Not now. They want this. Want us."

She growled, deep in her throat...and he licked her cheek. Her cheek, her forehead, her hair. He held her and she folded into his warmth and let his words roll over her, soft babbled truths about love and hard lies about survival. He smelled of wolf and fear and desperation, of love and comfort and worry. She let the change bleed out of her and sighed, exhausted.

Thunder-that-wasn't rumbled in the distance, and she ran her fingers down his cheek. "Thank you." They stood in silence a moment, but she couldn't help herself. "What do you think they're doing?"

"Felling trees. They're either going to make a battering ram or a giant bonfire."

They'd never get through the windows. The fort house had once been a frontier jail, and had thick iron bars in front of the glass, rusted and pitted with age but still thick. Behind them they'd nailed up thick hardwood boards and old tin sheeting. The hunters had tried to force the door, but the heavy steel held, and she'd shot three men through the mail slot to deter further attempts. She smelled them outside, the bloody bodies left as bait, but she couldn't risk opening the door. But God how she wanted to.

The hunters didn't know the wolves only had seven rounds left for the .308, the only reason they hadn't stormed the place.

She pushed him back with her fingertips, no longer claws. "Not a bonfire. They don't just want us dead, they want trophies."

"But they're cowards. If they breach the door or the wall, they know they're going to die. The first however many, anyway. They'll burn us out, just as soon as they're ready."

"No, baby, you're stuck in last century." Two centuries ago, really, but this one hadn't lost its baby teeth, at least in her mind. "They'll use grenades. A small hole, in it goes, and we're diving for cover or dead. They'll breach two places at once, split us up." She looked down, and wished she hadn't.

Their six pups dozed in the plastic laundry basket, heaped amongst dirty clothes and an old leather saddlebag, oblivious to the danger of their situation. Ears flat, they wouldn't open their eyes for another few days. Beautiful, fragile, helpless.

She hadn't eaten in two days, and hunger clawed at her ribs. The pups took from her what they needed and left her starving, and in a lean spring she'd be happy to give it. A pathetic cry tore at her heart, so she shifted, her once-sleek fur patchy with mange and malnutrition as she slipped from her human clothes. She tipped the basket and let her pups nuzzle against her, let them suckle. Weak from fear and starvation, she closed her eyes, head resting on the floor.

She didn't expect sleep to come, but pretending helped.

John waited for the sun to drop below the horizon before peeling back the board from the second story bathroom window. Campfires dotted the surrounding woodland, devoid of brush or cover. Roasting meat and beer and piss filled his nostrils, but his dry mouth wouldn't salivate. They'd cut the power, and with it the plumbing, and what little water they had left would go to Beth. For the pups.

He waited and watched, his human eyes more suitable for long-distance scanning than his wolf eyes, despite the darkness. A man sat on a log not far off, binoculars in his lap, a sandwich in his hands. He didn't so much look at the house as stare off into space in that general direction. A bullhorn leaned against his ankle.

Lightning flashed in the distance, and John caught a glint next to a haggard beechnut tree. He waited and watched, and in time the silhouette resolved itself into a prone man or woman with a rifle, eye scanning the house through a scope.

He ducked back, replaced the board, and licked his lips with a dry tongue. He'd seen two. How many more? How careful were they being?

The bloody, furry mess in the bathtub wouldn't answer him. Chet had taken a bullet in the chest, and while he'd made it into the house, it didn't take more than a minute for him to bleed out right through the bandage. At least it was too cold for flies.

John's stomach growled, and he turned away from the corpse. That path led to madness, and while his stomach didn't care, his mind still did.

They never should have come back for the pups.

Hayden looked up from the rifle, frowning. She'd expected another monster like she'd seen with her daddy, not a tired-looking man in overalls. He'd looked sad, worried, not hateful and violent. Not like a demon at all.

"The land ain't tame," Daddy had said. "Won't be, until the last of the monsters are gone."

Most people didn't believe in monsters. Her friends' parents taught them they weren't real. Her daddy had done the opposite, taught her and trained her, took her hunting and tracking from the time she could walk. And two weeks ago, for her fourteenth birthday, he'd given her a Ruger M77 .270 with a night-vision scope, and a trip to a "hunting safari" in western Montana.

Twenty men hunting five werewolves. It didn't seem fair.

The forward group harvested two before Hayden had even gotten into the truck, and the next few hours consisted of a harrowing chase through half-cleared woodland, bouncing over roots and creeks while her daddy lectured her on the technique.

"Like wolves'll run deer until they drop from exhaustion, you keep the weres on the run long enough and they'll turn and fight. They got way more endurance than you or me, but can't out-marathon a tank of gas.

"You hunt wolves like they hunt deer, not how we do."

They'd spotted their quarry just as they ran for a two-story brick fortress. Daddy'd fishtailed to a stop, and Hayden used the window as a bench rest. Huge beasts covered in dense fur, they moved so fast she had a hard time picking out detail. Humanoid, anyway, which told her all she needed to know. She'd trained on the front one, pulled the trigger just as he opened the door. His companions dove into him, carrying him through into the darkness.

"Dammit, Hay!" her dad had said as the door slammed shut.

"I got him." They locked eyes, but she wouldn't back down. "Solid shot, upper ribs. He won't make it."

He'd mussed her hair. "That's my girl."

Beth startled awake as a thunderclap rocked the building. John stood over her, human and dressed. "We need to go."

"What?" She sat up, naked and human, her pups mewling as they slid into her lap.

"They've got sentries, but the lightning'll blind them, and if the rain's hard enough it'll bog down their trucks."

She stood and pulled on her jeans, filthy denim covering legs clammy with old sweat. "They'll be watching the doors."

He nodded. "And the windows."

"So—"

He held up a finger to stop her, then pointed at the fireplace. "We go up."

She blinked in disbelief. "That's crazy."

"If we stay here we die."

She crouched, picked up her pups one by one and put them in the saddle bags. They didn't even have names yet, wouldn't until they were old enough to go on hunts with the pack—with their father, all that was left of their pack. Done, she pulled on a T-shirt and stood.

"Okay." Another peal of thunder rumbled through.

She crouched into the fireplace, rank with old soot, bat guano, and mold. Rain spattered her face as she looked up the chimney. Dark clouds blanketed the sky above the narrow opening, and claustrophobia tightened her chest. Wolves weren't meant for narrow brick crevices, weren't meant to climb.

She stood, just able to fit inside, and John cinched the saddle bags to her thigh.

"Go, baby. I'll meet you up top."

She pressed her forearms against the opposite side of the chimney and braced her back against the opposite wall. Her legs barely fit, and she dug her bare feet into the slippery gunk to keep any kind of purchase. John pushed from below to help her the first several feet, and a flood of lightheadedness struck the moment he let go.

"I can't—"

The saddle bags tugged at her leg, and she killed the excuse mid-breath. Her muscles screamed as she struggled upward, inch by agonizing inch, dragging her pups with her. Slick with ancient grime, she could just barely move one limb while supporting herself with the other three. Below her, John inched upward, supporting the saddle bags and their precious cargo with his shoulders.

Lightning flashed, and thunder slammed the breath from her lungs. She wanted to rest, to stop, to give up, but had nowhere to go. So she climbed. And climbed and climbed. Halfway up, John swore, and the rifle clattered to the bottom.

"Leave it," she said.

He chuckled, a harsh sound devoid of humor. "Planned on it."

For an eternity she played Sisyphus. Muscles locked, even a rest gave no rest, and the higher she climbed the worse the rain slicked her arms, legs, and the soot-covered brick. The space crushed her, squeezed her lungs, strangled her rational thoughts and left her chained in a cage. Thunder rumbled, lightning flashed, revealing John below, murmuring words of encouragement and comfort, though to her or the pups or himself she couldn't hear.

At last the sky broke above her, and she grasped the edge of the chimney with a cry of despair just abated. Tears lost in the downpour, she hauled herself out and then lay flat on the cold slate roof, saddle bags clutched in her arms. The pups whined and yelped, and she prayed the rain would drown out their feeble protests.

John dropped next to her and they lay there, frozen in place in the deluge, for several minutes. She knew she had to move again, but just wanted to close her eyes in the rain and let it wash her away into nothing. Her shredded muscles couldn't compete with the agony in her gut, the fire in her chest. But the sky, oh, how she'd missed the sky. Under the sky, in the rain, she could die happy.

"I can't do this," John muttered.

Anger fueled her, anger that he'd abandon her, that he'd give up on their pups. "You can. You will, dammit. We'll—" She caught his smirk in the lightning flash and wanted to kiss and kill him. "You son of a bitch, you got me."

As adrenaline sparked by anger burned through her, he smiled. "Next flash, to the edge."

She nodded, and tensed.

The sky lit and she rolled, arms tight around their precious bundle. She hit the wrought iron spikes on the edge of the roof and froze. Another flash, and she hauled over them, hung down as far as she could, and dropped.

Her stomach lurched. A tree exploded in a flash of white on a nearby hill. She hit the ground and cried out as her foot slid, wrenching her calf. Red-hot pain seared up her leg to her lower back, worse with every limping step to the shelter of the tool shed. John appeared beside her, and took their children from her arms.

Laughter and music rang out around them, the torrential downpour doing little to depress the spirits of their hunters. In every direction, campfires fought the rain, but no cries of alarm came from them.

"Are you all right?"

She shook her head, and kept her voice as low as his. "Landed funny. Hurts to walk."

"Okay. I'll help you." She shifted much of her weight onto his shoulders, and took a cautious step. "We'll go right through them. Just act naturally."

"No."

They whirled at the high-pitched voice, and John snarled.

A blond girl stood not ten feet from them, rifle slung across her back, hands empty and outstretched, palms up. Her pony tail stuck out from a Bass Pro baseball cap, and the water rolled off of her camo hunting suit. "Go South. Bill and Derek are drunk. I'll lead you."

John looked at Beth, deferring to the alpha female in this matter. Beth pressed her hand into his back, toward the girl. John stepped, she followed.

The girl smiled, pretty white teeth in perfect rows. "I'm Hayden. This way."

Beth grabbed her shoulder. "Why are you helping us?"

She shrugged. "My dad says you're monsters. You don't look like monsters to me."

They passed an unconscious man lying in a pile of beer cans. Beth snatched up his shotgun on the way by. Double-barreled, with six rounds tucked into a velcro-and-elastic holder on the butt stock, it weighed a zillion pounds. She put it over her shoulder without complaint and plodded through the mud between the child and her husband, gritting her teeth against the pain in her ankle.

They walked for twenty minutes, then forty, stopping at a small creek to drink and fill Hayden's water bottle. The girl picked her way with easy assurance, one foot in front of the other without hesitation or even a hint of nervousness, every once in a while stopping to check a GPS she kept in her pocket. She glanced more than once at Beth's limp, but said nothing.

Another ten minutes and Beth stopped, set the shotgun in the dirt. "Wait, please."

They stopped. Beth smelled the wariness boiling off of John, the jumbled discomfort of her pups.

Hayden smelled like soap and sweat and hot, bloody meat. She put her fists on her hips, an almost comical gesture in the pouring rain. "It ain't much farther." A pup whined, and Hayden looked at the bag. "Y'all got kids?"

John blinked. "Pups. Six. We need to get them to safety so they can nurse."

Beth hung her head, almost unable to speak. "I need food. Painkillers. I can't keep doing this."

Hayden smiled. "Safety's just around the corner."

"Where are we going?" John's voice projected distrust edged with contained hostility.

"A hunting cabin. The whole crew's supposed to meet up there tomorrow. After...after you're dead." She turned and walked, forcing them to lose her or catch up. They stumbled after her. Sure enough, they rounded an outcropping and in the distance saw a small cabin with a wrap-around porch, a single naked bulb shining out through the front window.

Beth cleared her throat. "And no one's there now?"

"Nope." Did she hesitate? Just for a split second? "They're all staking out your fortress. Plan to go in at sunrise, take you down. Hurry up!"

She took off at a jog.

Beth looked at John, read the desperate hunger there, felt it herself. She nodded. "Yeah."

He handed her the saddle bags on his way past. By his third step he'd changed, a seven-foot wall of sleek muscle, claws and teeth. He snarled as he leapt. Drool rolled down Beth's chin, and she almost fainted at the thought of fresh meat.

Hayden dropped prone, and John fell on top of her. He didn't catch himself, didn't land on his feet. Then Beth heard the shot, sharp and crisp.

She screamed.

Hayden grunted as the dead weight blasted the air from her lungs. Gushing liquid, so much warmer than the rain, ran down her face and hands, filling her mouth with the taste of iron and meat. The creature's musky scent overpowered the rotting leaves and new grass, and its thick fur almost blocked out the woman's scream.

A shotgun blast rang out. A rifle responded as she wriggled her way out from under the massive frame. Heavy footsteps stopped just behind her, and she rolled to her hands and knees and took the offered hand, rough with callouses and so, so strong.

Her dad hauled her to her feet.

"Did I do good, Daddy?"

He spat, a brown squirt of tobacco juice that disappeared into the carpet of dead leaves. "Yep. That male'll fetch us fifty grand, give or take. And ain't nobody else needs to know we got him."

"What about the female? She had pups."

He raised an eyebrow. "Pups, now? That's interesting."

"Six of them. Why interesting?"

He spat again. "I know a man's got a preserve up Ottawa way. You raise those pups right, you got one hell of a hunt in a few years." He took off her cap and rubbed her head, freeing strands of hair stained a muddy red-brown. "She's limping, and armed. You catch her, the pups are yours."

Hayden grinned, unslung her rifle and dashed after her prey.

THE END

To be continued in…

Demonic Visions 50 Horror Tales Book 7